cocoa beach
Bride

SWEENEY HOUSE
BOOK 7

CECELIA
SCOTT

Cecelia Scott

Sweeney House Book 7

Cocoa Beach Bride

Cover designed by Sarah Brown

ha Sweeney, and Taylor was under no obligation
any kind of relationship with him whatsoever.
g taking his pre-dawn phone calls.
y would he call her?
he know about Mom? Could he possible know
aylor had learned last night? Nah. Her mother
ping in the living room right this minute, after a
ht of trying to process the news that, at forty-
e was pregnant again.
This must be some other catastrophe.
aring her head, she slid her finger across the
of the phone screen and slowly raised it to her ear.
d?" she whispered, her voice quivering slightly
her will.
ylor! Wow! You answered."
frowned as the sound of her father's voice for the
e in nearly a year punched her in the gut.
y did he sound so *happy*?
ah, well, people don't usually call at this hour
omething's wrong." She could hear the edge in
, but she didn't care. Mr. Minx must have heard
ince her gray cat slinked up the covers to snuggle.
up?" she asked.
er she'd caught him cheating on Mom with Kayla,
-something nurse from his hospital, she didn't
deserved respect.
e's here, Tay!" he exclaimed, clearly unfazed by
py tone. "Your baby sister is here! Kayla had the
four this morning, and...wow. It's amazing. She's
l, and...and I wanted you to know."

Introduction To Sweeney House

The Sweeney House is a landmark inn on the shores of Cocoa Beach, built and owned by the same family for decades. After the unexpected passing of their beloved patriarch, Jay, this family must come together like never before. They may have lost their leader, but the Sweeneys are made of strong stuff. Together on the island paradise where they grew up, this family meets every challenge with hope, humor, and heart, bathed in sunshine and the unconditional love they learned from their father.

For release dates, preorder alerts, updates and more, sign up for my newsletter! Or go to www.ceceliascott.com and follow me on Facebook!

Chapter C

Taylor

Taylor Parker could barely
phone vibrated on the r
morning yet? The cats jumped fi
the bottom of the bed, equally bo

Seriously, *this* early?

She squinted into the beacor
from her ringing iPhone. Five
shocking than that was the name

Three letters burning into I
slack as she stared at the incomin

"Dad?" Taylor whispered,
surprise and, of course, the jolt o
with the thought of her father co

How long had it been since s
Long before she and her mo
Orlando to Cocoa Beach to start
best decision they had ever made

The last she'd heard from
Parker, was that his girlfriend,
Kayla's current status—was pr
enough for Taylor to cut the mar

He'd cheated on her mom,

Saman
to have
Includi
WI
Die
what 1
was sle
late nig
three, s/
No.
Cle
bottom
"Da
against
"Ta
She
first tim
Wh
"Ye
unless
her ton
it, too, s
"What'
Aft
a thirty
think he
"Sh
her snij
baby at
beautifu

An unexpected and, whoa, unwelcome wave of emotion crashed over Taylor, rocking her as she squeezed her eyes to fight the tears that threatened.

Great. Just...*great*. Her dad had a brand-new baby and her mom just found out last night that she had one on the way.

Couldn't Taylor's twenty-five-year-old life just be...normal?

"That's awesome, Dad," Taylor managed, her throat tight.

"Her name is Brooklyn," he said, like she'd asked, which she probably should have. "She's seven pounds, two ounces. Just like you were. And Kayla's doing great. She was a trooper, I tell you."

Taylor winced, shutting her eyes, stroking Mr. Minx and making room for Midnight, who also wanted love.

Had her father been this happy the day she was born? Twenty-five years ago, when he and Mom loved each other and before everything turned into a dumpster fire? Was he this overjoyed? He'd sure never acted like it.

"Congratulations. I'm really happy for you, and your new family."

"Taylor, can we just...wait. Hang on."

She heard some shuffling sounds from the other side of the phone call.

"Sorry, I'm walking out of the hospital room to get to a quieter spot. Can we just talk for a second? I haven't heard your voice in ages. I miss you, kid."

He missed her? Should have thought of that before he cheated on Mom.

"Well, you've got a new baby girl to love. And a new wife." Had he married her? She had no idea and a tendril of shame squeezed her chest. "And a new life, so...yeah. I don't fit in with all of that."

"Taylor, please just listen for a second, would you?" he pleaded. "Things have changed for me. I have a new baby now, and...well, I've made a lot of mistakes. I realize that."

You think? She managed to keep the sarcasm to herself.

"But I don't want to push you and Ben out of my life. There is no one that can replace you to me."

"Pretty sure there's a little someone who weighs seven pounds and two ounces down the hall that's basically the definition of my replacement." Yeah, she had some vitriol in her voice. But he *deserved* it.

"Taylor, come on. She's your half-sister. And Kayla is going to be your stepmom when we get married in the summer."

Oh, okay. First comes affair, then baby, *then* they get married. *Gotcha.* Then they'd live in the house where the Parker family once lived. They'd raise Brooklyn in the same rooms, no doubt adding her name to that special closet wall in the den where they'd measured and marked Ben and Taylor's heights and Mom had written words to describe their personalities at each age.

Resentment and jealousy and disappointment mixed like a bad cocktail hitting her gut.

"I'm just hoping..." Dad sighed, sounding more vulnerable than she'd ever heard him. "I'm hoping to patch things up with you and Ben before that happens. Especially you. I know you and your mother are close and I respect that, but it doesn't mean you can't have a relationship with me. Or Brooklyn. Or even Kayla. We're still your family, too."

Releasing the cats, Taylor stood up, walking over to the window, her second-story loft-style apartment giving her a lovely view of Merritt Island and the Indian River, calm and glassy before the sunrise.

Emotions rolled over her as her fingers grazed the textured sheers she'd hung after moving in here, gritting her teeth as he spoke about family—as though it meant anything to him.

And now with Mom's baby...whoa. That made this whole *family* thing a thousand times more complicated.

But she sure as heck wasn't going to tell Dad that.

"Tay?" Max asked when her silence lasted too long.

"I don't know, Dad."

"Why don't you and Ben come see your new baby sister, huh? Sometime next week or...or whenever you can. It would mean the world, Taylor, and we could, you know, start over."

Something in his voice sounded...soft. Not the same nasty, selfish man who'd chosen fun over his family and left them all in the dust as he forged his new life. No, he sounded like the father she remembered from childhood. The one who bought ice cream cones after school and taught her how to shoot a basketball in the front yard.

She'd loved that guy. But she was a kid then, and

didn't really know how off-kilter his moral compass really was.

"I'll think about it. I've got to go," she said quickly. "Congrats again."

"Okay, think about it. Thanks, Tay."

"Bye, Dad."

On a sigh, she sat on the bed and dropped her head in her hands, trying to understand it all.

Babies...for *both* her parents? How? Well, obviously, she knew *how*. But why? And what was she supposed to do? Act like it was normal that *both* her parents wanted... new families?

Even as she thought that, she knew, on some level, it was wrong. Mom hadn't tried to get pregnant, but she and Ethan, her fiancé...

She grunted. Yes, Mom was young, only forty-three. But still. There were just some things she didn't want to think about.

She pulled on a warm robe and slid her feet into a pair of leopard-print slippers, bracing to break Dad's news to Mom.

She tiptoed into the living room, fully expecting Mom to be sound asleep on the sofa where she'd left her last night, but instead she was up, curled in the corner of the sectional, reading her phone.

"Oh, hey, Mama. You're up." Taylor walked over to the galley kitchen, squinting at the sunlight pouring through the two windows. "I'd offer you coffee, but I don't have decaf and I'm pretty sure regular coffee is a pregnancy no-no."

"You'd be right about that," Sam said, punctuating the words with a nervous sigh. "Along with eight million other things, according to this Reddit thread I'm on."

Taylor made a steaming mug of coffee and sat next to her mother, craning her neck to read the screen. "You're on a subreddit called 'Geriatric pregnancies'?"

"Uh-huh." Sam nodded, her eyes wide. "There are a lot more risks at my age, and things I need to worry about, and..."

"Okay." Taylor reached out and gently lowered the phone away from Sam's face, giving her a smile. "Let's just stay away from Reddit rabbit holes for the time being, Samantha Sweeney. You've been pregnant twice before, and we turned out okay. Well, I did, at least. Jury's still out on Ben."

Sam chuckled. "I'm just nervous. This is the last thing in the world I expected to happen. I still can't believe it, Tay."

"Yeah. You and me both." Taylor sipped her coffee.

She wasn't *mad* at her mother, not really. On some level, she was really happy for her, and Ethan, who'd never had kids. But she couldn't help but feel a bit... perturbed. Don't people Mom and Dad's age know how *not* to get pregnant?

Not that the new baby would be anything but a blessing to the whole family. Even so, did both of Taylor's parents really have to go and have new babies later in life? Were she and Ben really not enough for either of them?

"Tay." Sam turned to her daughter, placing a hand on

her knee. "I know this is a lot to process, and I know it's got to be strange for you."

"Almost as strange as the fact that Dad called me this morning," she said softly, knowing this would be a difficult conversation under the best of circumstances. With Mom and her "geriatric pregnancy" search?

"What?" Sam drew back, her jaw falling open. "I thought I heard you talking to someone, I assumed it was Andre."

"Nope. Dad called."

"And you...answered?"

"Shocking, I know. But given the fact that it was five in the morning, I assumed there was a good reason for the wake-up call."

"And was there?"

Taylor looked at her mother, feeling a deep pang of sympathy for everything that Max Parker had put her through, and getting mad at her dad all over again. "Kayla had the baby," Taylor whispered.

"Oh...*oh*." Sam swallowed, nodding slowly. "Wow. The morning after I find out I'm going to have another baby of my own. How poetic."

More like how bizarre but, oh, Taylor was getting good at not speaking her thoughts this morning. "Yeah, so that happened. It's a girl, named Brooklyn."

"Sweet," Sam said, almost sounding like she meant it.

"He made some speech about how things are different now and he doesn't want to push Ben and me out of his life and wants us to come see the baby and... yada yada yada."

Sam sucked in a breath, glancing off toward the window as the words hit her and she processed them. "Wow. That's...wow."

"Yeah. I know." Taylor plucked at a thread on her robe, chewing at her lower lip.

"Are you going to?"

"I don't know. You know I've decided I want nothing to do with Dad and certainly don't want to forge a relationship with Kayla, but...the baby? It's not like three-hour-old Brooklyn ever wronged me. And she's as much my sibling as your little bun in the oven is going to be."

"That's very true." Sam pushed a lock of dark brown hair back, frowning a bit.

"What?" Taylor nudged her. "Say it."

Sam flicked her hand dismissively. "There's nothing to say, Tay. If you want to come to a good place with your father and find a way to have a relationship with him and your new half-sister, then I wholeheartedly encourage that."

"You do?" Taylor blinked.

"Of course I do. Forgiveness is powerful. Things change, life happens." She gave an apologetic smile. "At least that's what Ethan told me at three in the morning when I called him to unceremoniously announce he was going to be a father for the first time at forty-five." At Taylor's shocked look, she added, "I absolutely couldn't stand it. I had to tell him."

"What did he say?"

A slow smile pulled her mother's lips. "He cried happy tears. Promised to be the greatest dad ever. Was basically overjoyed and did his usual job of talking me off the ledge and convincing me this was the best thing since...ever."

"Oh, well, it is." Taylor sat back and drank her coffee, pondering it all. "I knew he'd be over the moon."

"I'm going over there in a bit to talk more. Unless... you need me to talk about Dad."

"What's to talk about? I'm not sure I want to mend that relationship. I'm not mad, just indifferent. And I have you, great enough for any two parents, not to mention the clan that just keeps growing in Cocoa Beach."

"You do have a big family here," Sam agreed.

And they were awesome people. Uncle John, her mother's older brother, had really become like a father figure to Taylor since she started working as an admin in his ad agency. Now she was a full-blown account executive and thriving, due in no small part to her uncle's confidence. She had fun and eccentric Aunt Julie, who was the new mayor of Cocoa Beach, and, of course, brilliant and driven Aunt Erica, the rocket scientist.

She had Grandma, Aunt Lori, Amber, a bunch of cousins, and Ben, her teenage brother, who'd really bloomed into a fine young man since they'd moved here. On top of all that? She had Andre Everett, her incredible boyfriend, whom Taylor adored more every day.

Honestly, she didn't need her scumbag of a father. But...the baby.

"I'm sorry, sweetie." Sam reached her hand out to

give Taylor's a loving squeeze. "This is a lot to put on your narrow shoulders."

"It's all good." Taylor straightened those shoulders as if to prove they could handle the weight. "I'm here for you, Mama. Whatever you need." She gave her mother a smile that only felt partially forced.

"I guess I'll need...everything. But at least I know I have you, and the family, and the world's best husband-to-be. Speaking of, do you mind if I skedaddle? He's dying to see me."

"Of course." Taylor reached out and gave her mom a loving hug, knowing this whole thing was going to take some getting used to, but nothing in this world could ever break their bond.

After Mom left, Taylor slumped down on the couch and buried her face in a throw pillow, trying to process the last twelve hours. It was all too much, so she was relieved when her phone vibrated with a call, and she saw Andre's name at the top of the screen.

Taylor answered with the first real smile on her face that day. "Hey, you."

"Morning, babe! I have some exciting news."

"Please don't tell me *you're* having a baby, too," she groaned jokingly.

Andre choked on a laugh. "Excuse me?"

"Long story."

"Care to talk about it over a celebratory coffee and chocolate croissant at Oceanside Cafe? Blackhawk Brewing's Cocoa Beach location got approval to put in a huge new back deck."

Taylor smiled, sitting up as her spirits and her boyfriend's voice lifted her. "That *is* good news! I'll meet you there in twenty."

"Can't wait. See you soon."

If one person in this world could calm Taylor Parker's spinning mind and ground her with laughter, support, and love, Andre Everett was the man for the job.

Chapter Two

Dottie

Jay Sweeney would call it a miracle. Dottie's husband, gone nearly two years now, had been given to hyperbole like that. Thinking of him, she smiled and bent over to pick up a tiny spec of dirt marring the otherwise perfect sand-toned hardwood floor of the Sweeney House lobby. But in this case, Jay wouldn't be wrong. The transformation of the family inn had been nothing short of miraculous.

With a sigh of pure satisfaction, Dottie scanned the inn's lobby to take in every detail of the nearly completed renovation that she and Sam had powered through for the last nine months.

Nine months! Had it been that long? The very length of time it took to grow a baby?

Yes, it had been exactly that long since her daughter had come home to Cocoa Beach with the goal of starting over after a heartbreaking divorce. Nine months since Sam persuaded Dottie to abandon her plan to sell the beachfront inn and cottage, and take her broken widow's heart somewhere away from Jay's memory. Nine hard and challenging—and fun—months and the reward for

their work was just as fulfilling as it would be to the
mother who'd just given birth.

With Sam's constant support and the love of all her
four adult children and her precious grandchildren,
Dottie had undertaken a monumental renovation of the
inn she and Jay had run for forty years. But Sweeney
House wasn't the only thing that had changed; the
process had helped Dottie heal and grow and transform
herself, inside and out.

With each passing day and every step along the way,
she could feel the fog of grief lift, replaced by hope and
optimism. She'd gone from feeling like an old and lonely
seventy-two-year-old widow to a healthy, happy woman
with a thriving business and a glorious family.

She took a few steps around the marble-topped
welcome desk to admire the grandfather clock that had
always stood exactly in this spot. The old, beat-up time-
piece that her husband had loved looked as different as
the rest of the place.

Sam's fiancé, Ethan, had used his carpentry skills to
refurbish and refinish the clock—and brought about
another change in the process when he'd found a birth
certificate and photo hidden in the back of the clock.
That ushered in a brand-new Sweeney offspring in the
form of Lori Caparelli, a child Jay had fathered before
he'd ever met Dottie.

Now, Dottie looked at the clock differently. Instead
of a source of pain when she thought about how much
Jay loved the old beast, she now saw the gorgeous
antique as the bearer of great news. Lori and her daugh-

ter, Amber, had easily captured Dottie's nurturing heart.

Since Lori had reconciled with her husband, Rick, and they moved here with Amber, a new branch of the family grew in Cocoa Beach, adding to the already solid Sweeney clan living in the small beach town.

"Another miracle," she whispered as she walked into the sunshine that poured through the glass doors and windows. On the other side was a stunning view of the beach from the sand to the horizon, the postcard vista enhanced by the darling cabana they'd built. That had been a spectacular addition—and the site of Sam's recent engagement.

Like the refurbished clock, the cabana would always represent change, possibilities, and, yes, miracles.

She turned and gazed across the small lobby, studying the double doors and hostess stand of Jay's American Bistro, the restaurant they'd literally fought City Hall to include on the property. That was the biggest change, and the irony was that the man they'd named the restaurant after had been no fan of change and had steadfastly refused the addition of an eatery at his "little B&B on the beach."

But this was another change that would be both profitable and exciting. Jay's American Bistro took Sweeney House from an aging but iconic Cocoa Beach landmark to a true destination for locals and tourists.

Warmed by the sun and the bright future ahead, Dottie continued her personal tour of the lobby, pausing at an oversized mirror placed to reflect the light and add visual space to the seating area. Looking into it, she smiled, patting the silver curls that her daughter Erica had encouraged her to wear around her face instead of pinned back.

Maybe it was because she was backlit by the sun, but Dottie liked the way she looked now. With some guidance from Taylor, her vivacious granddaughter, she'd gotten back into wearing a little makeup. She'd even secretly watched some tutorials for "women over sixty" to smooth away some lines and accentuate natural beauty.

Fit after almost a year of the physicality of renovations and her morning yoga classes on the beach with Lori, Dottie had improved her looks as well as her life. While not anyone's definition of a great beauty, there was a light in her eyes that came with inner peace and finally, *finally,* accepting the fact that her beloved Jay was gone and waiting for her in heaven.

Right now, at this moment in time—a month from a grand opening and on the precipice of something very exciting—Dottie truly felt like she'd been a witness to a miracle.

The sound of the double front doors opening brought her out of her reverie and forced her to turn from the mirror. She blinked in surprise at the sight of Sam and Ethan, arm in arm, entering Sweeney House on a gale of laughter with smiles as bright as the early spring sun.

"Well, look who's here." She strode toward them with open arms for a hug.

As she inched back, she smiled at Ethan, realizing it was the middle of the week and high school was in session, and there was no woodworking left for him to do at the inn. "I wasn't expecting you today, Ethan, but how nice to see you."

"I got a sub for my morning classes," he said. "So we could talk to you."

"Oh, okay." She looked from one to the other, suddenly sensing what her teenaged grandson, Ben, would call "a shift in the Force." Something was different with this couple. Something good, based on the glint in Sam's eyes and the smile on Ethan's face. "Oh, my goodness, you eloped."

"No!" they both assured her.

"Oh, good!" She pressed her hand over her chest, inexplicably relieved.

"You don't want us to get married, Mom?" Sam asked, misreading the reaction.

"Of course I do, but if you elope and we don't get to host the intimate wedding that you planned here at the inn, I'd be devastated. I know it's not until the fall, but I'm so excited about that."

They exchanged a quick look that spoke volumes. A look that Dottie could not read.

"Um, yeah," Sam said. "I'm sure you'll have plenty of lovely events like that here."

Dottie felt a frown pull. "But not yours?"

"Mom, are you in the middle of anything right now?" Sam asked, leading her toward the sitting area. "We want to talk to you."

"I was just doing the final punch list, although the lobby is done. I did schedule an interview with a chef, since that hire, along with one more housekeeper, will round out our staff. I know you said you wanted me to handle the first-round interviews this week, but..." Her voice faded out as she took in the expression on Sam's face.

Something was on her mind and it had nothing to do with the inn.

"What's going on?" she asked bluntly as she dropped into a chair and faced Sam and Ethan side by side on a love seat.

Once more, they exchanged that silent, million-words look that couples shared. Normally, that would make Dottie experience a pang of missing Jay but today, it didn't. Maybe it was the peace she'd just been thinking about, or maybe she was too curious to feel sadness.

"Mom." Sam reached to take her hand. "We have some surprising and exciting news."

Her mind whirred. If not an elopement, then—

"We're going to have a baby." The words tumbled out of Ethan's mouth as if he simply couldn't hold them back. "I mean, Sam is. She's pregnant. Sorry, Sam, I should have let you—but I'm so happy—"

Sam laughed at that and leaned into him, saying something, but none of the words actually registered in Dottie's mind. Instead, all she could do was gasp and cover her mouth as the pure joy nearly escaped in the form of a happy shriek from her throat.

"You're pregnant?" she exclaimed, squeezing Sam's hand.

"It must have been my last egg," she joked, glancing at Ethan. "And he, uh, scrambled it."

For a moment, Dottie merely looked from one to the other, overwhelmed with so many emotions she couldn't capture a single one and hold on to it. Joy and surprise and anticipation and disbelief and, of course, she waited for the pang of pain that Jay wouldn't be here to welcome another grandchild.

But that didn't happen. Instead, she felt nothing but unmitigated delight at the idea of Sam having another baby.

"How do you feel, honey? How far along are you?" she asked, trying to come back to Earth and get pragmatic about the challenges that came with this news.

"Great. Shocked. Elated. Terrified. And I think I'm about six or seven weeks, based on our best guess. Mom, I just found out a few hours ago. I haven't seen a doctor or anything. But we had to tell you first. Well, Taylor knows, too."

Dottie beamed from one happy face to the other. "I'm honored, you two. And excited. So, you're due in..." She lifted her hand to count months.

"October, I imagine."

Dottie's brows lifted. "Right in time for that fall wedding we'd planned."

"Yeah, well..." Sam lifted her shoulders. "Could we move up the timeline, Mom?"

"I don't want to wait," Ethan added, taking Sam's hand. "But we know you wanted to have the wedding here."

"Any chance we could pull that off?" Sam asked, squishing her face like a little kid asking for the impossible. "In, say, a month? I know that's when we planned the grand opening but—"

"That will *be* the grand opening!" Dottie exclaimed, practically jumping out of the chair. "We can do it, Sam! We could have a ceremony on the beach, then host a small reception inside."

"Are you sure?" Sam pressed. "That's not a lot of time."

"How fancy a wedding do you want?"

"Not fancy at all," Sam assured her. "Just family, close friends, good food, and some champagne. Well, not for me. I'll take sparkling cider. But I'd love to wear something...not maternity. I have no idea how fast I'll pop."

Ethan's face lit up. "You're going to be so gorgeous pregnant, Sam."

"He says that now," she joked, giving Dottie a look. "Wait until he sees me the size of a house."

"Baby girl, you deserve this," she said to Sam. "You both do."

"Another kid?" Sam raised a dubious brow. "I already have the two best kids in the world. But..." She leaned into Ethan. "Now I'm going to have a little math geek boy who can do carpentry on the side."

"Or a beautiful brunette princess with her mama's eyes," Ethan said.

Dottie smiled at the banter, but her mind was spinning. "How much time do we have for this wedding?"

"Let's pick a day that works for you, Dottie," Ethan

said. "Of course we want the sooner, the better, but you and Sam have to feel confident that the inn is ready."

"If I had a chef?" Dottie shrugged. "I think we could do it in a month."

"I'm here for you, Mom," Sam said. "Whatever you need. Punch list, push the last of the contractors, find that chef, anything."

"The chef is key, so we don't have to cater a dinner," Dottie said. "But I'll handle staff and the last of the punch list. You get everything else coordinated for a wedding, tell the family, and, oh my goodness, rest!"

She laughed. "Yeah, better sleep now, because come October? Sleep is a thing of the past." She gave Ethan a teasing look. "You ready for that, Daddy?"

"So ready," he assured her.

Dottie clapped her hands. "Oh, this is exciting. The first weekend in April are always the most beautiful days of the year here. It's a perfect time for a wedding."

For a moment, Sam and Ethan just looked at each other, and Dottie could feel another shift in their world.

"We're getting married in a month," he whispered, the elation in his voice unmistakable as he leaned closer for a kiss.

They talked some more, and did a quick walk-through of the restaurant, sizing up the space for a small reception.

"You have to nail down that chef," Sam said as they were leaving. "He's the key to pulling it off, so I hope that interview goes well. Who's coming in to interview today?"

"Somebody from up north who calls himself Chef Frank," Dottie said. "I recall his resume being very impressive but vague. I'll let you know after I meet with him."

They kissed, hugged, and said goodbye, leaving Dottie to head off to her office to start planning, but she wasn't quite sure her feet touched the floor.

Sam was having a baby.

She smiled up to the ceiling, shuttering her eyes. "You'd call it a miracle, Jay, and this would be no exaggeration."

FEELING like the interview should take place in the restaurant, Dottie arranged the two chairs with a pot of coffee and cups and ice water at the best table in Jay's American Bistro, with a beautiful view of the water. A review of Chef Frank's resume left her with two huge questions and she'd launch the interview with those.

One, why didn't he mention specific employers' names, only vague references to "a major New York restaurant" or "a Michelin-starred eatery." Was it because she couldn't or shouldn't check references? That was concerning, of course, but she was just as worried about issue number two.

Why would a chef who'd had this much experience want to run a small beach restaurant attached to a family-owned inn? Why not go down to Miami Beach for more Michelin stars or celebrity hangouts?

Once more, she flipped through the paper resume she'd printed out because the electronic version was... electronic. She was old-fashioned like that. The very thought added yet another layer of uncertainty. Would this whole operation be too low-tech for some hip guy who'd worked at big-name places? Would *she* be too old and outdated?

She glanced down at the resume again, her gaze landing on the name "Chef Frank" at the top. No last name? Really? But what really mattered were the years— nearly thirty of them—working in the food business. He had to be at least fifty, more if he didn't list the jobs from his earliest years.

She looked around, trying to see the place through the eyes of an applicant. The fifty-seat restaurant had a luxurious feel but retained the warmth of a coastal bed-and-breakfast. There was a very small bar, a row of booths, and four-top tables, plus a few strategically placed along the windows. Outside the French doors, a few more tables under an awning offered some al fresco seating that she knew would be popular on ideal winter evenings.

No. She refused to be ashamed of her modest but lovely bistro. Whoever got the job as chef would be lucky to work here, and as long as they got along, all would be well.

Holding that thought, she poured herself a cup of coffee, topped it with cream, and lifted it to her lips to sip just as she heard a man behind her clear his throat.

"Hello. Are you Dorothy Sweeney?"

She turned, blinked, and darn near spewed her coffee.

Was that Franklin Fox, renowned chef and Food Network superstar? Was her one and only celebrity crush standing in the doorway with one silver lock touching a dark brow and a look of pure mischief in deep brown eyes?

She nearly choked on the coffee but somehow got it down, already knowing there had been a huge mistake and a man who'd had his own cooking show, owned multiple restaurants, and was an Iron Chef would *not* be flipping burgers in Jay's American Bistro.

But for one brief and shining millisecond, she imagined what a game-changer that would be.

"Yes, hello," she said, standing and stepping closer. "I'm Dottie."

"Ah, then I'm in the right place." She noticed he wore a white linen shirt that accentuated his tanned skin, dress pants, and carried a silk case that she instantly recognized as what would be used to hold chef's knives. "I'm Franklin Fox."

She stared as he came closer, unable to miss the fact that he was even more good-looking than he'd been on *The Flavor Fox*, which she'd watched religiously. She could still hear Jay teasing her when the show came on, referring to Franklin Fox as her "TV boyfriend" whenever the show started.

She did the quick mental math, determining that Franklin Fox was likely just around her age, perhaps a year or two younger. He didn't look a day over sixty-five, though, and a young sixty-five at that.

"I know who you are," she said, clearing her head enough to take the handshake he offered. "And I'm sure you're in the wrong place."

"Jay's American Bistro?" He glanced around. "This is cute. I like the vibe." Then he looked back at her, leveling eyes the color of dark chocolate right through her. "And you are the owner I'm meeting today?"

"I'm...I'm..."

"Dorothy," he reminded her with a smile. "Like *The Wizard of Oz*."

She laughed softly. "I just go by Dottie," she told him. "And I don't know what you expected when you answered my ad, but I'm sure this isn't it."

His eyes flickered with surprise. "Am I in Sweeney House, on Cocoa Beach, and this is the inn's restaurant, just finished and opening soon?"

She nodded, vaguely aware that his voice was low and soothing, and that had always been one of the reasons she loved his cooking show.

"Then here I am, your new chef." He chuckled and lifted a shoulder. "Assuming you like me."

"Oh, I like you," she blurted out, then felt blood rush to her face at the admission. "I mean, I like your work. I'm a huge fan but I had no idea you were Chef Frank and if I had, I would never have been so presumptuous..." Her voice faded out as he walked by her, listening but just as interested in the surroundings and the view.

"What a location," he said. "Ideal, in fact. It's exactly what I'm looking for."

Of course. He wanted to buy it and add the place to his extensive portfolio of restaurants and businesses.

Disappointment weaved through Dottie's chest. "Oh, it's not for sale. We must have gotten our signals—"

"I don't want to buy it." He smiled and invited her to sit back down as he pulled out the other chair. "I want to be your chef."

He...*what*?

"Oh, I don't think so, Frank...er, Chef Fox. Or Chef Frank. Franklin." She gave a self-conscious laugh. "I mean, you're...you. Franklin Fox. You're an icon, a legend, and...and..." *So darn handsome.* "And way too accomplished for the job," she said instead.

"Is anyone too accomplished, Dorothy?" He sat down and rocked on the two back legs, crossing his arms and looking so cool it almost hurt to stare at him. But stare she did, slowly lowering herself into the seat across from him, not even sure this moment could be real.

"I *know*...you," she said, adding that nervous laugh. "You're famous."

"You know my PR company's image of me," he corrected. "And they no longer work for me. And I no longer own any restaurants, run any kitchens, or star in any TV shows. I'm here, a resident of Cocoa Beach, and I'm looking for a fresh start in a new restaurant that won't consume me, but still excite me. Is that you? Or, more specifically, your restaurant?"

He cocked a brow with just enough swagger to make her heart do something stupid. What was *that* all about?

She shook her head to clear the stars in her eyes and see this situation for what it was: crazy. "I doubt I could afford you, Chef."

"You name the price, Dorothy, and I'll agree to it."

Now she was really confused and had a hard time hiding it. "I don't understand why you'd want to work here. Isn't it quite a come-down from your life? I mean, I don't know everything about you, but I am a fan and I've watched your show for years and I know you own your own restaurants, have a place in the Hamptons and Miami—"

"Show is over, Hamptons is rented, Miami is on the market, and I sold my restaurants. Now, I live in a beach house about a mile down the road and I'm looking for a small restaurant where I can have fun cooking, maybe mentor some younger chefs, and help build a clientele without having my name on the door. That means I can take some days off, keep reasonable hours, and..." He took a breath. "Be a grandfather."

That last one threw her completely. "Oh...are you new to that?"

He considered the question, settling into his seat. "My grandson is fourteen, so not 'new' in the technical sense. But I haven't spent enough time with him—and by enough, I mean any. I'd like that to change." He winced. "I'm not exactly a, um, textbook grandpa."

She smiled, searching his face, getting past the good looks to catch a glimpse of something she would never have guessed would be hiding deep in a man as talented and famous as Franklin Fox—insecurity.

"Not sure there is anything 'textbook' about grand-parenting, which is as easy as it is fun. And I say that as a woman with seven and another one, I just learned, on the way."

He lifted a shoulder. "Not easy for everyone, Dorothy."

No one called her that—not anyone, ever, not once. But something in the way he said it kept her from correcting him.

"Trust me, grandparenting is a breeze compared to being an Iron Chef."

His eyes flicked as if he disagreed, then he slid his gaze toward the ocean, thoughtful for a moment. When he turned back to her, she could see that same air of vulnerability and self-doubt that had no place at all in the eyes of a man like Franklin Fox. But there it was, and, for some reason, it touched her heart.

"Would you like to offer high-end selections and a unique menu, attracting locals and guests to the loca-tion?" he asked, clearly changing the subject.

"Of course. That's exactly what we hope this restau-rant will do."

"Then I'm your man."

Her man? Her heart did that stupid flip again, prob-ably excited by the very idea of a celebrity chef at the inn. "I think you might be the man for a much bigger, more important restaurant."

"Big and important is overrated," he said. "I'm

looking for small, homey, easy to run, and a fun place to try some very exciting recipes. I'd love to help you build a following, get a juicy reservation wait-list, and establish Jay's American Bistro as a star on the beach. In return, I'd like a sous-chef of my choice and a decent staff. I want to set the menu, drive the team, try new dishes, and be able to take the weekends off and leave when there's a soccer game or school event."

As she opened her mouth to respond, he held out his hand.

"Look, I know you're looking for a full-time chef, but I can do the chef job in half the time or less. I want a place to work, and I need to anchor my life with a working kitchen. In return, I need to...I need time for family."

"No one understands that better than I do," she assured him, searching his face, hearing the determination in his voice but wondering...was it genuine?

As if he sensed her doubt, he leaned over the table and pinned her with his gaze. "I can't survive if I don't have a kitchen to run and recipes to create and a dining room full of paying customers," he said. "I need those things like other people need air and sleep. But no more cameras, no more interviews, no more cooking contests, and no more...attention. I'd prefer no one know who your chef is, and come for the food. Can you live with that?"

If it were true? Yes. But what if this was just a load of hooey, as Jay would say? It sure seemed too good to be true.

"I suppose I could," she said, purposely vague.

"And me taking family time when my family needs me, assuming I put a capable sous-chef in place?" he added.

If they were going to pull off a grand opening and a wedding? She needed an amazing and skilled chef. After that? Well, if he was really too good to be true, then she'd find someone else.

"Yes," she replied. "As a woman who is a grand-mother and mother first, and an innkeeper second, yes."

He sat up straight and reached his hand across the table. "Then do we have a deal?"

She hesitated. "Don't you want to see the kitchen first?"

His eyes glinted as he slayed her with a charming smile. "I've seen enough to know I could be very happy here."

Holding his gaze, she took his hand and shook. "Then welcome aboard, Chef Frank."

"Thank you, Dorothy. I think you'll be very glad you made this decision."

She hoped so. After all, what did she have to lose?

Chapter Three

Julie

The sting of last night's rant on Facebook was still fresh when Julie Sweeney opened the door to City Hall and walked to her office. After a month of being the mayor of Cocoa Beach, she really should be used to the trolls who had opinions about whether or not the single mother troubadour who used to scratch together a living making music was worthy of being the chief executive of the small town where she'd grown up.

She was.

She knew it, many on her staff knew it, the majority of voters who elected her knew it, and even the guy she beat knew it. But the need to *prove* it burned in Julie's chest every day when she came to work.

During her first month on the job, she'd made some small changes and big decisions. She'd built a working staff of trustworthy people, hiring and appointing people slowly over the past few weeks, but she'd inherited others and was still creating relationships with everyone.

She took home mountains of files to familiarize herself with mayoral issues and duties, scheduled back-to-back meetings to address what felt like an endless array of problems, and spent every waking minute with the single goal of improving life for the citizens of this sleepy beach community.

And still the loud-mouthed locals trolled on social media, which only made her more determined to succeed.

Stepping into the reception area of the mayor's office, she greeted some staffers, said good morning to the deputy mayor—a man she'd really grown to like as her second-in-command—and stopped to check in with the city manager.

But it was when she rounded the corner to her over-sized office and saw Amber Kittle, her niece and now administrative assistant, that she truly felt comfortable. Amber had been her campaign manager and proved herself to be invaluable, as well as the safest of safe places to fall when the demands of the day wore Julie down. But Amber was seven months pregnant, so that soft place to fall would disappear soon.

In the meantime, Julie felt blessed to have the young woman—who was not only family and a friend, but also had deep political experience—by her side.

"Jules!" Amber called, turning from her computer screen, her sweet face bright and her stomach kind of massive as she stood. "I have the most amazing news!"

"I hope it's that we're closing the Facebook page," Julie muttered, only realizing then how much the negative press was getting her down.

"Please," Amber scoffed. "Those keyboard warriors mean nothing. Anyway, wait until you hear this great news."

Julie led the way into her office, hanging her bag behind the door and walking to a desk the expanse of a queen-sized bed. Amber had laid out a schedule, key documents, a few resumes, some talking points for a meeting, and—God bless the girl—a double espresso with almond milk just because.

"You're a saint," Julie said, seizing it and dropping into the chair. "Hit me with this great news, girl."

Amber perched on the edge of the guest chair, her brown eyes bright and a smile looking ready to bloom.

"Two words, Jules. Two wonderful words: Wave Haven."

Julie frowned at the words, which of course she knew, but couldn't put into context. "Wave Haven as in the music festival in Tampa every year? I've been there and have the fried brain cells to prove it."

"Wave Haven as in the music festival that was just moved to Cocoa Beach and will be held on our pier, at our beach, with our local businesses reaping the benefits of ten thousand people."

She sucked in a breath, eyes wide. "What? Wave Haven moved here? That festival has been in Tampa for as long as I can remember."

"Not this year. Apparently, there was a shakeup and scheduling error, along with a change in Tampa's local government, and some new noise laws. Bottom line, they booted Wave Haven under pressure from the people who run Gasparilla and—"

"Geez. Is everything political?"

"Yes, and thank goodness, because one of the local

promoters worked some magic and got the festival here next month. Apparently, the previous mayor, Linus Pemberton, had signed some vague permitting agreements in conjunction with the city of Tampa in case this were to ever happen with any of their major events. And it has!"

"Next month?" She gasped. "Like in April?"

"First weekend."

Julie's jaw dropped as the news finally sank in.

"This is it!" she proclaimed, shooting to her feet. "This is the big win I needed. A music festival! I mean, if that isn't in my wheelhouse, what is?"

"Fair warning," Amber said. "It's a lot of work."

Julie dropped back to her seat. "I'm not afraid of that."

Amber nodded. "We can do it, you have the staff, you'll find the money, and I know you have the desire," she said. "But it's going to put everything else on the backburner for a while."

"Backburn it all," she said, underscoring that by sliding the pile of papers to the side of her desk. "Tell me everything about the festival and what needs to be done. Food trucks, dance stages, water stations, big speakers, and free parking for everyone." At Amber's look, she laughed. "Okay, no free parking. I need to think like a mayor, not a festivalgoer. Speaking of, who's the headline act?"

"The Space Kittens."

Julie's jaw dropped. "They're big!"

"Evidently, the promoter used the fact that Cocoa

Beach is in the heart of the Space Coast to get them here."

"Whatever it takes! Bliss loves that band," she said, referring to her teenaged daughter. "Nothing like a good all-girl band! This whole thing is going to be a blast!" She winked. "See what I did there? Blast. Space. Get it?"

Amber laughed. "Yes, I get it, and yes, it's going to be fun, but job number one is public safety."

"Absolutely!" Julie agreed, pressing her hands together. "How do we do that? Please don't tell anyone I asked that question."

Amber laughed. "You know you can ask me anything and I'll tell you how—with the help of Chief Brian Wilkes, who is the head of Cocoa Beach's finest."

Amber rolled her eyes. "Ah, yes. King Brian."

"Just *chief*...of police. He's a Cocoa Beach staple and you've already met him at your swearing in and the first all-staff meeting with your direct reports, of which he is one."

Julie shook her head. "I met him before that," she said to Amber. "But you gotta take the Way Back Machine to Cocoa Beach High School, class of '93. Brian Wilkes was the star quarterback, valedictorian, Homecoming king, and one really mediocre saxophone player."

"You knew Chief Wilkes in high school?"

"I knew *of* him," she said. "I seriously doubt he had any idea who I was, although we had one music class together. But we did not hang out in the same crowd. He was...popular, good-looking, cool, and squeaky clean and on his way to some big school to play football. I was unknown, skinny, more hot than cool, and on my way to living on a tour bus with a guitar in my hand. He was friends with John, of course," she said, referring to her far more sociable twin brother. "But not me. He was...*that guy*."

Amber laughed at that. "I get that he'd be *that guy*, based on what I've seen and heard. And *that guy* is the head of your police department, so maybe you should not remind him that his saxophone playing was only mediocre."

"Mediocre was being kind. Please, it was the one thing King Brian *couldn't* do. He even had the perfect head cheerleader girlfriend, Lanie Nordstrom." She curled her lip. "Five-foot-nothing of sheer adorable perfection. I bet he married her, popped out five perfect kids, and lives in a big house with a picket fence."

"You can ask him all about it when he comes in here this morning."

"Today?" Julie frowned and looked down at her schedule. "I'm meeting with him today? Why?"

"Wave Haven, which, as I told you, will push everything else to the side."

"Okay. What's the meeting about?" Julie asked.

"A big, beautiful budget request," she said. "His staff will handle the Wave Haven security details, but he's going to want you to find the money to fund it. And that means you'll have to rob Peter to pay...What did you call him? King Brian?"

"Not to his face. That's just what the stoners and

slackers called him. The rest of the school just bowed when he walked by."

"Practice your bowing, Jules, because he'll be here soon."

Julie nodded, putting her brain back in the present. "What do I need to prepare for a meeting with him?"

"Just listen to what he wants and needs, and promise him he'll get it. Then we'll all work together to figure out how."

Julie huffed out a breath of relief. "Amber, I would be totally lost without you."

The other woman lifted a brow. "Better start interviewing, because I'm eight weeks from delivery and I may not want to work the last two."

Julie didn't even want to think about that. "Just take it easy, sit as much as possible, eat healthy, and know that you're irreplaceable."

"No one is—" She picked up her phone as it rang. "Oh. King Brian is in the lobby."

Jules narrowed her eyes. "Don't call him that or I will."

Laughing, Amber scooped up her tablet and some outgoing mail from the box, blew a kiss, and headed out the door.

Julie stood, smoothed her flowing, patterned skirt, and forgot all about Brian Wilkes and his bad sax playing. All that mattered now was that this music festival went off without a hitch and her little town looked good to the world and made a lot of money. She needed a win, and

Wave Haven had all the hallmarks of Mayor Sweeney's first big victory.

WHEN AMBER BROUGHT Chief Wilkes into her office, Julie came around the desk and shook his hand, noticing again that the cute boy had aged into a handsome fifty-year-old man. Not her type, of course, with close-cropped salt-and-pepper hair, a broad chest covered with the official stars and bars of his police uniform, and a shave so close it was a miracle he had skin left.

She had to look up to meet the gaze of the man who was easily over six feet, and when she did, she caught his silver-blue eyes flutter over her as they shook hands and said hello. She was suddenly aware that *her* work uniform was a floral skirt that almost kissed her flat sandals and a silk shell with sleeves short enough that the wing of her butterfly tattoo peeked out.

She remembered the trolls on Facebook who mentioned those tattoos as often as possible. Was he on their side? She had no idea, since she'd inherited him as chief of police.

"Thank you for coming in, Chief Wilkes," she said, gesturing for him to join her at the oval-shaped conference table by the bank of windows. "I understand we have a big event coming to town."

He took a seat across from her, sitting directly so the sun shone on his face, which really did look good for his age. Probably a lifetime of clean living and the love of

Lanie kept him healthy. She resisted the urge to check his left ring finger.

"And that has you smiling," he noted, opening a tablet computer.

"Actually, I was thinking of..." She made a little whimper, because she probably shouldn't take this conversation back all those years, but how could she resist? "You probably don't remember this, but we went to high school together."

"Of course I remember," he said. "We were in Mr. Masterson's music class senior year where you sang like a bird and I played the sax. Badly."

She choked a laugh, weirdly relieved to have that out in the open. "Not *that* badly."

He lifted a dark brow with a dubious look. "Fortunately, I didn't pursue music, at least not professionally, like you did."

"I did, but no more. Music is merely a hobby now, and my heart is in City Hall."

He nodded, holding her gaze before looking down at the screen to tap it to life.

"Shall we talk budget?" he asked. "The police presence at this event will come under that indescribably gooey line item called 'contingency and unexpected expenses,' and you'll have to work mayoral magic to find the money."

"Oh, yes, of course." She scooted in and crossed her arms. "How much will all this fun cost the city of Cocoa Beach?"

He gave a soft grunt. "Fun for festivalgoers. Potential

nightmare for the police." He turned his iPad toward her. "This is the bottom line, but we can certainly discuss ways to reduce that number."

She looked down at the spreadsheet—her nemesis—and tried to find which of those bazillion squares would be considered the bottom line. It was just a sea of numbers.

As if he sensed she was lost, he pointed to one line on the screen. "That's what you need," he said. "The biggest number, but it doesn't take into account parking revenue, which will help offset the costs."

Whoa, it *was* a big number.

"Okay." She squinted at it and tried to think of where she could get that amount of money. When she looked up at him, she was surprised to find him staring at her with a funny look on his face. "Is there more?"

"No, I was just thinking..." His face deepened with the slightest flush, making him suddenly seem more human and vulnerable. "I always knew you were going places."

"Me?" she scoffed. "I can't believe you even knew my name in high school. After all, you were—"

"King Brian," he supplied with an eyeroll. "Trust me, I've heard the nickname."

She angled her head in a silent apology, since it was obvious from his tone that the name wasn't a source of pride. "Well, you were, uh, high-profile. I was one of the kids in the background. You were the one going to a big college. Which one was it again? Alabama? Auburn?"

"Georgia Tech, but I left after the first year. I got

injured and couldn't play ball and ended up coming back here, joined the Marines, and then law enforcement."

She searched his face, a little surprised by the resume. "And married Lanie Nordstrom, I bet."

All humor left his eyes. "Actually, yes, I did marry her, but it, uh, didn't last."

"Oh. I'm sorry. You were always such a celebrity couple."

He snorted. "Like most celebrities, we imploded. Made it ten years, but then..." He shrugged. "I think she finally accepted that she didn't marry the next Tom Brady. Or maybe she didn't accept that, which would explain our divorce."

The subtext of sadness touched her heart and made her remember that she never liked Lanie Nordstrom anyway. "Did you have any kids?" she asked, feeling a need to get the smile back on his face.

It worked. He beamed. "One. A son, Davis, who followed my footsteps into the Marines. He's twenty-five."

"Aww, that's nice. I have a daughter."

"I know." At her surprised look, he added, "You're the mayor. Got a lot of ink around here during the campaign."

This time, she was the one who rolled her eyes. "Oh, yeah, and nearly lost the election over an old picture of me smoking pot." She cringed. "Probably shouldn't bring that up with the chief of police."

He just smiled, and it softened his features and put a light in his eyes. "Well, it didn't cost you the election, no matter how hard Trent Braddock worked to ruin your name. You earned the votes fair and square."

"There are still plenty of naysayers, believe me. Half the time I'm scared to open Facebook to see today's anti-mayor tirade."

"There's always a loudmouth," he said. "Ignore them."

She smiled at that, grateful for the support. "Thank you, Chief."

"Hey, old music class buddies have to stick together. You can call me Brian."

"And I'm Julie," she countered, glancing down at the screen when the eye contact lasted one heartbeat too long. "So, this is the amount you need?" she asked, all business again. "It is awfully high."

"To do this event right, we need all hands, overtime pay, and lots of equipment to cover perimeter patrol, crowd control, health and safety, emergency preparation, criminal activity, drunk and disorderlies, and, of course, the very biggest potential problem at an event of this magnitude."

She tried to imagine what that would be, digging into her personal experience at music festivals. "Drugs?"

"Parking violations."

She gave a little laugh. "Oh, yeah, our secret weapon for covering the costs."

"Bingo." He flipped the tablet closed. "That's really all I needed. I'll submit the official budget to your office and if you have questions, you can ask me anytime."

"I really want this event to be a huge success," she

confided as they stood. "If only to shut up the, uh, loud-mouths, as you call them."

"Whatever you do, don't back off and let them own the page. Get out there and talk to people. I've been in Cocoa Beach long enough to know that the locals want to hear from their leaders all the time."

She frowned, considering how to do that. "Like press conferences?" She grimaced. "I really hate those."

"Of course, because the media is trying to trip you up. I see a bunch of small Florida town stuff on my feed because of my job. I saw one mayor get on and do a regular two-minute update with a cute name like *A Minute with the Mayor* and it struck me as a proactive way to get your message out and be louder than them."

She inched back, instantly liking the idea. "Just get in front of my phone and...talk?"

"Just be you, Mayor...er, Julie. Maybe bring in some staff person to explain a new program or answer questions. But you don't even need that. You have a pretty engaging personality and once you become a living, breathing human, the clowns might stop flappin' their lips and blowin' hot air."

She laughed, more at the good ol' boy way he said it than the idea.

"I could call it *The Mayor's Minute*." She rolled the idea around in her head, loving it like the perfect lyric for a song she was writing. "That's genius!"

"Hey, I stole it from another town, so not genius."

The humility touched her. "Will you be my first guest?"

"Nah, I'm not good on camera."

"Are you kidding? A big, tall, handsome chief of police? You're right out of central casting!"

A soft flush deepened his cheeks and right in that minute, King Brian seemed incredibly...normal. And she liked it.

"Thank you for coming in," she said again. "I will find your budget, and if you see me on the city Facebook page and don't like what you hear, you only have yourself and your good ideas to blame."

"Happy to help, Julie."

"You certainly did, Brian." As she walked him to the door, she had one more question about the past. "So, do you still play the sax?"

He gave a deep laugh that came from his chest. "You mean do I still play the sax so that it sounds like a sheep is being strangled?"

"It wasn't that bad. Okay, maybe a little, but the musician in me is curious."

"Yes, I do play," he said. "After my divorce, I decided to take lessons—much needed—and the music gives me great pleasure. I get together with a few of my cop buddies and we have a little jazz garage band, too."

She eased back, jaw loose. "That's so cool. Let me know if you ever need a singer."

Something brightened in his eyes. "I will. And I'll send that budget over this afternoon."

She said goodbye and stood in her doorway watching him saunter down the hall, a smile on her face.

"You look happy," Amber said, yanking her from her reverie.

"I am," Julie replied. "That man just gave me the best idea for social media."

"Really."

"Yes. Why?"

"Oh, I don't know. You're smiling like he gave you an idea for something a lot more interesting than that."

She wiped that smile away instantly. "You're imagining things." Wasn't she?

Chapter Four

Dottie

S pontaneous Sweeney gatherings—with no holiday, no agenda, no purpose but fun and a chance to catch up—were sometimes hard for Dottie to orchestrate. With the opening of the inn looming, the work schedules of her grown children and their spouses, and the demands of raising kids, it wasn't always easy to bring all four of her kids—and their families—to her house.

But Dottie and Sam had decided that not one more day should pass without sharing the big baby news. A few quick calls, some schedule juggling, and the decision to skip cooking and order Pub Subs, those insanely delicious hoagie sandwiches from Publix, and the whole process came together easily.

With too many people for the dining room table, they spread out all over the cottage, which was still decorated the way Dottie had left it when she moved permanently into the inn. But the beachfront home bore more and more of Sam's fingerprints as she and Ben made it their permanent home.

From a seat in the living room where she could see most of the downstairs, Dottie eyed her family scattered around as they unwrapped subs, shared bags of chips, popped open soda cans, and shared jokes and conversations.

Jay used to lean over at moments like this and say, "Take a mental picture, Dot. This is the stuff that life is made of."

The simple moments, the ordinary times. She waited again for that pang of grief—that twinge of sadness that she was having one of those moments without him—but it didn't hit. Was she healing? Was grief behind her?

Was it behind all of them?

She scanned the group, catching a glimpse of her son, John, and his beautiful wife, Imani, as deeply in love as the day they married. Even with three kids and John running a successful marketing business, the two of them made time to keep romance in their marriage and Dottie loved that.

Next to them, Erica sat on the floor in front of the coffee table with her daughter, Jada, and husband, Will, all of them spreading the deli paper as plates for their sandwiches while they chatted. Dottie's youngest daughter was thriving in her new role as a mother to adopted Jada, who, in turn, had come out of her shell as a bright and involved sixth grader.

Lori sat next to Amber, her maternal gaze warm as she put a hand on Amber's ready-to-pop belly and no doubt reminded her daughter to breathe, as a good yogi would. Over at the dining table, Sam and Taylor chatted, while Ethan was in a conversation with Ben, and Dottie knew why it looked private and serious.

Sam told Dottie right before everyone started to

arrive that she and Ethan had shared the news with Ben, so he didn't get blindsided this evening in front of his family and cousins. He'd been shocked, probably a little embarrassed—after all, it was his mother and former math teacher they were talking about—but he'd gotten about as excited about the baby as Ben could get. He'd settled in so well to life in Cocoa Beach, Dottie had no real concerns about Ben; he could handle what life threw at him.

With a look from Sam, Dottie knew it was time to make some announcements. She tried—and failed—to get everyone's attention. John noticed and whistled loud enough to bring all conversation and laughter to a halt.

Dottie chuckled at the reaction, thanked John, and held up her hands. "All right, Sweeney gang. This wasn't just an excuse to get Pub Subs. We have news to announce."

That got the appropriate amount of interest and reaction, bringing anyone who wasn't in easy earshot to the room as they all focused on Dottie.

"Must be good news, Mom," Erica said softly from her seat not far away on the floor. "You've looked unusually happy since we got here."

"Me? Well, yes, it is all good news, I'm glad to report." She looked across the room at Sam, who couldn't wipe the smile from her face. Nor Ethan.

"There's good news and...great news," she added with a tip of her head, waiting through the chorus of questions, comments, and jokes. "The good news is that we are officially re-opening Sweeney House in one month and our inaugural event will be..." She lifted her hand to gesture to Sam and Ethan. "A wedding day for Sam Sweeney and Ethan Price!"

The cheer was loud, with lots of clapping, but a few surprised looks.

"That's an accelerated timeline," Imani said, dabbing a napkin on her lips. "I thought you two wanted to wait for an autumn wedding."

Sam and Ethan exchanged a look, and a secret laugh.

"Yeah, so did we," Ethan said, holding her gaze. "But, uh, Mother Nature had other ideas." He put his arm around Sam and turned them both to face everyone. "You tell 'em, babe."

"Tell us what?" Erica asked, but her voice rose like she knew exactly what was coming.

Sam flushed and laughed and she lightly touched her stomach. "Looks like I'm not done giving birth to amazing children. Here comes one more!"

This time the cheer was deafening, with lots of people popping to their feet to clap and hug and high-five the new parents-to-be.

Dottie's gaze fell right on Taylor, who smiled and clasped her hands together. Something in her granddaughter's deep brown eyes looked troubled, and Dottie wondered for a brief moment if Taylor wasn't entirely thrilled about this news.

"Guys, it's early days," Sam said after the congrats died down. "I just didn't want to keep it from any of you

and Mom thought tonight was a good way to tell everyone. I'm due in October, so..." She glanced at Imani.
"That's why the accelerated timeline."

"So, wait a second," Julie said, tapping her phone. "A
month, Mom? The first weekend in April? I hate to break
it to you but that is the weekend of the Wave Haven
music festival and I'll be up to my mayoral eyeballs with
work."

"Both days?" Dottie asked.

"The festival is on Saturday."

"Then let's have the wedding on Sunday," Sam
suggested. "It's not going to be that big."

"We can do that," Dottie said, "if I can get the new
chef I just hired to work on a Sunday. Might be tough,
because, well, he's Franklin Fox."

For a moment, no one said anything, but Erica
choked softly.

"I thought you said Franklin Fox," she said.

"Me, too," Imani agreed.

"Wait... Didn't you?" John asked.

Dottie just nodded, fighting a smile. "Believe it or not
—and trust me, I didn't—Chef Franklin Fox came in
today to interview for the job as head chef at Jay's American Bistro and, well, I gave it to him."

A cascade of questions followed and Dottie brought
them all up to speed on the conversation she'd had with
the famous chef and her decision to hire him.

"Wait a second," Erica said, sitting up straighter.
"Dad used to call him your TV boyfriend. I remember

how he teased you about having a crush on that famous chef."

Dottie rolled her eyes and probably turned a deep red as everyone laughed at that. "Please. Your father had a nickname for everyone. There's no crush—except on the calendar. I didn't have any other great candidates and he's obviously qualified."

"Overqualified," John added.

"People change," Julie chimed in. "Plus, major coup for Cocoa Beach."

Dottie shook her head. "He asked to keep it quiet," she told them. "He said he'd rather make Jay's a destination restaurant because of the food, not the chef. And, honestly, I don't want a bunch of looky-loos coming into the lobby trying to get a glimpse of him. So, no public announcements from the mayor's office."

"Understood, but it's a shame," Julie said. "I could use him on *The Mayor's Minute*."

As Julie shared her idea for social media, Sam came across the room to perch on the armrest of Dottie's chair, putting an arm around her.

"Thanks for doing this for me, Mom."

"Oh, please. Ben did the hard work by picking up eighteen sandwiches at Publix."

"And snagging one for his lunch tomorrow."

"He's taking the news okay?" Dottie asked.

Sam nodded, smiling at her son, who was laughing with Ethan about something. "Aside from the fact of *how* the baby happened, he's cool. It's just a logistics thing now. Do we live here or with Ethan? We were going to move to Ethan's house, but he only has three bedrooms and uses one as an office."

"You should all live right here," Dottie said. "Turn Taylor's old room into a nursery and call it."

"Mom, this is your cottage."

She looked around one more time, all the years she'd spent here with Jay somehow both fresh and distant. "No, Sam. You can live here. I'm so comfortable in my suite at the inn and you're right here. Can Ethan sell his house?"

"He can, but he's more than willing to work it out so Ben and I can move in after the wedding. Again, logistics. We'll figure it out."

"Okay, my dear. The cottage is always here to be your home."

"I know." Sam smiled kindly. "Thank you, Mom."

She put a finger on Sam's lips. "Just promise me there won't be a big family fight over the house when I'm gone—"

"Shut your mouth, Dorothy Sweeney."

Dottie smiled. "Don't worry. I have too much to live for." She lifted a brow. "One more grandchild, and this one's going to be born with me living five minutes away."

Sam beamed. "Yes, he is."

"He?"

"I'm feeling boy, but who knows. Tell me more about the celebrity chef, Mom." Sam jabbed her shoulder playfully. "Do I have to worry about you getting cozy in the kitchen?"

Dottie rolled her eyes, but hated the fact that she felt something akin to butterflies at the thought of it. "You have to worry about that new reservation software I cannot figure out to save my life."

"Oh, yeah, I promised to look at that. I will, but—"

"But you're busy. Pregnant, and getting married. Please," Dottie said quickly. "I'll get to it tomorrow. The only thing I have on my calendar is an interview for the second housekeeper. I've got a girl coming in tomorrow."

"You want me to interview her?" Sam asked.

"I'll handle it. You have a wedding to get ready for in one month. On a Sunday. Not a problem?"

"Not at all. I love a Sunday wedding."

Julie joined them and they started chatting about the music festival and how much she wanted it to be a success.

"Well, you have to feel like you're in your element," John said, leaning in close enough to join the conversation and for Dottie to see the resemblance between the twins, the two oldest of her kids. "It is music, after all."

"If all I had to do was hang out in the mosh pit and dance," she joked. "My office is paying the police for crowd control, processing vendor permits like crazy, and I'm already stressing about meeting with the promoter, because apparently they want us to do some of the promotions and I don't even know what questions to ask."

"We would know," John said, using the corporate "we" to refer to his marketing agency.

"We can help you prepare," Taylor added, coming in

not just as Julie's niece, but one of John's top account managers.

"Would you? Could you?"

"I ran the Ron Jon Invitational, remember?" Taylor reminded them. "I can definitely help you, Aunt Julie."

Julie's sigh of relief was audible. "I'll take all the help I can get," she said. "Anything to shut up the trolls on Facebook."

They talked about that, and Julie shared her insights on the chief of police, of all people, and pretty soon they were diving into chocolate chip cookies—another Publix delight—and then saying goodnight.

Hours later, as Dottie walked the path between the cottage and the inn to get ready for bed, she paused and looked out at the moon hanging over the Atlantic Ocean, giving the water a silver line down the middle.

Jay loved that moonbeam, she remembered. He'd sit out on the cottage deck and watch for it every night.

Once more, for the third or fourth time that day, she braced for the wave of pain, but all she felt was...good. Life was good, and that didn't mean she no longer missed Jay. It just meant she still had a good life and that's what he'd want for her.

Inside the inn, she passed the entrance to the restaurant and peeked inside the glass doors to the empty space. He'd never wanted a fancy restaurant at the inn. How would he feel about the fancy chef? Would he laugh or scoff or...be jealous?

Surely he had nothing to be jealous of, she thought as she walked toward the stairs that led to her suite.

That said, she was kind of excited about Franklin Fox. If nothing else, he added a little whitewater to her otherwise calm life. And that, she realized, made her feel very much alive.

DOTTIE GAVE up on the software instructions after too many YouTube how-to videos that didn't really tell her how to do anything. Happy to see it was nearly time for her interview, Dottie moved from her cramped office to the restaurant, opening the doors to the empty dining room.

She'd told the candidate to meet her here for the interview, settling in at the same table where she'd met Franklin Fox to read another resume. Emily Preston, according to the document in front of Dottie, had three years of commercial housekeeping experience.

That was a plus. Most applicants with experience wanted to work for a major hotel chain to get better health benefits and some other perks that an inn as small as Sweeney House couldn't offer.

Hopefully, the size would be a benefit to this candidate. There was one other housekeeper, Bella, but with ten rooms and now more foot traffic from the restaurant, they needed two.

Dottie was optimistic that today's interview would give her the last hire she needed to get this show on the road.

She unlocked the restaurant doors and checked her

watch. Emily wasn't due for ten minutes, so Dottie returned to her growing to-do list and started a whole section for wedding planning. It was—

"Um, hello?"

Looking up at the barely whispered word, Dottie squinted at the young woman hovering in the doorway, silhouetted in the light behind her.

"We're not open yet," Dottie said. "Can I help you?"

"I'm, um, Emily Preston."

"Oh!" Dottie stood immediately and walked toward her. "You're early."

"I'm sorry, I can—"

"No, no. Early is good. Early is great!" Dottie extended her hand. "I'm Dottie Sweeney, and I own Sweeney House. Come in and sit down, Emily."

She got a tentative shake in response. The woman followed Dottie to the table and sat on the edge of the other chair as if she might up and run at any moment. Her gaze dropped to the paper on the top of the table and Dottie could have sworn the young woman shuddered at the sight of her own resume.

"Well, thank you for coming in, Emily," Dottie said as she scooted her chair over the wooden floor. "Did you have any trouble finding it?"

As the girl—although based on the high school graduation date on her resume, she was in her late twenties—gave a standard answer, Dottie took in the waif of a woman in front of her.

It wasn't that she was small. In fact, she might have

been five-seven, but extremely thin and narrow. She had porcelain skin and hair so black it looked freshly dyed but badly cut. She wore a simple gray sweater over black pants that fit poorly, as if she'd borrowed them for the interview. Her eyes were blue—and did not go with the black hair at all—but it was the nerves in her gaze that made Dottie want to put this young woman at ease.

"So, is this your first visit to Cocoa Beach?" Dottie started. "I see you worked down in south Florida for a few years."

"Um, yes." She gave a quick smile.

"And what brings you up here? Love? Family? Or just a chance to try something new?"

She nodded, looking like she would seize the last option. "New. I want...new."

"Did you have a bad experience at..." Dottie looked down at the resume. "Marriott?"

Emily swallowed and shook her head. "No, I just...I like it here," she said.

"Do you have friends here or..."

"I just think it's really pretty and I wanted to work right on the beach."

"Well, that's Sweeney House." Dottie searched her face, getting a weird sense that something wasn't right. It wasn't wrong, necessarily, but Emily seemed shy to the point of nervous. "So, let me ask you, Emily. What do you like most about working in a hotel?"

She blinked as if she hadn't been expecting an open-ended question. "I guess..."

"Helping guests?" Dottie suggested when her face went blank.

"Cleaning," she said. "I love to clean. I'm a great cleaner."

"Oh, well, that's job qualification number one," Dottie said brightly. "So few people really like the process."

"I love it," she said. "I find it very...satisfying."

Dottie smiled. "Nothing like a good vacuum line on the rug, huh?"

She didn't smile back, but nodded. "I like things in order," she said. "That gives me peace."

"I fully understand. This job requires an early riser. How are you in the morning?"

"Great. I usually get up around five and walk my dog."

"Oh, you have a dog? What kind?"

"A little mix of terrier and beagle and...I don't know." Her face brightened for the first time. "Her name is Ruthie."

"Well, that's very sweet and if you get up early, that takes away my biggest worry."

"Oh, I'm never late for anything, Mrs. Sweeney. And I've never stolen anything or...or done anything wrong. I just really need a job. I can start tomorrow."

Dottie laughed, her always maternal heart folding at the low-key desperation in her voice. "Well, I can't start you tomorrow, since we don't open for a month."

"I can do anything," she said. "Not just clean. I can... help you. I can file and I'm good on a computer and I...I don't have a car, but I can walk anywhere. That's kind of my superpower."

"You don't have a car?" Dottie frowned. "How did you get here?"

"I walked."

"Where do you live, Emily?"

She swallowed and shifted in her seat. "Not far. Easy walking."

"In...an apartment?"

She started to answer, then stopped, closing her eyes. "I'm staying in a short-term motel until I can get a job," she said. "I'm...starting my life over. I don't know if that makes sense—"

"Complete sense," Dottie said quickly. "And I really shouldn't pry. I probably broke every rule in the Florida employee handbook, but—"

"It's fine. I just want to get my feet on the ground and I love to clean. I can work any hours at all. And I'll do whatever you need, not just cleaning. I can work in an office, run the desk, anything you need."

Dottie laughed. "Well, all I really need now is a housekeeper, unless by some miracle you can help me figure out some new reservation software."

"Oh." Emily sat up. "I know my way around technology. I'm not a programmer or anything, but I used...I'm...I'm good at that kind of stuff," she finished with a dash of uncertainty.

"Really?" Dottie's brows rose, and not just because she desperately needed someone to explain that software to her. If Emily was good at computers, why be a maid?

For reasons Dottie shouldn't be digging into. It wasn't her business, and if the girl needed a job that desperately, she'd probably be a good hire. Jay always said wanting a job was more important than the qualifications—skills could be learned, motivation was ingrained.

And she certainly seemed motivated.

Instead of asking more personal questions, she leaned forward. "I actually don't need a housekeeper for a few weeks, but if you can start right away, I sure could use some help with some of the technical stuff that's giving me headaches. Plus, now that construction is done, there's a deep-clean needed for every room before we can open the first weekend of April."

Emily gave her a real smile this time, all the way up to her blue eyes. "I'd love to work here."

"Okay, then." Dottie laughed. "I can offer you a good salary, above minimum, and you should be able to get out of that motel quickly."

"That'd be good, since Ruthie barks all day and the management already complained."

"You can bring her to work!" Dottie told her without hesitation. "I love dogs and, assuming she doesn't bite, she could be a great addition to the inn."

Her eyes widened and maybe misted at the offer. "Really? That would be so awesome. She's super good, completely trained, and great with strangers. You will love her."

"I'm sure I will," Dottie said.

"Thank you!" Her whole face softened with pure joy.

"I'm so happy. Thank you." They shook hands, agreed on a salary, and Emily promised to start the next day.

She thanked Dottie profusely before heading to the door. On the way there, she paused and turned. "Oh, Mrs. Sweeney, one more thing."

"Honey, it's just Dottie. What is it?"

"Would you mind paying in cash?"

Dottie inched back, surprised at the request. Especially from a young person—she knew from her grandkids they never carried so much as a dollar in cash. "I'm sure I could, but can I ask why?"

"A bank problem. Someone hacked my account, some scammer from the internet, and the bank flagged my account and won't let me open another one. I'm sure once I've been here for a while I can get that all squared away."

Really? Was that the reason? "I'm happy to help if I can," she said vaguely, but the request was a red flag she couldn't ignore. "Just to make things easier, can I take a picture of your ID and information?"

For a moment, she could have sworn Emily paled, but then she reached down to her bag—which, it had to be noted, wasn't inexpensive—and pulled out a wallet. "Sure. Here's my license. I can't use my social anymore because I'm waiting for a new card. The hackers and all..." She handed Dottie her license, which was Florida, with a Fort Pierce address.

Dottie snapped a picture of it, then held it back out to her. "Thank you, Emily."

"Sure. And I'll get the bank stuff sorted out, but if I start right away, it would help to have cash."

"Of course." Dottie gave her a warm smile, which was returned, then watched her leave.

When she sat down again, she eyed the resume and picked up her cell and dialed the number for the Marriott in Fort Pierce that was on the first line. It clicked immediately to a computerized message.

The number you have dialed is not in service...

Huh. Maybe she typed it wrong. Checking the internet on her phone, she found the listing for the hotel and called, but it sent her to Marriott corporate. After a few tries, she reached an HR department and explained that she was checking on a reference from one of their housekeepers.

"We can't give performance recommendations," the woman said.

"Could you verify employment?"

"Of course. Name?"

"It's Emily Preston," she said. "Worked in the Courtyard by Marriott in Fort Pierce, Florida, for the past three years."

She heard clicking in the background. "I have a Josh Preston at another location, no Emily."

Dottie's heart dropped a little. Could she have lied?

"Thank you," she said. After she hung up, she studied the next line, which was high school graduation. What had she done for the last seven years, especially if three of them were not at the Marriott?

Sam would not be pleased with yet another hire of questionable background. Not overqualified, like Franklin Fox, but maybe...dishonest?

Emily didn't strike Dottie that way. A little shy, maybe scared. Whatever she was, Dottie had to trust her instincts and, in this case, she felt like she was helping out a young woman who desperately needed it. Plus, she was starting over. If Sam didn't understand that, who would?

Chapter Five

Emily

Ruthie was already barking when Emily walked down the open-air walkway to her room at the optimistically named Sandcastle Resort.

Emily.

The most bizarre part about her whole bizarre experience over the past two months was that Amelia had started to think of herself as Emily. Well, that's who she was now.

Amelia Rosetti, twenty-nine-year-old wife, daughter, dog-mother, former administrative assistant, and current woman-on-the-run, had ceased to exist the day Emily Preston was born on a fake ID.

"I'm home, angel," she called to the dog as she used her key to get in. "Not that it's *home*, but it'll have to do for now."

And for the foreseeable future, she thought as Ruthie leaped into her arms, fourteen pounds of quivering excitement.

"I know, I know, baby," Emily crooned, hugging the little creature who'd somehow kept her sane during the most insane journey imaginable. Could she have gotten from Denver to Florida—without a car, credit card, or legitimate cellphone—without this little darling?

"No, I couldn't have." She buried her face in Ruthie's short tan fur, squeezing with love and affection. "But guess what? I think I got a job, and that's not the best part. You can come to work with me! Yes, you can!" She laughed at Ruthie's swinging tail. "I met the nicest lady and she gave us both a job, Rutheroni!"

She set Ruthie on the bed and sighed, looking around the dark, miserable room that smelled like mold and...she didn't even want to think what else. The Sandcastle Resort was a dump, but it was an inexpensive dump that accepted cash, and that made it perfect for Emily.

Of course, it wouldn't be so dark if she'd open the blinds and let some Florida sunshine in, but habit and fear kept Emily in the dark and her curtains perpetually shut.

Checking to be sure no one was around, she took Ruthie out to a tiny patch of grass, then came right back inside. There, she poured out some dog food and heated up a cup of noodles in the microwave for herself, then finally took out her laptop to do her daily search of missing persons and news from her hometown.

Triple-checking her VPN and getting online via an incognito browser that hid her IP address, she dove into a list of websites and news outlets, bracing for a mention of her name. One of these days, she'd see the headline...

Castle Rock Woman Missing For Two Months

But there was none. No mention of Amelia Rosetti, no suggestion that she'd left town in the middle of the night, no implication that her husband, a highly-regarded FBI agent, could have anything to do with her absence.

By now—seven weeks after running away while Doug was on an overnight assignment—she shouldn't be surprised that he hadn't yet announced to any authority that his wife was missing. He'd be under the spotlight so fast his hair gel would melt. He'd never go to the authorities. After all, he *was* the authority.

And he made darn sure she knew that.

Special Agent Rosetti was too smart to tell anyone his wife had disappeared. They'd look for a body, they'd look for evidence, they'd look into their happy, *happy* marriage.

But they wouldn't find anything, because Doug had found ways to hide his abuse—and the marks he left on her arms and back—and had cut Emily off from every person in her world.

So not only was it possible, it was probable that no one had noticed she was gone. She knew her husband—a cocky, arrogant overachiever—was counting on finding her before anyone realized she'd disappeared.

And she didn't want to think about what he'd do to her when he did.

Still, it had been nearly two months and he hadn't pounded on her door and threatened to kill her...again. Yes, she'd moved a lot, traveled by bus, and followed the plan she'd created. She'd cut her long blond hair, dyed it black—yes, clichéd, but it totally changed her look. She stayed in the background, spoke to almost no one, kept moving, and protected the pile of cash she'd been hiding since Grandma Gigi told her where it was and made her take it.

That had been, what? Close to a year ago when Gigi died.

She groaned and pushed away the laptop, taking Ruthie to the bed to lie down with her while she thought. With Gigi gone, no one—not her mother or father or a single person she knew—really cared that Amelia Rosetti was MIA.

Was that possible? Surely Nancy the Nosy Neighbor noticed that Emily didn't take Ruthie out anymore. Maybe a FedEx guy wondered why he didn't drop off packages for her. She'd missed a dentist appointment. Didn't they wonder where she'd gone?

The sad truth was no one knew Amelia Rosetti well enough to miss her. Only Doug, and he could find her all by himself. And would, no doubt, if he looked long and hard enough. After all, an FBI agent with connections all over the country? A man who was considered "the investigator's investigator," frequently brought onto cases around the country for his uncanny ability to track down baddies on the run?

Who could really escape Doug Rosetti?

"Well, we can and we did," Emily whispered as she stroked the dog on her lap with one hand and scrolled through local Denver news with the other. "We outsmarted the smartest guy on Earth."

The conversation with Mrs. Sweeney had given her the first real glimmer of hope that she'd felt since...well, since she'd first cooked up this plan. It had started after

Gigi died, and Doug knew there was really no one left to love his wife. He'd gotten rougher, and hit her more, threatening her constantly.

She'd thought about getting help—but she didn't trust any cop, not anywhere. They all knew Doug. She'd considered going to a church or a women's shelter, but couldn't stay locally. So when Doug left a file in his office that profiled a man who made illegal IDs, she started cooking up her escape plan.

Yes, she'd watched *Sleeping with The Enemy* and every other movie about an abused wife who got away, and that helped her formulate this plan. None of them ever took a dog, though. Well, she couldn't survive without Ruthie. She knew it might have been a mistake because a woman with a dog was a lot more memorable than a woman alone, but as long as she kept a low profile, no one would need to remember her.

The ID guy had given her an address in Fort Pierce, Florida, so she decided to head in that direction. When she created a fake resume, she picked an employer in that town, but never even got that far south. The bus stopped in Cocoa Beach, which sounded chocolatey and delicious, so she'd stayed here, found this heinous motel, and, today, got a job.

She was darn near two thousand miles away and as long as she stayed off any radar, didn't use her real name, only had a "burner" phone from Walmart, and got paid in cash, she could make enough money to get out of the country.

That was her ultimate goal, but it would take at least

six more months of no car, no expensive rent, and no...attention.

She closed her eyes and thought about Mrs. Sweeney, who'd given her plenty of attention.

Petting Ruthie, she whispered, "She reminded me a little of..." She didn't finish, not really wanting to go down that sad rabbit hole.

But something called her to reach down into her backpack and dig up that old, yellowed letter that Grandma Gigi had dictated for her nurse when she was on her deathbed.

She pulled out the lined notebook paper and took a deep breath, running her fingers along the stiff edges.

My Dearest Amelia,

First I must tell you that raising you has been one of the greatest joys of my whole life, and I am so proud of the young woman that you've become. I know my departure from this world is going to bring you sorrow, and for that my heart aches, but I must remind you that I know exactly where I am headed, and I'm frankly quite excited to go there.

I know with every bone in my body that my Savior awaits my arrival, along with my wonderful husband, your grandfather, and my only daughter. Yes, I am excited indeed.

EMILY DREW BACK, thinking of the only daughter that Grandma Gigi was referencing. Her mom—well, adoptive mom—Joanna Painter, who'd passed away tragically when Emily was only three.

Grandma Gigi took in her departed daughter's adopted child and raised her as her own, forging a deep and unbreakable bond between the two of them.

It was my greatest honor to become your mother, though Joanna would have loved to have that role. God needed her home a bit early, as we know. She was so excited when she finally adopted you, and I know she's been smiling down on you for all these years.

Amelia, there are some things I must say to you before I move on to the next life, and I pray you listen.

Emily shuddered and closed her eyes. This was the part that always hit the hardest when she read this letter.

I want you to leave that man. I've seen the bruises, I know the signs. He is not good to you, and it is my greatest wish that you would walk away and find yourself a new life. In our secret spot in my basement, you'll find the key to a safe deposit box. You know I don't believe in banks, so there's about $15,000 in cash in that box. Take it, and run. I beg you. Do whatever you have to do to protect yourself, and the Lord will guide you and light your path.

Emily sniffled and wiped a tear. He had.

Lastly, I want to give you the name of your birth mother. With me heading onward to Paradise, I think that you should have it. Her name is Vanessa Young, and she lives in Burbank, California. When you feel alone, look her up. You need someone in this world with you, Amelia, and this is the woman who brought you into it. Don't keep yourself alone forever. You know I always say, a trouble shared is a trouble halved.

"A trouble shared is a trouble halved," she whispered, realizing she had no one on this planet left to share her troubles with.

Emily didn't know much about her birth mother. Just that she'd had a daughter at age sixteen, tried for about six months to be a mother, but decided to give her baby up for adoption to Joanna, another single woman.

And that Vanessa had named her Emily, which was why when Amelia Painter Rosetti had to cease to exist, Emily was the perfect new name to choose.

And one more thing, perhaps of the greatest importance. Please take my dear little Ruthie. She loves you so much, and she will prove to be great company, even in the darkest of times.

I love you, my sweet granddaughter. Life on this earth is fleeting, you mustn't spend one more minute of yours living in terror and pain. Remember that God did not give you a spirit of fear, but of power, love, and a sound mind.

Until we meet again.

Grandma.

With slightly quivering hands, Emily lowered the letter onto the faded colors of the ugly bedspread, feeling another tear fall and splash onto the paper. Rereading Grandma Gigi's letter always had a way of transporting her back to that night. The night Gigi died, and the nurse gave her this letter.

That night, after reading this letter, she began to plan. With some digging and her competent computer skills, she'd gone through Doug's files and figured out how to get a fake ID. She got Grandma Gigi's money out of the safe deposit box and began to map out her journey.

Finally, when the night was right, she took Ruthie and left.

And now, here she was. Nearly two months later, and she had followed just about all of Gigi's instructions to a T. Except for one.

Her eyes lingered on the name Vanessa Young. With some digging on the computer, Emily had been able to acquire a phone number for her birth mother pretty easily, but she'd been far too scared to dial it.

But the loneliness grew stronger every day, the desperation for love, support, guidance, connection... It was becoming too much to bear. And after today, meeting the lovely Mrs. Sweeney, Emily ached for her grandmother more than ever.

But she was gone, and so was her adoptive mother, and there simply wasn't anyone else on the planet who knew or cared about or missed her.

Emily lifted the cheap disposable phone she'd been using this week. She swallowed nervously and keyed in the number she'd scribbled on the back of Grandma Gigi's letter when she found it a few weeks ago.

As the line crackled with a ring, Emily felt her blood run cold and her body shake with nerves.

This woman, this Vanessa Young, only knew her as a baby, and...gave her away. Why would she want anything to do with Emily now?

Suddenly, the ringing stopped and a woman's voice answered the call.

"Hello?"

Emily froze, unable to breathe or think or speak.

"Hello? Is anyone there?"

That was her. That was her real mother, the one who brought her into the world and named her Emily.

In a moment of panic, she smashed the red End Call button and threw the phone onto the other side of the bed.

She wasn't ready. Not yet. Maybe not ever.

"Oh, Ruthie." She clung to the dog. "I hate living like this, but now we have a job and soon, very soon, we'll figure out a way to leave this country. We'll go to Paris or Spain or Greece. Somewhere far, far away where we can never be found."

It was probably a stupid dream and a useless plan. But it bought her hope and freedom, and she needed those more than a person needed air and water.

Chapter Six

Taylor

Taylor blew out a breath as she forced herself to focus on her computer screen, narrowing her eyes at the budget breakdown for her newest client at the ad agency.

Work was her solace, her peace, her constant in the midst of her crazy and ever-changing life. Work made sense. A whole heck of a lot more sense than both of her divorced parents having babies within a year of one another, that was for sure.

But today, the numbers on the spreadsheet seemed to run together, her head spun, and she couldn't seem to drown out the distractions and zero in on her exponentially growing to-do list.

No matter how hard Taylor tried, her father's words on the phone bounced around in her head and bugged her like a buzzing gnat she wished she could just smack away.

"Focus, Taylor," she whispered to herself, expanding the budget sheet for Spotless and Sparkling, a cleaning service that Coastal Marketing had just acquired as a local client.

She began to write up a list of budget allocations—

online advertising, local sponsorships...

The ringing of her desk phone jolted her out of her thoughts. "Coastal Marketing, this is Taylor Parker."

"Taylor, it's Janet," the cheerful voice of the receptionist replied. "There is someone in the lobby here to see you. A handsome young man."

Now *that* made her smile more than budget spreadsheets ever could.

"Oh, yay," Taylor said on a soft laugh. "I could use an afternoon coffee break. Tell him I'll be right down."

Welcoming the opportunity to procrastinate with her boyfriend, Taylor grabbed her phone and purse and headed out of the Coastal Marketing office and into the elevator, riding it down to the first floor.

Andre always knew when she needed him the most. She didn't even have to tell him. How sweet of him to surprise her at work!

As the elevator doors slid open, Taylor felt herself grinning as she walked into the lobby and saw...

Her younger brother.

"Ben?"

"Hey." Ben Parker, who had recently turned seventeen and looked more and more grown up every day, it seemed, stood in the lobby holding two cups of coffee and wearing a nervous smile. "Wanna hang?"

"Benjamin." She walked over to him and gave him a hug, ruffling his silky straight hair. "Since when do you visit me at work?"

"I just got out of school and baseball practice was

cancelled because the lightning alarm went off, so I thought I'd pay my favorite sister a visit."

She glared at him, taking one of the coffees and motioning for them to go sit at a little table by the window. "You can't say that anymore. You have another sister now, remember?"

"Yeah." Ben ran a hand through his hair and gave a crooked smile. "That's actually kinda what I wanted to talk to you about."

Taylor studied her brother, noticing that his shoulders had gotten broader and his little bits of teenage acne had cleared up. He was going to be a senior next year, and would be going to college soon and, *wow,* life happened fast.

"Brooklyn." She sipped her coffee, leaning back and folding her arms over her chest. "You want to talk about Dad's new baby?"

"Taylor." Ben looked up, his expression serious as he set his jaw. "I want to go and see them. Dad and the baby. And I want you to come with me."

Taylor felt her eyes shutter closed, and she glanced away. "Ben, I'm sorry. I can't do that. I'm sure Mom will let you take her car to Orlando this weekend if you want to go and see him and you're welcome to. But I'm not going to—"

"Seriously?" He drew back, a frown pulling at his face.

Taylor let out a soft breath. "Yes, seriously," she whispered.

"What, so you're just never going to talk to him

again? Even though we have a new baby sister and he's making a huge effort to reach out and possibly make things better?"

She pursed her lips. "It's more complicated than that, Ben."

"How?"

She leaned in and lowered her voice. "I *caught* him cheating on Mom. I watched him destroy this family when I walked into the kitchen and there was some stupid bimbo in the bedroom. He never cared about us, he never—"

"Dude." Ben shook his head, cutting her off. "You have got to let go of all this anger. It's not hurting him, it's only hurting you."

"I...I don't have anger," Taylor protested, calming her voice and patting down her hair. "I'm not angry. I'm simply indifferent toward him. He broke Mom's heart, and he broke up our family. I want nothing to do with him."

"I agree. I know he did that. And believe me, I hated it, too." Ben shrugged. "But look at Mom, now. She's doing great with the inn and now she's engaged to Ethan and *she's* having a new baby. See? She's moved on."

"Is that weird for you?" she asked with a soft chuckle, welcoming a tangent in the conversation.

"What, Mom having a baby with my old calculus teacher?" Ben laughed. "Yeah, it certainly wasn't on my bingo card for the year, but, hey—they're happy. It all seems like it worked out for the best."

"Maybe. I guess." She shrugged, glad he was so cool, but kind of wishing they were more aligned on this.

"He's still our father, Tay," Ben insisted. "And he's having this whole new chapter in his life, and it kinda seems like he wants us to be a part of it."

Taylor leaned back and took a deep drink of her coffee, touched that Ben remembered her favorite Starbucks order.

"He could ditch us and forget about us," Ben continued. "That would be the easy way out, but he's not taking it. He called you, and he wanted to talk."

"And I talked to him," she insisted.

Ben smirked. "Nicely?"

"Sort of nicely."

He reached out and grabbed her arm, giving it a light shake. "Come on, Taylor. Let's go this weekend, on Saturday. We can leave in the morning and be back by the afternoon."

The thought of coming face to face with Max Parker this weekend made Taylor feel cold and nauseous. She wasn't ready. Not after what he did to Mom. She wasn't ready to forgive him and be buddy-buddy with his new wife and coo over his baby. He didn't deserve it. He'd broken her.

"I'm sorry, Ben. I'm too busy right now. Work is crazy, I'm up to my eyeballs helping Mom and Grandma with the wedding, I just... I can't. You go."

Ben's face visibly fell, disappointment shadowing his gaze. "Can you just...think about it?"

Taylor pressed her lips together and swallowed,

nodding stiffly. "Sure. I'll think about it. Thanks for the coffee, and...I'm sorry."

"'Sokay." Ben stood up, patting Taylor's shoulder as he walked around the table to leave.

"We'll talk," she said to him as he headed out through the doors of the office building, guilt pressing down on her chest.

Even if Taylor had any desire whatsoever to see her dad or his new baby—which she didn't—that would be so brutally unfair to Mom.

Taylor always had her mom's back, through the cheating and the divorce and the starting over that ensued afterwards.

They were best friends, and the closest of confidants. If Taylor wanted to have any kind of relationship at all with her dad, that would be an unthinkable betrayal of Mom.

She couldn't do it. She wouldn't do it.

But the more she thought about things, she did realize that her little brother was right about one thing. It would do her some good to let go of her anger. She just didn't know how.

SURELY THERE WAS nothing that could fix a mood like wedding cake tasting at Annie's fabulous bakery, The Cupcake Queen. Sam and Taylor were already deep in a sugar coma as the two of them sampled Annie's brilliant creations.

Ever since she opened her doors to her dream business several months ago, Annie Hawthorne—Sam's bestie, who was like a second mother to Taylor—had thrived in every way.

Taylor was beyond happy for sweet Annie, who now ran a successful business and was madly in love with the adorable hunk of a gym owner next door, Trevor, and his daughter, Riley.

"Okay, what's next, ladies?" Annie floated around the pink and blue checkered tiles of her bakery, beaming with joy. "We still have yet to try the raspberry vanilla buttercream and the dark chocolate peanut butter ganache. Oh!" She glanced down at her printed list of possible cake flavors. "And the blueberry lemon cream. Can't forget that one."

"Oh, my gosh..." Sam leaned back in the high-top chair, pressing her hand to her belly. "I think if I eat any more cake, little baby here is going to turn into ganache."

Taylor laughed, lifting her fork. "I'll try more, Annie. Keep 'em coming."

"What's with you?" Mom asked Taylor, her head angled with concern. "I can tell something is bugging you, girl."

Taylor scraped the remnants of frosting off her plate as Annie brought out samples of something with red jelly filling and white clouds of icing. "Ben came to my work today."

"Ben did?" Sam frowned, drawing back. "Why?"

"Is he all right?" Annie asked as she gave them each a

sample size of the newest cake flavor and sat down in the third barstool at the high-top.

"Is he taking the news hard?" Sam asked. "When I told him I was pregnant, he seemed surprisingly cool about it, actually. But you know Ben. He hides his emotions sometimes."

"No, no. It wasn't your pregnancy he wanted to talk about. I also noticed that he was surprisingly chill and minimally weirded out by the whole thing."

Sam let out a soft sigh of relief. "Good. That's good to hear."

Annie turned to Sam. "It's because he's your son, and he sees how happy you are, so it doesn't matter if it's weird to him. Anyone with eyes can see how you're glowing."

"Aww." Sam pressed a hand to her heart. "Thanks, Annie."

"It was about Dad," Taylor said softly, picking up a small bite of raspberry white chocolate heaven. "He wanted to... Okay, wow, this one has to be in the wedding cake. Are you kidding me?"

Annie chuckled and waved a hand. "I've perfected that one."

"Add it to the list," Sam agreed. "It's a must."

"Anyway," Taylor continued, "Ben wanted me to come with him to go see Dad and the baby this weekend." She studied her mom's expression, waiting for a stab of pain in her eyes or a shadow of hurt and disappointment.

But Sam just looked at her, still as glowing and bright-eyed as she was thirty seconds ago. "Max asked you to go, too, right? When he called you the other morning?"

"Well, yeah, but..." Taylor swallowed. "I'm not going to."

"Tay..." Sam sighed softly. "Are you sure?"

"Am I sure? Mom." She leveled her gaze with her mother's. "This is Max Parker we're talking about. Evil, selfish, horrible, cheating narcissist Max Parker. Remember?"

"Of course I remember, honey, and believe me, I'm certainly not in his fan club and never will be again. But...I've moved on. That anger and hatred I felt towards him has faded a lot. I think if you want to be in his life and the baby's life...then you should."

Taylor blinked back in surprise, studying Sam.

Had she really just let go of all that rage and pain? Had falling in love with Ethan and getting engaged and pregnant just wiped away all the residual sadness and anger toward the man who ruined her life?

Taylor thought back to what Ben had said earlier, about how it all worked out for the best.

Looking at the glow in Sam's eyes, maybe he had been right.

"But that would be, like, a total betrayal to you, Mom," Taylor said. "I am on your team, your side, one hundred percent. And because of what he did to you, I have no interest in talking to him."

"If I may interject..." Annie lifted her fork tentatively. "Taylor, sweetie, I don't think anyone on this planet would ever, for a millisecond, question whose team you're on."

Sam laughed, nodding in agreement. "Tay, I don't think this is about me. I think this is about you."

Taylor inhaled, stress tightening her chest. Had everyone let go of this hurt besides her? When did that happen?

"Honestly?" Sam reached across the table and took Taylor's hand, giving it a squeeze. "I think it might be good for you."

"You do?"

"Yes. I told you that the other day, when he called."

"I know, but..." Taylor lifted a shoulder. "I figured you were just being, you know, diplomatic."

Annie snorted.

"No, I was being genuine. Grudges don't do anyone any favors. You have a new baby sister and who knows? Maybe your dad has turned over a new leaf."

Annie leaned in. "You've got to free yourself of the anger, Tay. You don't have to be best friends with the guy, but forgiving him would do you a world of good."

"I've forgiven him," Taylor protested, crossing her arms and frowning. Would *no one* take her side on this?

"You have?" Sam notched a brow. "Look, sweetie. No one resents Max Parker more than I do. But letting go of that resentment has brought me so much peace. It's what's allowed me to move on, open my heart to love again, and now carry a brand new little blessing for this new chapter of life."

"It's just..." Taylor clenched her jaw. "It's not that easy for me."

"I get that," Annie said with a nod. "But maybe you could go with Ben, for his sake if for no other reason. And at least tell us if the baby is cute or not."

"All babies are cute," Sam said.

"Not Satan's," Taylor grumbled, making them laugh. "Yeah, okay," she added glumly. "I guess I can do that."

"It'll be good for your soul." Sam smiled. "And for your brother."

With the decision stirring in her heart, they finished out the cake tasting and eventually decided on three incredible flavors for Sam and Ethan's wedding cake.

Annie cooked up an adorable design with all-white frosting and little black hearts decorating the whole thing.

Taylor's heart felt lighter as she headed out of the bakery and climbed into her red Honda and started the engine. Before driving away, she sent Andre a quick text to see if he still wanted to come over for the latest install-ment of their *Lord of the Rings* binge.

As she pulled out of the parking space, she caught a glimpse of Trevor heading next door to the bakery for a little rendezvous.

Trailing behind him, clinging to his hand, was little Riley, a seven-year-old fireball of sweetness and personal-ity. While Trevor walked up to the bakery, he grabbed his little girl and swung her over his shoulders.

Riley laughed and squealed as her daddy carried her

in, and Taylor watched the scene through her windshield.

Like a movie reel, she thought about being that age with her dad. She thought about riding around on his shoulders like that. She was his little girl. And he screwed up, terribly, horribly, darn near unforgivably.

But maybe part of him still thought of Taylor as that little girl on his shoulders.

She groaned to herself, yanking out her phone to call Ben.

"Hey," Ben answered after two rings.

"Fine. We'll go on Saturday."

Chapter Seven

Julie

Julie was beyond grateful that John had agreed to meet her early this morning in his office and help her prepare for this afternoon's festival planning meeting.

As much as the former musician loved her new role as mayor of Cocoa Beach, this brand-new monkey-wrench of a music festival presented both a huge mountain to climb and a major opportunity for growth.

As she strode into the spacious office of his ad agency, she took in the wall-to-wall ocean views, looking over the empty desks for employees who, unlike John doing her a favor, didn't come in at seven a.m.

The sun had only just risen over the horizon, casting an orange glow on everything it touched and filling Julie with a new sense of hope and excitement for the big day ahead of her. She had to lead and direct the Wave Haven planning meeting, and, whoa, that was going to be a challenge for a woman who lived in a van and played rock gigs until less than a year ago.

Thank goodness she could enlist the big guns at Coastal Marketing for help.

Julie knew that there was no one who could run a

corporate meeting better than her dear, sweet twin brother, who she lovingly brought a latte to thank him for going above and beyond.

"Here you are, brother of mine." She handed him the steaming hot cup as she walked into his glass-walled office.

"Much appreciated." John blew on the coffee before taking a sip. "It's not my first time arriving at the office with the rising sun, but I'm willing to bet this is new for you."

Julie wrinkled her nose and gave her brother a playful glare. "I may be new to the whole 'normal job' thing," she said with air quotes, "but I have to say I'm enjoying it a lot."

"You seem really happy, Jules." John smiled, and it reached his eyes. "Grounded."

She nudged him playfully. "Never thought you'd describe me as grounded, did you?"

"There are many adjectives that you've embodied over the years." He shook his head with a soft chuckle. "Reckless. Wild. Spontaneous."

"Unorthodox," she added with a notched brow.

"Sometimes, maybe. But now...you are grounded. You're the mayor. And I am exceptionally proud of you."

Julie drew back, touched by the compliment from her brother. Historically, Julie and John had always represented the classic twin opposites—she was the rebel, and he was the rule-follower. They'd butted heads at every turn and found their lives mostly in completely different places over the years.

To hear him say he was proud of her and to feel that she'd grown so much and come so far? Wow. It stunned her.

"Come on, let's take this in the conference room and be official," he said.

She followed him to a room with a long table, pulling her laptop out of her canvas tote bag as they settled in.

"You didn't think I could actually win the election, did you?" she asked as she flipped the computer open.

"Honestly?" John placed his palms flat on the table. "I could see how passionate you were about it, but I thought you were in over your head. I was wrong. And I'm sorry for doubting you."

"Not entirely wrong," she remarked. "I do feel in a bit over my head with this whole Wave Haven thing."

"Really?" He cocked his head with surprise. "A music festival? I would think this is your bread and butter."

"Yeah, *attending* them," she scoffed. "Or opening them. Not planning parking regulations and security measures."

"Oh, that's easy stuff." John waved a dismissive hand. "Besides, you're the mayor. Don't you mostly just delegate that sort of thing to the people in charge of those specific departments?"

Julie straightened her back and lifted her chin jokingly. "Look at me. A *delegator*. Yes, that's the goal, and also kind of the whole point of this meeting. I need to decide who does what, how they do it, how much money comes out of the budget for them to do it with, and make it sound like I've done this a hundred times before, and that none of them should question my authority."

"Okay." John laced his fingers together and furrowed his brow. "Who all is going to be at this meeting?"

"So, I'll be leading it, and then there are two representatives from the Cocoa Beach Department of Leisure Services, the head of the city event coordination staff, an executive promoter for Wave Haven, and the chief of police, Brian Wilkes." Julie raised a brow. "Remember him? King Brian? You guys were buds in high school."

John tilted his head back and cracked up.

"What?" Julie leaned forward. "What's so funny? You guys totally ran in the same AP class perfectionist circles."

"Of course I remember him," John said through his hearty laughter. "We were good friends in high school, yes, and I totally forgot you'd be working so closely with him, since he's the chief of police here, but of course. It makes sense."

"Right." Julie studied her brother, pressing on. "But what is so funny about that?"

John shook his head, scratching the back of his neck as he leaned back in the office chair. "It's just funny how life happens in a small town sometimes. Brian had the worst crush on you in high school, and now the two of you are mayor and chief of police."

She drew back, surprised and admittedly tickled by this tidbit. "Brian had what? You're wrong. He absolutely did not."

"Jules." John gave her a 'get real' look. "He always

asked me about you. Constantly. He would try to play it so cool but it was completely obvious. All the guys on the baseball team would tease him about it."

Julie choked on her shocked laughter, still totally stunned by this twenty-five-years-late revelation. "Me? King Brian didn't even know I existed. He was being crowned on the Homecoming court and I was likely behind the bleachers smoking and strumming my guitar."

"He most definitely knew you existed. You guys had music class together, remember?"

"Yeah, I do. It's hard to forget saxophone playing that horrendous."

John chuckled. "Brian was good at everything but music. He tried, though. Heck, I think half the reason he signed up for that music class was that he knew you'd be in it."

Julie rolled her eyes, stifling a smile she was unable to hide. "But what about Lanie Nordstrom? He had the cutest cheerleader girlfriend ever."

"Yeah, he liked Lanie, and she liked him. They ended up married."

"Divorced now."

John pressed his lips together. "I heard. Sure, they had a typical high school relationship, but he always had a thing for you. It bugged me to no end."

"Huh." Julie leaned back, biting her lip. "A thing for me. Well, I'll be darned."

She thought back to high school, how she'd sing in music class and sometimes she'd catch him looking at her. Judging her, she'd always assumed. Thinking about how low her SAT scores were and how she and her perfect twin brother could have possibly been so different.

But maybe that's not what the high school superstar was thinking at all. He...liked her.

Suddenly, Brian Wilkes, chief of police, didn't seem quite so intimidating.

"Okay, John, get me ready for this meeting. I don't want to disappoint...my secret admirer."

JULIE BEAMED around the conference room, all seven faces looking at her with approval and respect, or at least she hoped they were.

"So, there you have it." She let out a small exhale. "If everyone does their jobs and we're all able to implement these measures and procedures, Wave Haven should be a safe, fun, and highly successful event." John's words flashed in her mind. "Safety, of course, is the top priority," she repeated for probably the tenth time, but whatever.

"This all sounds great." Brian was the first to speak after Julie closed the meeting. "I think we have an awesome team here in Cocoa Beach, and I have all the faith in the world in our ability to handle this event." He nodded, his gaze locking with Julie's for a brief second.

"Thanks, Chief." She smiled, trying not to think about the fact that he had a crush on her in high school but, oh, it was just so juicy and funny she couldn't *not* think about it. "Any other questions or concerns at the moment? We'll be in touch, of course."

All the attendees of the meeting shook their heads, and the head of the Department of Leisure Services, Linda Westbrook, stood up and gathered her things. "I think everything is under control, given the last-minute timeframe of this event. I'll get going on my part ASAP." She walked up to Julie and held out her hand. "Thank you, Mayor."

Linda had been around Cocoa Beach forever, with a well-established reputation for running a ship as tight as her hair bun. But as the head of Leisure Services, she took fun seriously, and she was someone Julie wanted to impress. From the look in her eyes as they shook hands, Julie had nailed it.

As the conference room cleared out, Brian lingered in his seat, typing some notes on a laptop.

Feeling buoyed by her success—and just a little bit sassy from the crush news John had shared—Julie took the seat next to him, raising her brows as she looked at Brian expectantly.

"Yes?" He turned to her slowly, a smile pulling at his cheeks.

Julie shrugged casually. "How are you feeling about all of it? Does everything suit your safety protocol, Chief?"

Brian leaned back, shutting his laptop and placing his palms flat against the closed computer. "Actually, I think the way you're handling this is brilliant."

"Really?" Julie inched back in surprise, her cheeks warming at the flattery. Or was he just saying that because of an old infatuation?

"Yes, really. I have to admit, I had my initial doubts when you were elected."

Julie snorted. "Join the club."

"But you're really on top of your game. You know exactly what needs to be done and by whom and with these instructions and this breakdown, I can get my team where they need to be and help this whole shindig run smoothly."

"Well, thank you." She smiled. "I really appreciate that. Like we talked about before, I'm working on my, you know, image."

Brian laughed softly, studying her face. "It'll just take some time. Those decades-old reputations are hard to overcome."

"You would know, King Brian," Julie teased. "Who wouldn't want *that* as their reputation?"

"Someone who gets accused of having peaked in high school and is now just a lame ol' small-town cop." He gave her a self-deprecating half-smile.

"First of all, you're the chief of police, not a lame cop. And secondly, I'd take 'peaked in high school' over 'weirdo angsty burnout chick who could hardly get through Algebra Two.'"

"But you aced Mr. Masterson's music class."

"I was inspired by the sweet sound of your sax playing."

Brian laughed, shaking his head. "Speaking of that, do you have any plans right now?"

Julie glanced at her watch. It was nearly six, and normally she would head home to hang out with Bliss, but she knew that Bliss was going over to a friend's house to study after soccer practice and wouldn't be home until late.

"Well, I should probably look over some more of those special event checklists. I want to make sure the personnel management is—"

"Julie, come on. You've worked your butt off today. What do you say we have a little...musical fun? For old times' sake."

She leaned in, her interest piqued. "Musical fun?"

"Come to my place, just for a little. My band is getting together tonight, and, well...we don't usually have a vocalist."

She felt her eyes widen as the idea of playing sent a chill of excitement up her spine. "You want me to jam with you guys?"

"We'd love it. I'll send you the address and you can meet me over there. I'm sure the guys are already in the garage."

Julie opened her mouth to object because, well, she felt like she had to. But why? Was there anything wrong with hanging out with Brian Wilkes outside of work?

"Are you sure that's..." She glanced around. "You know...appropriate? *Chief?*" she added with a playful smile.

"Sure." He shrugged nonchalantly. "Just two old high school friends playing some music after work."

"Friends?" She arched a dubious brow.

"Okay, acquaintances."

Julie laughed. "I didn't think you wanted to be my friend, King Brian."

"Well, I'd like to now." He smiled, the glimmer in his eye making her heart nearly skip a beat. "If it's not almost thirty years too late."

Julie inhaled slowly, a very unexpected flutter tickling her belly. "All right. Let's play some music."

By the time Julie arrived at Brian's house, the sun had nearly set, and the remainder of daylight was cast into his open garage, where there was, indeed, a full band.

She pulled her car up to the curb and got out, laughing as the sound of electric guitar and drums hit her ears. It was a real *garage* garage band. Talk about authentic.

"You made it!" Brian walked out to greet Julie in the driveway. He had changed out of his police uniform and into a CBPD T-shirt and black sweatpants. It was probably the most laidback Julie had ever seen him. High school days included.

"You guys have quite the setup here." Julie walked into the garage, instantly feeling at home among the instruments and music equipment. She patted the top of a big black amplifier, admiring it. "The Fender Mustang. A classic."

"Julie, this is Keith, Tony, and Rob." He gestured at the guitar player, drummer, and keyboard player respectively. "We work together on the force."

Tony, the drummer, a bald man with a big, friendly smile, lifted his drumsticks. "Welcome, Julie. I hear tell you've got vocals."

"Thank goodness," Rob chimed in, leaning against his electric keyboard. "Our lack of a singer is pretty much the only thing holding us back from quitting our day jobs and making it in the big time."

"Really?" Julie drew back.

"Absolutely not," Rob replied quickly with a hearty chuckle. "We love being police officers. This is strictly a passion project."

Keith strummed his red Ibanez. "But a darn fun one at that."

Julie let out a deep breath, joy washing over her as she took in every single detail about the moment, all of which were just awesome.

For so long, she'd been determined to make music her career and her livelihood. She felt that as a true, passionate artist, there was simply no other direction her life could go, and if she was doing anything other than music full-time she'd never be fulfilled.

But she had been so, so wrong. There were a million other things in life that fulfilled her, and that didn't mean music couldn't be a big part of it. She was finding her balance, and, even at almost fifty years old, still finding her way.

"A microphone for the great Julie Sweeney." Brian handed her a mic and grinned, his eyes lingering on her.

"Oh, so we're just jumping right in then, huh?"

"Absolutely." Brian swung his saxophone around from his back to in front of his chest, positioning the mouthpiece at his lips. "Pick a song, any song."

"And there's about a ten percent chance we know it," Rob chimed in.

Julie laughed, running her fingers across the microphone. "'Livin' on a Prayer' by Bon Jovi has a sax part, right?"

"Are you kidding?" Brian's face lit up. "One of my all-time favorites."

"Let's do it." She tapped the mic to test it. "We'll see if you've gotten any better in the last twenty-eight or so years."

As Keith's guitar hummed the first few notes of the rock-and-roll classic, the world melted away, and Julie sank deep into her element.

Through laughter, harmonizing, a few missed notes and entirely too much fun, they played all of "Livin' on a Prayer," and Julie got to belt out the chorus with abandon.

As she sang the final hook, dancing and laughing with Keith and his guitar, she glanced at Brian, who was looking at her with a certain glimmer in his steel-blue eyes from behind his sax.

Well, what do you know? There was quite possibly a decades-old crush that never fully went away.

As Julie watched him play the alto sax part—which he actually nailed, she had to admit—she wondered if that crush just might go both ways.

"Okay, that was awesome," Tony declared as his cymbals rang out the final crashing note of the Bon Jovi song.

"Whoo!" Julie threw her hands up. "You guys, we totally nailed that!"

Keith reached out for a high-five. "You're awesome. What a voice!"

"Thank you. Well, you guys played it right in my octave range, so it worked out." She turned to Brian, who walked closer to her, lowering his saxophone. "The years have really refined your talent, Julie. I mean, wow."

"Uh, hello—you, too!" She gestured playfully at the saxophone. "You're incredible. This is so much fun."

"See?" Brian teased. "Even uptight cops can have fun sometimes."

Julie grinned, her heart fluttering. "Let's play some Foreigner!"

Without missing a beat, Keith hit the first few notes of "Urgent," and they were off.

Chapter Eight

Dottie

Dottie Sweeney often wore lipstick and a touch of blush. A swipe or two of mascara, perhaps. So today's beautification had absolutely nothing to do with the fact that Franklin Fox was coming by the inn to discuss menu planning and kitchen arrangements in a few minutes.

Heavens, no. She was simply a put-together woman who enjoyed looking her best. The lipstick and the blush —and her pretty sweater and most flattering jeans— would be slipped on no matter who was coming to the inn, handsome celebrity chef or not.

With an extra bounce in her step, Dottie headed down to the lobby of Sweeney House and rounded the corner toward the restaurant.

Jay's American Bistro was now the crown jewel of the inn, with every last detail of the place perfect.

What an unbelievable joy it had been to share the creation of this new endeavor with her dear daughter, and now planning to open the whole place on that very daughter's wedding day? A true treat.

And although Dottie was slightly hesitant to trust the famous TV chef who'd won every competition on the

Food Network and opened multiple high-end starred restaurants, Franklin Fox would be running the kitchen. By a hilarious and wildly unforeseen turn of events, that was for sure.

"Dorothy!" Franklin's voice in the dark restaurant startled Dottie, and she jumped a bit, glancing around.

"Oh! Franklin, you're here."

He flicked on a light switch as he walked out from the kitchen, looking even taller than she remembered. "Got here a tad early. A young woman working on the computer system in the back let me in."

Emily, Dottie figured. Of course.

The mysterious but sweet girl who Dottie hired as a maid had been working the past few days setting up the new, state-of-the-art software to run the website, registration system, and bookkeeping for the inn and bistro.

"Oh, right, well then." Dottie nodded and stepped forward, unsure why she was a tiny bit nervous. Sure, he was famous, but it was *her* restaurant. "It's good to see you again, Franklin. I'm glad you're here."

"You as well." He flicked a smile. "You look lovely, Dorothy."

Warmth burned her cheeks, and she nearly laughed with embarrassment at the flattery. Good heavens, she was seventy-two. And he was a rich TV guy with an ego.

Still, the compliment was undeniably charming.

"Thank you." Dottie cleared her throat and gestured to a table in the corner of the restaurant, by a window overlooking the ocean. "Shall we talk menu?"

"The greatest kind of talk there is," he said playfully,

pulling one chair out at the table and gesturing for her to sit down.

Just being a gentleman, that was all.

"As you know," Dottie started, pulling out a folder with papers and notes, "the opening event for both the inn and Jay's will be my daughter's wedding, the first Sunday in April. We're expecting a crowd of about forty to forty-five, and of course there will have to be multiple menu options. Can you do that?"

"Can I do that?" Franklin laughed, his dark eyebrows rising as he folded his arms over his chest and leaned back in the chair with just enough arrogance to be annoying.

But Dottie wasn't annoyed, she was wildly amused. "I'm just making sure." She held her hands up defensively. "I don't know how much of that TV stuff is planned and doctored."

"Doctored?" Franklin gave a gasp in mock offense. "Are you questioning my cooking skills, Dorothy Sweeney?"

She laughed, flicking her fingers. "I would never."

"Good. Don't. Because those forty to forty-five guests will be served quite possibly the most well-thought-out, balanced, flavorful, creatively unique dinner they've ever had, and they'll go tell everyone they know that Jay's American Bistro at Sweeney House is the best of the best. Of this, I can assure you."

Dottie sucked in a breath, studying the man's eyes. Surely, he wasn't completely trustworthy. How could he be? And yet, there was something about him that was so genuine, so passionate and real, Dottie could hardly deny that he seemed as authentic as can be.

What then, was his real reason for being here? Why on Earth would someone of his status—and ego, for that matter—want to cook anonymously at a no-name startup restaurant?

She simply couldn't buy that there were no ulterior motives beyond wanting to mend relationships with his grandson. But here he was, as real as anyone could be. Puzzling, truly.

"That sounds wonderful, Chef. Where should we start?"

"Entrees, and build around them. Of course, there must be a seafood."

"Agreed."

"But not your generic, run-of-the-mill salmon filet, or even whitefish. Whitefish is becoming so overdone. The sea bass craze is overrated and out of hand. What we need is—"

The loud ringing of Dottie's cellphone interrupted him. "I'm so sorry." She grabbed her purse and dug through it for the phone. "Let me just see who this is."

She pulled it out and glanced at the screen, seeing the name Bliss Sweeney as the incoming caller.

"Oh, boy. It's my granddaughter." Dottie held up a finger. "Just let me take this really quick and make sure everything is okay."

Franklin smiled. "No problem."

"Bliss, sweetheart, what's going on?"

"Hey, Grandma! Are you busy right now?"

Dottie laughed softly to herself. "Well, yes, a bit, actually. Is everything all right?"

"Yeah, yeah everything is fine. It's just that my school is doing a '70s themed day for spring spirit week next week, and I thought it would be so cool if I could go through some of your old clothes in the attic and find some actual, real vintage stuff to wear instead of the fake fast-fashion crap that everyone gets online."

Dottie glanced up and met Franklin's gaze. By the way he laughed and shook his head, it was obvious he'd heard the entire exchange.

"I will absolutely help you find something fabulous, Blissy. How about you come over tomorrow morning before school?"

"Sounds good! Thanks so much, Grandma."

"Of course, hun."

"Love you! Bye!"

"Love you, too." Dottie hung up the phone and shook her head apologetically. "Sorry. Grandma duties."

Franklin lifted a shoulder and smiled, but something about it seemed shadowed. He glanced away, then back to Dottie. "So, the seafood."

"Right. Yes, yes. You were saying that whitefish is overdone."

"Terribly so." He pressed his lips together, thinking harder and more seriously about food than Dottie had ever seen anyone do it. "I'm thinking scallops would be nice. It's hard to beat a good scallop."

"Ooh, I love scallops! And so does Sam. She always

gets the bacon-wrapped scallops for an appetizer over at Sharky's Sea Shack down the road."

Franklin stared at Dottie, blinking with his jaw slack. "It's a miracle she doesn't get a side of food poisoning."

Dottie couldn't help but laugh. "Don't diss Sharky's. It's a local landmark."

Franklin flicked his brows playfully. "My apologies. Well, these scallops will be pan-seared in a brown butter sauce, with—"

Again, Dottie's phone blared out her loud ringtone, cutting him off.

"I am so sorry!" She pulled it out of her purse to see who was calling now.

Damien, John and Imani's oldest son.

"Another grandkid." She gave an apologetic grin. What could Dame want? "I better just take it real quick."

Franklin waved a hand. "By all means."

"Hi, honey," Dottie said after answering the call. "How are you?"

"Hey, Grandma!" The cheerful voice of the sixteen-year-old superstar warmed Dottie's heart. Damien was always such a light. "How goes it?"

"Actually I'm a bit of a busy bee right now," Dottie said with a laugh. "Working on planning your Aunt Sam's wedding and getting the new restaurant up and running."

"That's awesome," Dame said. "Well, I won't bug you too much. It's just that my dad's birthday is coming up in a couple weeks—"

"I remember. I was there," Dottie teased.

"Right." Damien laughed. "Anyway, I was wondering if you could help me pick a gift? I don't think he needs another necktie or coffee mug, and Liam, Ellen, and I want to all go in on something together, just from us kids."

"Oh, Dame honey, I think that's a wonderful idea! Yes, I can certainly help you, but I'm a bit in the middle of something..." She grinned and gave Franklin yet another apologetic look from across the table. "Let me think on it and get back to you."

"Of course! Thanks so much, Grandma."

"Anytime. Love you, buddy."

"Love you, too! Bye!"

Dottie slid the phone back in her purse, clicking the side button to silence the ringer. "I am truly sorry. No more distractions, I promise."

"Your, uh, grandma duties are pretty demanding, huh?" Franklin asked with a smile.

Dottie laughed, rolling her eyes. "They never leave me alone."

"Right." Franklin swallowed, his eyes flashing as he glanced to the side.

Dottie could instantly sense some sort of sadness in him, and it worried her. She saw how jazzed he'd been about the food, so she knew to quickly bring things back to the main focus.

"So, scallops."

"Ah, yes. Scallops indeed."

They continued to discuss the menu, planning the

ins and outs of not only Sam's wedding, but the menu of the bistro as a whole.

Franklin insisted it must change seasonally, and Dottie thought that was a wonderful idea to keep people excited and always looking for the newest menu items.

His food visions were revolutionary, and Dottie sat and listened in amazement as Franklin pondered side dishes, wine pairings, sauce complements, and used the term "mouth feel" more times than she'd ever heard in her life.

After an hour with Franklin Fox, Dottie still didn't quite know his motivation or agenda for being here, but she did know one thing with certainty—this guy was the real deal when it came to cooking.

"I suppose that's it for now." Franklin patted the table as they finished up their discussion. "I'm going to need to get in touch with whatever locally sourced grocers and fishermen are in the area."

"There's no shortage of fresh fish." Dottie smiled. "This was truly a delight, Franklin. Thank you very much for how much thought and care you're putting into all of this. I can imagine it's probably one of the smallest-scale events you've worked on."

Franklin smiled, giving a casual shrug. "Dorothy, I believe that every meal in life is a gift, a treasure to be savored and enjoyed. Whether that's cooking for a panel of judges on *Iron Chef America*, or here in your fine little restaurant for your family and friends. Food is...love."

Dottie was a bit awestruck by his sincerity once again, amazed that the man on TV Jay used to tease her about having a thing for was so incredibly genuine. "That's beautiful."

As they were wrapping up, Dottie heard footsteps coming from the lobby and looked up to see Ben standing in the entrance of the restaurant.

Franklin turned around and tipped his head. "Who's this?"

"Oh, Benjamin! What a surprise!" She glanced at Franklin as she stood up to go hug Ben. "This is my grandson, Ben."

"You've got to be kidding me," Franklin mumbled with a chuckle of disbelief. "You got grandkids coming out of the woodwork."

"I'm very blessed." Dottie smiled, walking up to Ben and giving him a tight embrace.

"Hey, Grandma, sorry. Are you..." He craned his neck to look past Dottie, his eyes widening when he saw Franklin Fox sitting at the table. "Busy?"

"We're just finishing up." Dottie waved him over as she walked back to the table. "Come meet Franklin!"

"Yet another grandkid," Franklin said with a chuckle, standing up to shake Ben's hand.

"Wow, it's really cool to meet you," Ben smiled, pushing his hair out of his face awkwardly. "I just needed to—"

"Let me guess—talk to your grandmother," Franklin answered with a soft laugh.

"Uh, yeah, actually." Ben gave a sheepish smile. "But I'll let you guys finish up. Grandma, I'll wait for you in the lobby?"

"Of course, dear. I'll be there in two minutes."

"Awesome." Ben turned to Franklin. "It was great meeting you, Mr...uh, I mean Chef..."

"Just Franklin is fine." He smiled.

"Franklin. Right." Ben waved as he headed out of the restaurant and back into the lobby of Sweeney House. "See you around."

"Don't feel rushed," Dottie said kindly. "He's got a lot going on with his parents both having babies, separately, and his sister doesn't want to go visit their dad and... yeah." She waved a hand. "Family stuff. I'm sure he's just looking for a listening ear."

Franklin sighed, this time visibly bothered.

"Is everything all right?" Dottie asked, noticing his bright eyes darkening as he glanced down at the floor. "Are you having second thoughts about the scallops?"

"No, no. It's not the menu. For once." He chucked dryly. "It's just..." He sat back down at the table, slumping into the chair.

Dottie got the feeling that he, too, might need a listening ear, and she joined him across the two-top once again.

"Your grandkids..." He shook his head, running a hand through his salt-and-pepper hair and dragging it down his face.

"I'm so sorry they were a bother." Dottie pressed her lips together. "I don't want you to think I don't take this seriously. I will keep my phone silenced from now on, and tell them not to—"

"No, no, Dorothy. Gosh, no." Franklin let out a sigh.

"They all just...they love you so much. They need you and rely on you and come to you with every little thing."

Dottie laughed softly, shrugging. "Yes, that they certainly do. Pesky buggers, but I love 'em," she joked.

"It's not pesky. I'd give anything for my grandson to be that close with me. To call my cellphone and willingly want to spend time with me and ask me for advice. But he hardly even notices me, wants nothing to do with me."

She inched back, surprised. "Really? After you moved here to live closer and spend time with him?"

"Well, it's complicated," he admitted on a sigh. "I'm divorced and barely spoke with my daughter, who sided firmly with my ex during the...messy stuff. She and I have barely talked for many, many years. My fault, all my fault."

She nodded with sympathy, getting a little clearer picture of this man.

"So I hoped when I moved here, I could change that. I'm seventy, have no one close in my life, and Henry? That's my grandson. He's a corker of a kid, spunky and fun. But I have absolutely zero idea how to relate to a fourteen-year-old. And I'm failing miserably."

"Oh, Franklin." Dottie felt her heart soften as she saw this man of wealth and fame and TV shows truly had a struggle of his own.

Maybe his answer in the interview was the actual whole truth, that he wanted to be close to his daughter and grandson. Maybe there wasn't an ulterior motive to this bizarre career move of his.

"Well, I mean, I've written some fat birthday checks," he added with a dry laugh.

"And I'm sure that your grandson was thrilled to receive those..."

"You could have fooled me."

"Well." She gave her head a thoughtful tip. "He's fourteen? Until they're older and driving, money doesn't hold quite the same appeal as, say, time doing something special."

"Doing what? Henry wants nothing to do with me. I'm his rich old grandfather he used to see on TV, but now I'm just a washed-up Food Network has-been."

Dottie couldn't help but laugh at this, and Franklin laughed, too. "Not exactly a has-been," she said, considering his problem. "Have you tried to spend quality time with him since you've moved here?"

"I tried to teach him how to make a decent roux without breaking the sauce."

Dottie drew back and arched a brow. "Just what every teenage boy wants to learn."

"Just what every teenage boy *should* want to learn."

"Maybe Henry isn't interested in cooking. Or maybe that interest will come in time."

He gave her a pleading look. "Can you help me, Dorothy? I came here to be close with them and I feel like I'm doing an absolutely miserable job. All I'm good at is cooking, and Henry's favorite restaurant is Chipotle! Which is criminal, truly."

Dottie snorted. "How could *I* help you?"

"Just...teach me how to be a better grandparent? Give me some of your sage wisdom?"

Intrigued, she leaned a little closer, wanting very much to give him that advice, which seemed as simple to her as a roux did to him.

"Why don't you plan an activity with him that's more Henry's speed? Something the two of you can do together, that isn't about food or cooking, but rather something that he enjoys."

"Hmm." Franklin leaned back. "I assumed it was my role to teach him what I know."

"Well, sure, to an extent, but you should also get to know him. What makes Henry tick?"

"I know he's big into cars, plays all kinds of racing video games on the TV and stuff."

"Go-karts," Dottie answered, snapping her fingers and pointing at him. "There's a driving-themed park not too far from here called Andretti's and you can race go-karts. Maybe you two could do that?"

Franklin lit up, grinning from ear to ear. "That's a great idea! Henry will love that. Sounds a bit out of my comfort zone, but I'm willing to try."

"Fair warning, though—you might have to eat a hot dog or chicken tenders or something." Dottie lifted a playful brow. "Talk about criminal."

He grimaced, but then laughed. "Small price to pay for time with Henry when his face is not in his phone. Thank you for a great idea. I'm going to call my daughter now and see if I can set something up."

"Good! And remember." She tapped the table to

make her point. "You can learn from Henry, too. Don't try to teach him. The teaching and advice-giving will come naturally, in time."

Franklin nodded, taking this seriously and looking as if he was making mental notes. "I really appreciate it. And we'll be in touch, of course, about the menu. I've hired my sous-chef and a server, so I'll brief them on everything. If we need more staff for the event, I can handle that for you."

"Wonderful," Dottie said, and meant it. An experienced chef meant he knew how to run a restaurant, which was a godsend right now.

They both stood and she extended her hand, but Franklin opened his arms and opted for a hug, which was unexpected and so authentic.

When he left, Franklin walked with a bit more pep in his step and she was left to marvel at how someone so successful could struggle with something that came so naturally to her.

And maybe, if things worked out for him and Henry, he'd stay for a while. As one of her many grandchildren might say, she was *here for that*, she thought with a smile and a little pep in her step, too.

Chapter Nine

Emily

Emily had to admit that working on the new software system for Sweeney House was a welcome distraction from the messy state of her life, and she was grateful for the income.

With the added bonus of having Ruthie next to her and wandering about the inn as Emily loaded and ran the new programs for Dottie, Emily was the closest thing to "secure" she could remember for two months.

She could feel herself relaxing and not jumping at the sound of every door opening or ringing phone. Even in public, she didn't look over her shoulder or avoid eye contact with every stranger as she had been doing since she launched her life on the run.

Although when she'd heard loud voices and a commotion in the parking lot of the motel last night, she decided it might be time to switch to a different one. Her rule was to never stay anywhere more than a few weeks.

Having to brush away another wave of sadness, regret, and fear for her life, Emily focused on the dashboard in front of her, and the system for tracking reservations.

Technology was her comfort zone, where things did

what they were supposed to do at the click of a key, and when they didn't, there were answers online. She didn't know the first thing about being a hotel maid, but she knew a lot about cleaning—Doug made sure their home was immaculate...or else.

A knock startled Emily more than it should have—so much for relaxing. She

whipped her head around to the office door, only to see sweet Dottie standing there, looking quite elegant and beautiful with her silvery hair in soft waves and a notice-able dash of lipstick.

"Oh! Dottie." She pressed her hand to her heart to feel it racing. "You, um, you startled me."

"My apologies, Emily. I just wanted to check in and see how it was going with the new software installation." She walked over and pulled up a chair from the corner of the room, dragging it closer and taking a minute to love on Ruthie, who was curled under the desk. "I just finished up my meeting with the new chef."

"Oh, yes, I met him. I let him into the building earlier because the front door was locked, and he was banging on it."

It had been Emily's mild heart attack of the morning, but once she walked up to the glass doors, she realized it wasn't Doug. In fact, it was an older man she thought she recognized.

"I know we're not open officially, but we don't normally lock the front door of the inn during business hours," Dottie said. "In case there's a walk-in for reser-vations."

Emily's eyes widened. "And...anyone can walk in?"

"Well, Cocoa Beach is not exactly a hotbed of crime," she teased. "But whatever makes you most comfortable."

"I'll have to get used to this small town," she replied with a smile, wanting to change the subject. "And that man who came? He looked familiar but he's not in your family, is he?"

"Goodness, no. He's Franklin Fox, from the Food Network."

Emily gasped and felt a grip of panic. "Are there cameras coming? Is he doing a special or something?"

"Oh, no. He's going to work here but has asked to stay very much off the radar. No press, no celebrity attention. He's cooking for fun and a chance to be near his family."

Relief swamped her, knowing she couldn't stay somewhere that would even have a remote chance of catching her face on camera. Doug would sniff her out in a heartbeat.

"I'm surprised you recognized him," Dottie said. "He doesn't really appeal to the young crowd."

"Well, I was raised by my grandmother," Emily said hesitantly, thinking through every word so as not to reveal too much. "She loved the Food Network and HGTV. That's all she watched, honestly."

"Well, your grandmother has good taste. I was also a fan." Dottie's brows drew together. "Past tense?" she asked gently.

Emily nodded. "She, uh, passed away a few months ago."

"Oh." Dottie placed a loving hand on her arm. "I am

so sorry to hear that. No wonder you're out starting all over. Were you close?"

"Thank you, and yes, we were close, but she was very sick in the end. Until that, she taught me everything I know. She gave me everything I needed."

"That's wonderful."

But talking about Grandma Gigi would lead to questions, and Emily wanted to avoid that and any personal conversations, even though Dottie was so kind, and Emily desperately craved friendship. "So, what's Franklin Fox like in person?" she asked brightly.

"Well, obviously, he's a skilled chef. But he's also a very kind and genuine man. Handsome, too, actually," she added on a laugh, her cheeks turning slightly pink. "I mean, for his age. Not that I'm one to talk about age, but... you know. But, yeah, he's...very nice."

Emily found herself smiling. Did Dottie have a crush? "You guys would be a cute couple," she said, only half teasing.

"Oh, good heavens!" Dottie tilted her head back and flicked her hand dismissively. "Now *that* is crazy talk. I'm a one-man woman and my man, my Jay, is waiting for me in heaven."

Emily gave a sad smile. "With my Grandma Gigi." And the minute the words were out, she could have kicked herself. She shouldn't be saying real names! What was wrong with her? "Oh, I better get back to this booking software. It isn't going to manage itself."

"Just so I don't have to manage it too much," Dottie

joked, her gaze lingering on Emily, as if she wanted to ask a question or say something else.

Emily swallowed, glancing away.

She didn't know Dottie Sweeney well, but she knew she wasn't a dumb woman. Dottie was bound to figure out that there were some weird circumstances surrounding her newest hire, and she was not the type of woman who appreciated being lied to.

Nor did she deserve it. Emily hated the guilt that came with her secretive life, but she continued to remind herself that it was a necessary part of her escape plan, and it was all a means to an end.

"Alrighty, then." Dottie patted the desk and stood up. "It looks like you've got everything under control."

Emily nodded. "It's going well."

"Good. Be prepared—you're going to have to teach Sam and me a big ol' lesson when you're all finished setting it up."

She smiled. "I don't mind."

"Thanks, Emily." She walked to the door, placed her hand on the handle, and turned around, a glimmer in her eyes that reminded Emily so vividly of Grandma Gigi. "And, honey, if you need anything, and I really do mean *anything*, I'm here for you, okay?"

For a moment, Emily just studied her, thinking about how long it had been since anyone had called her "honey." Since Gigi died.

But she couldn't let herself get swept up in Dottie's warmth and kindness. She couldn't let this dear woman pull the truth from her, and something told Emily that she might try—she'd want to help. And help could lead to...being found.

She swallowed a lump in her throat and forced a smile. "I'm all good. Thanks, Dottie!"

"You bet."

But just as Dottie was about to open the office door and head out, they heard a loud bang and a crash from somewhere else in the inn, probably the lobby.

With a soft shriek, Emily's heart leapt into her throat and the instant surge of adrenaline and white-hot terror washed over her as she automatically reached for Ruthie.

It's him. He's found me. He just broke into the inn and is coming for me.

"What..." Emily's voice trembled. "What was that?"

Dottie didn't look nearly as terrified, of course, but she did have a concerned frown on her face. "I'm not sure. Let me go investigate."

Emily let out a shuddering breath, squeezing her eyes shut and clutching Ruthie in her arms.

"Honey..." Dottie angled her head, clearly confused by Emily's seemingly bizarre overreaction. "It's okay. I'm sure something just fell or a vendor came in and made a sound. This is a very safe area."

Nowhere was safe. Not really.

"No, no... You don't understand..." Emily cleared her throat, forcing her quivering hands to still as she buried them into Ruthie's coat.

But she couldn't control her rapid-fire heartbeat and hyperventilating.

"I'll be right back, okay?" Dottie headed out the office

door and back down the hallway that connected it to the hotel lobby. "Let me go see what happened."

All the while, Emily desperately searched for escape routes. There was one small window on the back wall, but it looked right out at the parking lot, where Doug would undoubtedly see her trying to run away.

She couldn't very well go out into the lobby, because he was there.

He's here...he's here...

She realized she was frozen in place, and her best plan was to just stay put in the office and remain as quiet as possible.

She listened hard, expecting any second to hear his angry, booming voice, the growl of his temper, which was enough to send her crashing even further into fight or flight.

Which, out of those two options, Emily always chose the latter. But she could only flee so far.

He was an investigator, after all, and a darn good one.

But then a sound floated through the building, one she certainly didn't expect.

Laughter. Dottie's laughter.

Of course, Emily thought to herself. He'd charmed the sweet older woman, probably convinced her that he'd accidentally wandered into the wrong place, or that he was just some nice, innocent guy who knew Emily and wanted to see her at work.

Everyone loved Doug. He was charismatic and outgoing and exceptionally likeable. He was a master at his game, and could talk his way out of just about anything.

Emily gritted her teeth, holding her breath and listening hard.

Now, a male voice. Laughing, too. Talking to Dottie. But...it wasn't Doug.

She clung to Ruthie, letting out a sobbing sigh and shutting her eyes. Still trembling with residual fear, she ran a clammy hand through her hair.

The office door swung open, and Emily shuddered, but it was just Dottie. "Oh, hi. Is...is everything okay out there?"

"Yes, yes." Dottie waved a hand. "That was my future son-in-law, Ethan. He came by to bring over some materials for the wedding arch he's building for the big day and dropped a giant pile of wooden two-by-fours all over the lobby." She chuckled and rolled her eyes.

The final stage of relief set in, and Emily let herself fully and completely let go of the horrible thought that Doug was in the building.

"Now." Dottie walked over to the desk, sitting back down in the chair next to Emily, and leveling a very knowing gaze on her. "Do you want to tell me what the heck is going on, and why you got so scared just now?"

Well, Emily was right. Dottie Sweeney was not dumb.

And, wow, she wanted to tell Dottie. She wanted to emotionally dump all of her trauma onto this loving, sweet, gentle-hearted grandmother and let her make her hot tea and cookies and tell Emily how everything was going to be okay.

She wanted someone to know. She wanted someone to care. Her heart ached for the companionship and closeness she'd had with Grandma Gigi.

Emily looked into Dottie's impossibly kind blue eyes and pressed her lips together. "I just...startle easily. It's nothing."

"Emily, dear." Dottie sighed softly. "I've been around a long time. I've raised a lot of kids and grandkids. I've had countless employees at this inn over the years, and I must warn you that I treat each and every one of them like my own family. That means that if I see one of my people showing signs that something is wrong, I'm going to ask, and I'm going to care. You simply haven't a choice, my dear. You're at Sweeney House now, and you're loved by default."

Tears stung behind Emily's eyes as a quivering lump rose in her throat. She wanted to cry, she wanted to scream, she wanted to fall into this dear, dear woman's arms and tell her how scared she was.

"It's nothing..." The lie was so obvious it hurt. "There's nothing to tell."

"Emily." Dottie placed a hand on Emily's arm. "I saw how scared you were. You're fearful, and if you're worried about anything or you feel that you're in danger, you can tell me. I really don't—"

"No." Emily looked up and met the older woman's eyes, feeling a tear slide from her eye. "I can't...I can't talk about it. You're very sweet to notice, and to care, but...I can't."

Dottie nodded slowly. "When you want to talk about it, whatever it is, you come to me, okay?"

She nodded, feeling that tear meander down her cheek. She just couldn't take any chances.

But something in Dottie's sincere, concerned eyes, her warm and loving smile... Emily couldn't help but wonder if she had it in her to hide the truth from this woman for that much longer.

Chapter Ten

Taylor

The drive from Taylor's apartment to Dad's house—once known as "their" house, where Taylor and Ben were raised in Winter Park—was exactly one hour and nineteen minutes. Taylor hated every second, spending all of them questioning her decision to visit in the first place.

Ben sat in the passenger seat of Taylor's Honda, messing around on his phone, playing music on the radio, and fidgeting. Clearly, he was nervous, too.

Taylor had to remind herself that she was doing this for Ben. She was going to support Ben and be by his side through a potentially difficult and emotional situation. She, herself, was determined to stay far removed emotionally, and simply get through the day.

The sun was blasting through the clear blue Florida sky as they cruised across the Beeline to Orlando, then they crawled through side streets to get to the residential area of Winter Park. Before she knew it, Taylor was at the gated entrance of the upscale neighborhood where she'd grown up.

Suddenly, her heart rate picked up and her palms were slick against the steering wheel.

"This is so beyond weird," she mumbled, slowly inching up to a gate she'd driven through a thousand times.

Ben sighed and ran a hand through his straight hair. "Yeah, I still kind of can't believe Dad and Kayla live in our old house."

Taylor wrinkled her nose, taking a slow, calming breath as she drove up to the guardhouse and rolled down her window.

Just get through the day, Tay.

A burly man Taylor didn't recognize walked up to her window and crossed his arms, looking more like he worked for the Navy than the guard gate at Hibiscus Landing.

"Name and ID please?"

Well, hello to you, too, Taylor thought to herself as she reached into her purse and pulled out her driver's license. "Hi, I'm Taylor Parker. I used to live here, at 375 Sunrise Lane."

"Doesn't matter if you used to live here, Miss. Are you visiting as a guest today?"

Taylor swallowed, a pang of sadness and weird nostalgia hitting her as she stared at the entrance to the neighborhood where she'd become everything she was.

Thousands of shopping trips with Mom, getting picked up for her first date in high school, coming home from med school for winter break the day she found Dad in the house with...a woman.

All of this was so deeply a part of her. When in the world did she become a "guest"?

"Ma'am?" The Navy Seal-Wannabe's voice snapped Taylor out of her thoughts.

"Oh, yes, sorry. Yes. I'm a guest. Visiting Max Parker at 375 Sunrise Lane."

He walked back into the guardhouse, held up her ID and typed some things into the computer.

"They've gotten strict," Ben remarked.

"No kidding."

"Dad knows we're coming, though," Ben said. "He put us on the list."

"The list." Taylor rolled her eyes. "To get into our own house."

"It's not our house anymore, Tay." Ben leveled his gaze with hers. "You have your own apartment, and I'm going off to college soon. This place is in the past."

How was he so mature about all of this? How had Ben become so wise, while Taylor was still so bitter and childish?

"You're right." She turned to him and pushed a smile onto her face. "Thanks, Benny."

The guard walked back up and handed her ID. "Here you go, Ms. Parker. You can follow that road and then take a right at the stop sign—"

"I know how to get there," Taylor said with a soft laugh. "Thanks."

With nerves prickling and anxiety humming, Taylor pulled the car into their old driveway, and she and Ben sat quietly together as they looked up at the house that held a storybook of memories.

The beautiful, Spanish-style, five-thousand-square-foot Floridian home had been Sam's pride and joy, and often the only thing that got her through the roughest times of her marriage.

Taylor recalled how much time and energy her mother put into making that home the perfect balance between a stunning showpiece and a cozy family sanctuary.

A family that should have been happy, but someone had to...*have an affair with a nurse.*

Taylor looked up to see her old bedroom window, to the left of the two giant columns that flanked the grand entryway.

Flooded with memories and nostalgia, Taylor shook it off and looked at the house a different way.

"It's just a house, right?" she whispered to Ben.

He looked at her and nodded, his brown eyes wide. "It's just a house."

"All right, kid. You ready?" She turned the key and pulled it out of the ignition, her head buzzing and her stomach turning as they walked up to ring the front doorbell of their childhood home.

As they waited for someone to answer, Taylor's heart was pounding so loud she couldn't hear anything else, and her knees felt like liquid and why, why, *why* did she care so much?

Why was she so horribly nervous to see a man she didn't give a crap about? She should be ice-cold and indifferent, the picture of apathy.

But she was not apathetic; she was terrified.

Suddenly, the front door swung open and...there he

was. The villain of Taylor's life. The bane of her existence. The man to blame for all of her pain and sadness and the brokenness of her family.

Her father.

He stood in the doorway looking like...Dad.

"Taylor, Ben. You made it." Dad gave them a soft, sincere smile. "Come on in, guys. I'm really glad you're here. Both of you."

"Hey, Dad." Ben reached out his arm, opting for a side-hug.

Taylor stayed back, giving a quick wave and making it clear that hugs were not on the table.

"Hey, bud. Wow!" Max drew back and looked at Ben. "You're my height now!"

Ben laughed and shrugged a shoulder. "Just about, I guess."

Max turned, his eyes darkening with visible sadness as soon as he looked at Taylor.

Shadows formed around his gaze and a hollow weakness filled his expression. "Taylor. Good to see you."

She locked eyes with her dad for a single heartbeat before looking away. "Yeah, well, Ben needed a ride."

Ouch. Even she could hear how slicing that was. Mom would say she had a razorblade for a tongue when Taylor was nasty like that and she instantly regretted it. Even if he did deserve it.

"Well, either way." Max stepped closer to Taylor. "I'm really glad you're here."

Inside, Taylor did a double-take at the entry and living room beyond. Every trace of Sam's soft coastal

décor with teal and cream accents had been replaced by...
what did they call this wood and iron look? Organic
modern or some such thing.

"Wow," Taylor said softly. "The whole house is so
different."

"Yeah, we've, uh, done some updating, you know. But
the upstairs TV room is still the same."

Taylor knew exactly why her dad mentioned that
specific room. The upstairs TV room, which they'd
grown up calling the "playroom" and later on "the den,"
was a sacred place in the happier days of the Parker
family. They'd watched movies and played games in
there, a place that Mom let be an explosion of toys, video
games, and teenaged posters.

Off to the side was a large walk-in storage closet
with the wall marking their heights and distinct personality traits like "sometimes shy" and "loves to dance" and
Ben wrote "picks her nose" next to Taylor's once
—in ink.

She still hadn't forgiven him for that.

Taylor glanced up the dramatic stairway, filled with a
bittersweet hope that she'd get to see the wall today, like
Sam had said.

As Max led them into the living room—as if they
didn't know the way through their own house—Taylor
took a moment to study her father.

It had been nearly a solid year since she'd laid eyes on
the man, and he definitely looked...different. Not older,
necessarily, but more relaxed. He was wearing gym shorts
and a T-shirt, which was bizarre, because Taylor could

hardly remember seeing him in anything but a button-down and slacks or his surgery scrubs.

His hair had grown a bit, and had some more silver mixed in with the brown. He looked tan, and, dare she say...in shape.

"Kayla!" Max called as the three of them walked down a hallway that used to be lined with their school pictures. "Taylor and Ben are here."

"Oh!" The voice of her dad's mistress sent a chill up Taylor's spine. "Oh, good! She just woke up when the doorbell rang."

"Sorry about that," Ben said, walking side by side with Dad into the two-story living room.

The furniture was all different, too, with that same super contemporary coldness that Sam would absolutely hate. But the good news was it didn't feel like the same house and while that was wrong on every level, it did eliminate a lot of memories.

In the living room, Kayla was lying in the recliner, holding a bundle wrapped in a pink blanket in her arms.

"Hi, Kayla." Taylor waved a hand, smiling awkwardly at the woman who broke up their parents' marriage.

"Taylor, sweetie. How are you?" Kayla looked up at her, big blue, model-like eyes blinking with ridiculously long lashes. Her skin was creamy and perfect without a drop of makeup, and her blond hair fell in effortless waves around her stunning cheekbones.

"I'm, uh, you know."

I'm standing in my childhood home staring at the

woman who slept with my dad while he was married and is now holding this baby I'm supposed to love. How did Kayla think she was?

"Fine."

"Good." Kayla nodded. "That's good."

Ben walked up and stood next to Taylor. "So, this is Brooklyn, huh? She's so tiny."

"Yes! This is her." Kayla beamed, turning the baby outward so that Taylor and Ben could see their new half-sister.

"Oh." The sound slipped out of Taylor's lips when an unexpected hammer of emotion hit her. She looked at that tiny face, with a perfect little nose, big blue eyes and soft, round cheeks and...and...and all the resentment evaporated.

"I have a...sister," she whispered out loud, smiling. "And she's beautiful."

The baby cooed, the sweetest little sound.

Ben stared at her like she'd been dropped from another planet. "Wow. Hi, there, kiddo. You're...small."

Kayla laughed, looking up at him. "But wait until you hear how big her voice is."

"That's...fine. Not sure I can handle a crying baby?"

"Hey, Ben." Max stepped closer. "Let's give the girls some baby time. I'm restoring a '67 Mustang that's in the garage. I'd love to show it to you."

"A Mustang?" Ben's eyes lit up as Taylor rolled hers.

Of course he finally got his dream car. And dream woman. And dream daughter.

"Cool." Ben said, clearly not fighting any of the jealousy and resentment that Taylor felt, following his dad out of the room and leaving the three "girls" alone.

Taylor forced herself to look at nothing but the baby, who was so easy on the eyes it wasn't right.

"Do you want to hold her?" Kayla asked, her expression looking hopeful.

"Oh, I don't..." Taylor glanced around. But, yes. She really did want to hold her. "Okay, why not?" She leaned down near the recliner as Kayla sat up and slowly handed her the tiny bundle that couldn't weigh as much as Mr. Minx.

"She's a little fussy right now, but she'll calm down," Kayla said. "I just fed her, so she might have a little gas."

"Gas, huh?" Taylor took the baby in her arms, holding her close to her chest and watching her blink her eyes and move her arms around. "You're too cute to have gas."

Kayla barked a laugh. "You wouldn't believe what she's capable of."

Taylor couldn't help smiling. For one thing, Brooklyn was impossibly cute, with the tiniest little hands that reached out and grasped at the air. Her precious pink lips made a circle as she cooed and whined, and her eyes were closed tightly shut.

For another, she couldn't believe she had a sister. She'd wanted one her whole life, and remembered being devastated when her mother told her the new baby would be a boy. She'd loved Ben unconditionally, but...a sister.

Okay, half-sister. But still.

Perching on the end of the sofa, Taylor held Brooklyn

against her chest, awestruck by the adorable sweetness of this perfect little human who looked right into her eyes and—wham! *Bonded.*

"She loves you!" Kayla smiled, and they laughed awkwardly through the weird tension in the room.

Taylor kept her eyes fixed on her new little sister, already excited to see her grow up and get to know her as she did.

"Taylor, I, uh..." Kayla scooched up in the recliner, pushing some hair out of her face and locking eyes with Taylor.

"Yeah?"

"I just..." Kayla let out a nervous breath. "I know how weird this must be for you. I know how awkward and strange and uncomfortable this all is."

Taylor scoffed sarcastically. "Slightly."

"But can I just be real with you for a second?"

Taylor looked at the other woman and braced for the wave of hatred. But maybe it was the baby, or maybe Kayla, despite her natural beauty, was feeling as vulnerable as Taylor. For some reason, Taylor simply looked at her and saw, well, another woman. Not an evil witch homewrecker who'd ruined their lives.

"Sure." Taylor stroked Brooklyn's soft little head. "You can be real."

"I'm so sorry for how everything went down. Sometimes I feel sick about the way all of this unfolded with Max and your mom and you guys. I've..." Her voiced cracked, and she shut her eyes to fight what appeared to be real tears. "I've made a lot of mistakes. I have regrets that keep me up at night like you wouldn't believe, but...all of it led me to her." She nodded at the baby. "And I really do love your dad. I'm so sorry, though, Taylor."

An unexpected tightness gripped Taylor's throat, severe enough that she didn't trust herself to talk or even hold Kayla's gaze. She looked down at the baby and tried to steady her next breath.

Was this a genuine apology? And, more important, should she accept it? Dang, she really didn't want any part of the high road, but here it was, wide open and waiting for Taylor to take it.

She slowly lifted her eyes and looked at the woman, her dad's fiancé, and more of that raw vulnerability written all over her pretty face.

"Look," Kayla continued with a shuddering voice. "I know you guys feel pushed out, but I don't want you to. This baby has changed everything for me, and for your dad, too. Could we maybe try to...I don't know...start a new chapter? I want to get to know you."

Taylor swallowed, still not trusting her voice.

Maybe it was her gorgeous baby sister in her arms, or maybe it was the nostalgia of being back at 375 Sunrise, or maybe it was just plain old humanity, but Taylor looked up at Kayla and smiled.

"Sure."

Feeling a bit softer and considerably less bitter than she had that morning, Taylor agreed to have a cup of coffee with her dad while Ben held Brooklyn in the living room.

Taylor knew her dad wanted time alone with her to say whatever pathetic attempt at an apology he was going to conjure up, but she didn't protest when he asked her to join him on the back porch.

There was no need to be a brat, she decided. She was grown up now, with a job and an apartment and an amazing boyfriend, and was mature enough to handle her father with at least a small amount of grace.

That's the example she wanted to set for Brooklyn, anyway. Now that she had a little sister.

"Taylor Ann." Max looked at her, emotions swirling in his dark eyes as he took a sip of coffee. "You're so grown up."

Taylor laughed dryly, looking out at the backyard. The home backed up to one of the many small lakes dotting central Florida, with a smattering of mangroves and pepper trees along the grassy shore.

Taylor used to sit out there with Mom and Ben when she was young, waiting for turtles to show up so they could feed them.

"That's what happens, I guess." She shrugged, feeling the warm breeze lift her hair off of her shoulders, smelling the familiar scent of the water and hibiscus trees that lined the yard.

"You're liking your job, huh?"

Taylor glanced at him, noticing the genuine interest in his gaze, the desperate attempt to connect.

Once again, her mind flashed to the scene in the bakery parking lot, of Trevor, Annie's boyfriend, throwing his little girl over his shoulders while she giggled wildly and clung to him.

Her father still saw her as that little girl, and she had to remember that.

"It's awesome, I really love it." She let out a soft sigh and smiled. "The office is right on the beach, so there's ocean view from my desk. The work is amazing. I manage over sixteen active accounts now, and continue to take new ones every month. I've even had a couple of really big ideas that made for super successful marketing campaigns."

"Taylor." Max clasped his hands together, beaming with pride and maybe some relief that he'd cracked her wall. "That's awesome. Good for you."

"Thanks, yeah. I mean, it's not a hospital residency..." Because she'd quit her path to medical school when he'd broken up their family, crushing his dreams far more than hers.

"Eh. Doctors are overrated," he said, flicking his hand in a way that told her he'd forgiven her for ending that dream.

Encouraged, she added another smile. "And work is how I met my boyfriend, Andre, so...good things all around."

"And how is that going? With Andre?"

She felt warmth rising in her chest as she thought about the man she'd grown so deeply in love with. "It's just perfect, to be honest. We started out as really good friends, because we were working on this project together to get his brewery up and running in Cocoa Beach. But then, I don't know, we got to know each other so well and one day I think we just realized we were crazy about each other."

Dad held her gaze, a warmth in his eyes that Taylor almost forgot he was capable of. "I'm so happy for you. You seem really grounded and stable and...I'm just glad to see it, Tay. I'd, uh, love to meet him sometime."

Once again, Taylor Parker surprised herself when she met his gaze and said, "I'd like that, too."

It was like dropping a weighted vest, losing that first layer of bitterness and resentment. They talked a little longer, watched an egret take a stroll over the grass, and actually laughed at a few things.

She told him about Mom's upcoming wedding and the grand opening of the inn and how Franklin Fox was the chef. He asked more questions about the Sweeney family, at least acting like he cared, even though he'd never been a huge fan of that side of their family tree.

Maybe he really had changed. Maybe she had. With each passing moment, she felt lighter and realized...she'd missed him.

"Hey, Tay." Ben popped his head out through the sliding glass door, a wide smile on his face. "Kayla is gonna take a picture of you, me, and Brooklyn if you wanna come in."

"Siblings pic, newest addition included." She stood up. "Can't miss that."

"Thanks, Taylor," Max said, getting up to follow them in. "Thanks for this."

Taylor nodded. "Of course."

She and Ben held the baby in front of the fireplace—where the brick had been torn out and replaced with giant, shiny tiles that Mom would pronounce "hideous"—and smiled into Kayla's phone.

"I'm going to take her up to bed," Kayla said. "You want to see her room?"

"Do I?" Taylor asked on a laugh. "Because if it's mine..."

"No, we actually redid the guest suite for her. Yours is a guest room now, and Ben's is an office."

"My old room's an office?" Ben said. "Cool. I want to see it."

They all headed up the stairs while Kayla prattled on about how she would be changing the wooden railing to something called "oil-rubbed bronze," which sounded... not fun to slide down.

But Taylor stayed quiet as they got to the top of the stairs and rounded the corner, passing the huge den, which did look exactly the same.

"This room is next," Kayla said as they peeked in. "Probably looks familiar to you now, but I've got new furniture on order and we're getting a built-in..."

Her words faded as Taylor walked toward the storage closet door, aching to see that old wall again. In fact, she wanted to take a picture of it, because Mom had left in such a hurry, she surely hadn't remembered to do that.

"Her nursery is this way—"

"Just a sec." Taylor pulled open the door and touched the light switch, turning to the family wall to...to let out a grunt of sheer disappointment.

The wall was bright white, freshly painted...and blank. "It's...*gone*?"

"Hey, where are our heights?" Ben asked, poking his head next to her, then muscled by, moving a storage bin and garment bag to reveal...more white wall.

Getting closer, Taylor realized that it had been painted over and rather sloppily. As if someone took a paintbrush and whitewash, willfully erasing the last living memory of Taylor, Ben, and Sam in this home.

The names. The numbers. The words and smiley faces and hearts and...memories.

She smashed the light as she walked out, feeling the same kind of switch flip in her heart. Forgive her? Have a relationship with them? Come back and...*be a sister*?

After the snapshot of their lives *was painted over*?

Dad was standing in the den, his face communicating that he knew exactly what was going on in her head.

"You painted over it?" Taylor barked, tears threatening. "Seriously? You couldn't even keep one thing—one wall hidden behind a closed door? Everything in this house is different, you and...and her...you've wiped away every memory of our family, and you couldn't even keep that one little wall with pencil marks on it when you knew how special it was?"

"Taylor, listen, please..." Max held up a hand, but she pushed past him into the hallway, striding toward the staircase.

"I knew this was a mistake. I never should have come here."

"It was not! Taylor, please, wait." He followed her down the stairs, but Taylor was already storming to the front door, angrily wiping a tear as she tried to shove her feet back in the sneakers she'd left by the door, because there was a No Shoes rule in Mom's house. This one? Apparently there was a No Former Family rule.

Ben slinked down last, silent. Kayla was behind him, still holding Brooklyn.

"What happened?" Kayla asked as she reached the bottom of the steps. "Taylor, what's wrong?"

Taylor ignored her entirely and turned straight to Ben, locking eyes with him. "You're okay with this? That they just eliminated our childhood memories."

Silent, he walked to his own sneakers in the entryway.

"Taylor, I'm sorry," Max said breathlessly. "It's not that we wanted to erase you guys or anything—"

"It's not?" Crouched over her sneaker, she looked up at her dad. "Because you didn't even bother to match the paint color, you were in such a hurry."

Max pressed his lips together.

An old, familiar pain stung in Taylor's gut as she swung her purse over her shoulder and dug for her car keys.

"It was me," Kayla said abruptly, standing between her and the front door. "I painted over it. Your dad was out of town and didn't know about it, but he was..."

"Furious," he finished for her.

Taylor looked back and forth between the two of them. "I don't really care which one of you was holding the paintbrush. That doesn't take the pain away. Nothing does." She looked sternly at her brother. "Come on, Ben. Let's go."

"Please, just let me explain," Kayla said desperately. "It was a moment of weakness and jealousy and insecurity, and I was so ashamed but couldn't get it back."

It didn't matter. Taylor's head was pounding and she didn't want to hear about how it happened. They were both fakes.

With a hurried goodbye, she and Ben got into the car and she whipped out of the driveway and out of the neighborhood.

They rode home in silent sadness. One hour and nineteen minutes of silent sadness.

Chapter Eleven

Julie

In an effort to upgrade her image to one that was more professional, serious, and, well, *mayoral*, Julie had asked Erica to take her on an evening shopping spree. The two set out on a hunt for some business attire that looked the part, but didn't completely kill Julie's nonconformist vibe.

Was there such a beast at the Merritt Island Mall? If so, Erica could find it.

"Thanks so much for doing this," Julie said to Erica as they perused the women's section of Dillard's, and Julie did her best not to cringe at the "office" clothes that really looked like "school principal" clothes to her. "I know you're so busy with work and Jada and everything."

"Are you kidding?" Erica glanced over the rack of Calvin Klein jackets and smiled at her sister. "Up until several months ago, I barely saw you once a year, Jules. The fun of getting to hang out with my coolest older sister anytime I want has not worn off."

"Coolest?" Julie gave a fake gasp. "Don't tell Sam."

"She'd agree, trust me," Erica teased.

Julie smiled, holding up a hideously ugly brown blazer before quickly returning it to the rack and cringing. "Well, I brought you on this little escapade because I need to tone down my coolness a bit. I want to appear more, you know, mature and serious. My image could use some help now that I'm the mayor."

"First of all, I love the way you dress, but I definitely get where you're coming from. There comes a need for professional attire. Professional...with a flair."

"Exactly," Julie said. "And you, Miss Rocket Scientist, are the woman for the job. You always look so sharp and put together, but never dull."

Erica laughed, looking down at the clothes she'd worn to work that day. A silky turquoise blouse tucked into neat black slacks with stylish, closed-toe shoes with a low heel. "I like my business casual that's not too casual. Fine line, you know? But, Jules, do you really think you'd be comfortable in clothes like mine? It's so not you."

Julie fluttered yet another one of her long, flowing floral skirts, which she'd paired with a bright pink knit tank top and white sneakers. "There's somewhere in the middle, don't you think? Then I can save my Aging Rock Star wardrobe for the weekend."

Erica snorted. "Aging? You look amazing. Oh, check this out." Erica held up a plain black blazer. "It's a good staple item you could make fun with a pop of color."

"Fun?" Julie wrinkled her nose. "As in funerial?"

Her sister cracked up. "Funerial? You love black!"

"Yeah, hip, cool, statement black. That is hide-your-self-from-the-world black."

"Okay, okay. So you want something serious but with

a little spunk," Erica said, browsing a rack of tops. "Give me a chance to look."

"This is cute." Julie held up a leopard print tank top with a hopeful grin on her face.

"Yeah, for a nightclub."

"Really?" She reracked the shirt and shook her head.

Erica guided her over to another section and they continued to shop. "So, aside from the missing wardrobe pieces, how are mayoral duties going?"

"Actually, pretty well. It's a ton of work, but I don't mind that. There are good people in the office and I've learned a ton just in this first month and a half. Like... yeah." She laughed. "Mostly I learn and pray I don't make a massive mistake."

"I'd imagine it's like drinking out of a firehose at first," Erica said. "So much to absorb."

"Definitely. And don't get me wrong—I still love new and exciting things, so the learning curve doesn't bother me. The Facebook comments, on the other hand... Those can go away at any time."

"Still?" Erica rolled her eyes and made a face as she sifted through a rack of button-down blouses. "Ignore people. They hide behind a keyboard and say mean things to feel better about themselves."

"Ignoring them is easier said than done." Julie sighed and shook her head. "They aren't just random people, they're locals. They're Cocoa Beach residents who voted against me and actually care what I do in this job and how I do it. They don't take me seriously."

Erica met her gaze, her brown eyes filled with

sympathy and understanding. "They just don't know you, Jules. They don't know how awesome you are."

"They think I'm still the artsy loser who barely made it out of Cocoa Beach High."

"That is not true." Erica pointed a stern finger at her sister. "But a more mature and serious wardrobe could definitely help your case."

"Exactly. Let's look at long sleeves." Julie widened her eyes jokingly. "Cover up these bad, scary tattoos."

"Speaking of Cocoa Beach High— Oh!" Erica held up a peach-colored cotton sweater with a V-neck and a longer cut. "Beautiful over tapered black pants. Leather pants," she added quickly. "Nice ones."

"Okay, okay. Now we're talking. And what about Cocoa Beach High?"

"How's it going with King Brian Wilkes?" Erica asked.

Julie felt a smile pulling at her cheeks. "Fine. Great, actually. He's chilled out a lot since high school."

"Does he still have a crush on you?"

Julie whipped her head around, drawing back with surprise. "How in the world do you know about that?"

"John told me," Erica said matter of factly, without even looking up from the clothing rack. "It's the latest Sweeney family buzz."

Julie looked skyward with an exasperated sigh. "Well, I wanted to move home to the family."

"And we buzz," Erica added with a laugh. "So...Brian?"

"I don't know. I can't imagine he noticed me when his

girlfriend—now ex-wife—was cute as a button and a total sorority-girl type." Julie ran her fingers across a flowery blouse that she kind of liked. "We're complete opposites. He's a clean-cut, rule-following cop and I'm..." She made a face. "Stoner Mayor, or so they say on Facebook."

"You know who you are," Erica replied. "Plus, you are currently shopping for clean-cut, rule-following clothes. People change." She fluttered a bright pink, knee-length skirt with a little ruffle at the bottom. "How about this?"

"I like it!"

Once they'd made it to the dressing room with a fairly solid array of what Julie called "grownup clothes," she began to try things on and find her place in the world of serious attire.

"It's perfect!" she said, twirling around in a floral blouse with a pair of cute slacks. "Still fun, still me, but serious me."

"Mayor you! You look great. I'm so proud of you." Erica beamed.

"Don't get sappy on me yet." Julie pointed at her as she headed back into the dressing room.

Suddenly, her phone vibrated in her purse, and Julie dug it out to see that Amber was calling. "Hey, Amber! What's going on?"

"Hey, so, not to be too alarmist or anything, but I just got off the phone with the Space Kittens' security manager."

Julie propped the phone against her ear with her shoulder, sliding out of the pants and back into her own clothes. "Okay, is everything cool? I emailed him yesterday and explained all the security plans for Wave Haven."

"Yeah, that's sort of the issue," Amber said with an annoyed sigh. "Apparently, Trina Tribelli, the lead singer, is an absolute nut about security and she's demanding twenty-four-seven officers at her hotel for the entire weekend. Many of them."

Julie let out a frustrated sigh as she slid her feet back into her sneakers and gathered up the clothes in the "yes" pile. "Seriously? How many enemies does this chick have? There will be tons of security at the venue and backstage, and we've already arranged for their transportation."

"I know, and I explained all of this to their representative, but he wouldn't budge. Apparently, Trina is a total nightmare to work with and is threatening to pull out of Wave Haven entirely."

"What?" Julie nearly shrieked the word. "Okay, let me deal with this. I'll keep you posted. Thanks, A."

"You bet. Good luck, Jules."

Erica frowned with concern as Julie walked out of the dressing room with her bundle of clothes to buy. "Work problems?"

"Musician problems." Julie rolled her eyes. "It's okay, I'll handle it. I've got the chief of police on my team."

"And he likes you." Erica wiggled her brows.

Julie opened her mouth to protest, but didn't bother. He *did* like her, and she wasn't mad about it.

"Thank you so much for dealing with this so late." Julie smiled gratefully at Brian as he opened the front door of his house, looking at-home casual in a black T-shirt and shorts. "I wasn't even sure you'd see my text."

"I'm the chief of police," he said, ushering her in. "The clock never stops. And certainly not for you. I mean, the mayor."

She smiled at the slip and walked through the entry into his living room. She'd been to his house the other day, but only actually stayed in the garage playing with the band.

"I hope you don't mind meeting here. I didn't want to deal with going into my office, but we could if you'd be more comfortable."

"This is fine." She glanced around the one-story house that was probably built deep into the last century, but had been lovingly remodeled into a more modern, open concept. She could see into a pristine kitchen without so much as a glass next to the sink, and around a comfortable living room with most of the leather seating facing a massive flat-screen that she just bet played a lot of sports.

"Your place is awesome," Julie said, looking around as she made her way to the sofa, noticing that the tables were clear of clutter, and even the books in the wall unit were neatly stored.

"Thanks." He scratched the back of his neck and

laughed softly. "It's, uh, you know...a bit too quiet at times but I like it."

Julie guessed that this was the house he moved into after the divorce with Lanie Nordstrom, since it was masculine, sparsely decorated, and didn't have a single personal item in sight.

"Hey, it's a bachelor pad," she teased. "The world's neatest bachelor pad, though, I must admit."

Brian shrugged. "Curse of a military man," he said. "Can I get you anything?"

"Actually, do you have any—"

"Diet Coke?" Brian finished her sentence, and correctly. At her surprised look, he added, "Another curse. A memory that never fails me." At the fridge, he pulled out a silver can and held it up to her. "You used to always have a can of Diet Coke with you in music class. So, no glass, no ice?"

She laughed and nodded. "Color me impressed." She took the can and kept her gaze fixed on him, fascinated and intrigued. "How in the world do you remember that?"

He sat down in a recliner that faced the sofa, unscrewed the top to his water bottle and took a swig. "I don't know. I just, uh, noticed you, I guess."

So John wasn't kidding. Huh.

The idea made her want to laugh and tease Brian relentlessly, but there was something too honest and sweet about him, and she didn't want to yank his chain about it. Instead, she leaned back and put her can on the table, using the one and only coaster she could see.

"I actually don't drink that stuff," he said.

"You just keep it for company?"

"I bought it before the band practice because I knew you were coming over."

She stared at him, inexplicably touched by that thoughtfulness.

"So." Brian leaned forward. "We've got a diva on our hands."

"Ah, yes." Julie reached into her purse and pulled out her tablet. "Trina Tribelli, lead singer of the Space Kittens and, evidently, total high-maintenance nightmare."

"Well, based on what you told me on the phone, she wants a squadron of local security personnel at her location at all times, right?"

"Two in the lobby, two in the parking lot, and one outside each band member's room." Julie groaned and rolled her eyes dramatically. "And she wants at least five escort cars when they go anywhere."

"Well, that's not happening," he said flatly. "At least not with the Cocoa Beach Police Department alone. We don't have that size of force, especially with so many officers at the festival and working overtime, and we certainly don't have the budget to bring in outside help."

"I was afraid of that." Julie took a drink of Coke and pondered the issue. "Now I'm not sure what to do."

"Tell her no or hire bodyguards. We do have security arranged for all the bands, but nothing in those numbers. Just one officer at the hotel, one escort, one on stage."

Julie grimaced. "She's threatening to pull out of the

festival entirely if everything isn't exactly as she wants it. She claims she doesn't 'feel safe.'" She held up dramatic air quotes.

"Maybe she doesn't, given that she's a rock star, and I don't want her not to feel safe. We can give her the numbers of several private security firms based in Orlando who'll send bodyguards over here. Trained, top-notch men. So, done and done."

Julie had exchanged a few texts with the Space Kittens' manager and already knew Trina wanted cops, not private security, because she claimed they didn't do their job.

"What about this..." Julie locked eyes with him. "What if you get help from a neighboring police department? Is that a thing that police departments do?"

He chuckled. "Help each other? Of course. But we've already booked backup from multiple PDs. Satellite Beach, Merritt Island, Indialantic. They're all coming and, man, it's tanking the budget. So, I can't call for more."

"Brevard County Sheriff's Office?" Julie suggested.

He nodded. "I talked to him, but his price tag for backup is astronomical. Maybe I'll dangle celebrity babysitting in front of him and see if he has a few deputies who want extra cash. Then they can manage for Trina Trumpet or whatever her name is."

Julie laughed. "Tribelli, and that could work." She tapped on her tablet, making notes for tomorrow. "I appreciate your help so much, Brian. I'd be beyond over-whelmed trying to manage all of this on my own."

"Hey, I'm glad to do it. But don't sell yourself short, Julie." He lifted a shoulder, his gaze glimmering as he winked. "You're a rock star. Literally."

Her cheeks warmed at the compliment. "I'm a *retired wannabe* rock star mayor, to be exact."

"What was that like?" Brian asked, leaning forward with genuine interest. "Life on the road all those years? I can't even imagine."

"It was..." Julie sighed wistfully. "Exhilarating. Fun. Impulsive. Thrilling. Until it became...exhausting. Difficult. Unstable. And, at times, scary." She winced, remembering the day they received Bliss's diagnosis and she knew her daughter needed a kidney.

"Did you just grow tired of it one day or... What changed?" he asked. "I never pegged you for one who'd ever settle down."

"I never thought I would," she admitted. "Staying in one place used to scare me. Roots were my enemy. I had my daughter sixteen years ago and, for a long time, raising her on the road was easy and fun."

"That must make her one cool kid."

"Oh, believe me, she is." Julie beamed with pride. "So, we had a blast, you know? Seeing the country, playing music, bouncing from town to town. She did homeschool on the road and got her musical education from me. But then, right before her sixteenth birthday, she, um, she got sick." Julie swallowed and shifted uncomfortably on the sofa. "And that just sort of changed everything. I realized that I needed roots that I never planted. I needed the family I'd left behind. I needed the very community I tried too hard to run from."

"Wow." He considered all that, nodding. "Bliss is okay now, right?"

"Totally healthy," Julie assured him. "My saint of a mother donated her kidney and they both came out stronger and weirdly bonded."

"That's amazing, and shared organs will do that, I suppose."

She laughed, instinctively leaning forward, closer to him, as they talked.

"So, that's what brought me back here. At first I was ashamed of how distant I'd been all those years, but I quickly realized that all I wanted to do was stay here, change my life, and make up for it."

"And now you're the mayor." Brian nodded slowly, as if he was very much enjoying putting together the pieces of Julie's crazy life. "That's incredible."

"It's quite the turn of events." She sipped her Coke. "But I love the unexpected."

"And, um..." Brian cleared his throat, his brows furrowing. "Bliss's father...is he..."

"Not even remotely in the picture." Julie sighed. "We were on again-off again while she was growing up. He'd show up, hang with us in our van for a week or two, play some gigs, then disappear. He had some addiction problems that he could never quite kick."

His face darkened with sympathy. "I'm so sorry to hear that."

Julie waved a hand. "I heard through the grapevine

that he's doing better now, so that's good. But to be honest? I never minded being a single mom. She and I are so close, it was more like hanging out with my best friend all the time."

"I can't believe how you handled that, Julie." He exhaled sharply. "That's such a hard experience, and you came out of it so tough. It's seriously impressive."

"Thanks," Julie said, smiling. "I guess I realized that I'd been chasing some unachievable dream my entire life, and when Bliss got sick, it occurred to me that I'd already achieved my dream, and it was her. Now that she's better, I want to give her that stability and comfort she deserves. And honestly? I'm loving it here. For the first time in forever, my feet are planted."

For a few moments, their eyes locked, and Julie felt her heartbeat kick up a notch.

She wasn't usually so vulnerable and candid about her past, but something about Brian made her feel warm and safe.

"You're a parent, too. Tell me more about your son. Davis, right?"

Brian lit up at the subject of his kid, which, of course, Julie could totally relate to. "He takes after me a lot, and I'm so proud of him. Like I said, he's in the Marines, but he'll be home on leave next month."

"That's awesome!"

"It is. Things are weird now, with the divorce. He had to split his time and all that...you know." He flicked his hand and sighed. "Divorce garbage. But he handles it, and Lanie and I are on fine terms."

"I'm so sorry about that." Julie pressed her lips together, furrowing her brow. "My sister Sam went through a divorce two years ago and it was awful."

"It's tough, but not as tough as kidney disease." He glanced at her, the sadness in his eyes quickly disappearing.

"We've both been through a lot since those old Cocoa Beach High School days, that's for sure."

"Yes, Julianna Sweeney, that we have."

Brian using her full name gave her an unexpected thrill. He knew her full name? So few people did.

"But one thing is certain, and you have to promise me you'll never, ever doubt it again."

She angled her head. "And what is that?"

"You, my friend, are a rock star."

And for the first time in a really, really long time, Julie felt like one.

Chapter Twelve

Dottie

"It's perfect." Sam turned to Dottie with misty eyes and a smile as radiant as the morning Florida sun. "It's absolutely perfect."

They stood side by side in the backyard of Sweeney House, looking out at the simple, elegant, and gorgeous ceremony arch for Sam's intimate wedding, which was now only three weeks away.

Ethan had almost finished it last night, and was waiting to add one final coat of white paint to the rustic wood finish.

"He did an amazing job." Dottie clasped her hands together. "Now, just picture all the chairs lined up, six rows of four on each side, all with a big satin ribbon tied flawlessly around the back."

"And a long carpet going down the aisle." Sam nodded toward the sand.

"Oh, yes!" Dottie stood up taller. "I have a beautiful aisle runner being dropped off later this week. I sent some feelers out in the antique community for a unique and elegant runner for a beach wedding, and got just the most beautiful piece. I hope you don't mind I chose it without asking you first. If you hate it, of course, we can—"

"Mom." Sam took Dottie's hands in hers and squeezed them. "It's going to be beautiful. I trust you."

Warmth filled Dottie's chest as she recalled the planning process of Sam's first wedding, and how sad she was when she'd gotten essentially pushed out of the whole thing.

This was a wonderful do-over.

Dottie smiled. "And I spoke with Tillie—"

"The florist?"

Dottie nodded. "Yes. She and her team are very excited, and they were able to put an expedited order on your white lilies. They'll be everywhere."

Sam drew back, her smile growing even wider. "I always wanted white lilies."

"I remember." Dottie wagged a finger as they walked back through the French doors and into the lobby area of the inn. "But mean old Max wouldn't let you have them."

"His mother insisted on red roses." Sam curled her lip. "She said lilies were too *pedestrian*."

Dottie chuckled and shook her head at the memory that seemed to be lifetimes ago. "Never liked that Max."

"Really?" Sam raised her brow in sarcasm. "I had no idea. Always thought you were a big fan."

Dottie rolled her eyes and laughed. "You have come a long, long way, my dearest Samantha. I am so proud of you, and I am *so* happy for you. And, selfishly, I'm just so glad I get to do this with you."

"Mom." Sam gave a tearful laugh as she wrapped Dottie up in a hug. "I love you. Thank you for everything you've given me this past year. Even after I spent all those years focused on him and pushing you away... I'm just so grateful."

"Honey." Dottie squeezed her daughter tightly and shut her eyes. "You kids are my world. There's no mistake that any of you could ever make that would be enough to drive me away."

"I'm so glad for that," Sam whispered, slowly pulling back. "And this!" She gestured joyfully around the stunning inn and pointed at the fabulous new restaurant. "*We* did this! It's done."

"It's finally done," Dottie said on a laugh of disbelief. "I can't believe it. The planning, the thinking, the decorating—"

"The laughing."

"The crying."

"All of it." Sam rested her head on her mother's shoulder and sighed deeply. "There's no one else in the world I'd rather have tackled this wonderful and challenging project with."

"And now"—Dottie turned to her—"we get to have your wedding, and run the place!"

"The real fun begins." Sam pulled her long dark hair back and walked over to the couch in the lobby, sitting down. "Man, this whole growing-a-baby-at-forty-three thing really wipes you out. I'm *beat*."

"Oh, honey, take a rest. We've been wedding planning for hours."

"And we're almost done." Sam placed her feet up on the ottoman. "What's left on the checklist?"

"Well..." Dottie pulled out her phone and her reading glasses, sliding them onto her face. "Your darling daughter insisted I keep the wedding planning checklist in *digital* format so we can collaborate on it—not that I know how that works."

Sam laughed. "Oh, Taylor."

"Speaking of our Tay..." Dottie lowered the phone and met Sam's gaze. "How is she feeling about her newest baby sibling?"

"Which one?" Sam retorted.

"The one you're currently creating," Dottie said slowly with a confused frown. "Unless, of course, you found out it's twins and are holding out on me."

"Oh, she's fine with it. Maybe a little freaked out by the whole thing. But Max's new baby?" Sam sighed, but even that thought wasn't sad enough to dim her pregnancy and bridal glow. "Different story."

"Oh, of course. I almost forgot that what's-her-name just had the baby. But Ben did stop by the other day and tell me he was worried about the whole situation. Poor kid."

"Yeah." Sam pressed her lips together. "He's having an easier time of it than Taylor, though. They went together to go visit Max and Kayla and the new baby yesterday and, from what I heard, it didn't go too well."

"Oh, no." Dottie drew back. "What happened?"

"I don't have any details. Taylor just wanted to hang with Andre when she got back last night, but she did text me and said it was...not good." Sam shrugged. "I imagine she'll fill me in later."

"She's a tough cookie, that Taylor," Dottie remarked. "But I do think it would do her a bit of good to try and forgive her father. For her own sake, if nothing else."

"So do I, actually." Sam pressed her hand to her belly. "I've healed so much since the divorce, and I really do think that everything happened the way it was meant to be. I'm not sure Taylor sees it that way yet. She can't seem to fully let go of the anger."

"She'll get there." Dottie smiled. "Just like you did. Say, this is a bit of a random tangent, but you know that maid I hired? Emily?"

"Yeah, I've only met her once. She's working on the computer stuff right now, right?"

"Yes, and she's quite good at it, which is surprising, since her resume doesn't mention a lick of computer experience."

Sam shrugged. "Just young and tech-y, I guess."

"Right, well, she's a bit of an odd bird."

"How so?"

"She seems...frightened. More than just shy. It's like she's scared or paranoid. There are some inconsistences with her history, and...I don't know. Just a bit of a mystery cloud around the girl."

"Really?" Sam frowned, leaning back on the sofa. "Like what?"

"Like she requested to be paid only in cash, rather than direct deposit."

Sam curled her lip. "Definitely kind of weird, I'll give you that."

"And I just wonder what's really going on." Dottie chewed her lip, glancing around the lobby. "I can't put my finger on it, but I just have a sense that she might be hiding something. A big something."

"Your instincts are never wrong about these things," Sam said. "Maybe try to talk to her again, get her to open up. If she really does need someone to talk to, there's no one on this planet more trustworthy and safe than you."

Dottie pressed her hand to her chest. "You're sweet. I think I will."

"Good. And let me know if there's anything I can do. Okay, back to the list." Sam motioned. "What's next for this rapid-fire wedding planning?"

Just as Dottie was scanning her phone screen, the front doors of the inn swung open, and a bright-eyed, energized Franklin Fox came barreling into the lobby.

"Franklin." Dottie stood up, suddenly very aware that she hadn't put makeup on or fixed her hair. "I didn't think we had another meeting until—"

"Dorothy Sweeney, I simply must hug you right this second!"

Dottie kept her eyes fixed on the man striding toward her, vaguely aware of Sam's shocked laughter and gaping jaw from the couch beside her. "You...what..."

Franklin reached her and held out his arms, giving her a genuine and wonderfully warm hug that Dottie did not want to end.

He smelled like expensive cologne and was surprisingly strong for his age.

"Well, looks like the celebrity chef really is excited to work here," Sam quipped from the couch, standing up. "I'm Sam. Pregnant bride."

"Pleased to meet you, I've heard such marvelous things." Franklin held out his hand and shook Sam's. "And I *am* excited to work here, of course. But I just had to stop by and let your incredible mother know how much she helped me."

Dottie drew back, completely lost and confused. "Me? What did I do?"

"The go-karts," he said plainly, his eyes dancing as he locked gazes with Dottie. "I took Henry to the go-kart park, and we drove all day. He loved it. We must have raced a hundred times. It was quite a thrill, actually. And..." He raised his brows, pausing for emphasis. "I ate a hot dog. And it was delicious."

"Oh, wow!" Dottie clapped her hands together, warmed by the true joy on the man's face. "That's wonderful news, Franklin!"

He turned to Sam and pointed a finger at Dottie. "Grandmother of the year, right here."

"And mother," Sam added, winking at her mom.

"Oh, goodness. You flatter me." Dottie pushed a soft wave of hair out of her face. "I'd love to hear more about it."

"You two chat." Sam gave Dottie a sneaky look and a half-smile. "I'm going to head back to the cottage for a nap. I'm exhausted."

"It was great to meet you, Sam." Franklin smiled at her. "Rest up."

Sam waved a hand as she headed out of Sweeney House, leaving Dottie alone with her celebrity crush.

"You should have seen it, Dorothy." Franklin sat down on the couch and she joined him, turning to face him. "He was so excited. His face lit up like the sun when I told him where we were going, and he barely looked at his phone all day. He was engaged, and every time I worried he might be getting bored or having a bad time or wishing he was anywhere but with his old grandpa, he would say, 'Let's race again!' or, 'We should check out that other track!'"

"My goodness, it sounds like a fantastic day!" Dottie smiled, inching closer to him.

She couldn't help but marvel at the fact that this man, who seemingly had everything one could want out of life —riches, fame, wealth, legacy—just wanted to connect with a fourteen-year-old boy.

It clearly brought him more joy than any of those career endeavors had, and that fact alone made Dottie trust him and like him just a smidge more every minute.

"It was spectacular. And I owe it to you." Franklin studied her, his dark eyebrows raising as he came up with an idea. "I have to make you dinner!"

"Oh, Franklin, please." Dottie laughed and waved a dismissive hand. "It was just an idea that I'm sure you could have come up with on your own. You owe me nothing."

"Nope." He shook his head. "I insist. Friday night. A

special, private dinner, here at Jay's, just for you. A thank you for being a wonderful boss and an even better... friend. Plus, it'll give me a chance to test drive some of these menu items for the wedding."

Dottie tried her best to hide the butterflies of excitement rising in her belly. Was this...some sort of date? No, certainly not. He was just being kind.

But it also sounded quite a bit like a date. And in that case...was she ready for that? Did she trust this celebrity chef? Did she have it in her seventy-two-year-old heart to even look at a man that way?

She'd had her one love, her forever soulmate. What silliness it was to even consider having feelings of any kind for a man!

But then...here he was. Making her have feelings that she didn't completely hate.

Thoughts swirled around in her mind as Dottie frantically tried to sort out her emotions. But as she looked at the man in front of her, there was simply only one thing to say.

"Okay." Dottie smiled. "That sounds lovely."

Chapter Thirteen

Emily

It was a shockingly beautiful morning, picturesque enough that Emily was inspired to bring Ruthie and her journal down to the beach and enjoy the sunrise.

It had been a long time since Emily had truly enjoyed anything without looking over her shoulder every five seconds or constantly making sure she had an escape route ready and clear.

But today, Emily felt the tiniest bit calmer and more at peace. Maybe it was the salty ocean air and the soft pink sunrise, or maybe it was that weeks had passed, and he hadn't found her yet. Maybe she was just...finally feeling safe.

The motel she'd been staying at, despite its massive shortcomings in the luxury department, was just a block from the beach, and for that, Emily was grateful. The inn was about a mile away, so she could get to the only two places she wanted to go: work and the water.

Today, she walked out barefoot toward the ocean, feeling the cool, wet sand squish between her toes. The Atlantic was still and calm this early, sparkling with the reflection of the rising sun.

Emily sat down on the sand, and loyal Ruthie

plopped down right next to her, giving her knee a loving lick and taking a long sniff of the salt-sprayed air, her pink tongue hanging out to the side.

"I know, baby." Emily scratched adorably scraggly fur on the back of Ruthie's neck. "I like it here, too. But we can't stay. We can't stay anywhere for very long, at least not yet."

The beach was silent and nearly empty but for a few intrepid surfers and the occasional morning walker. Taking in the peace, Emily closed her eyes, attempting to let it soothe her ever-churning soul.

She opened up the worn college ruled spiral notebook she'd snagged at Walmart one of her first nights after running away and flipped through the pages, covered front and back in her handwriting.

She'd preserved every detail of this experience, days and nights of her harrowing journey, recording her fears, her hopes, her anxieties, her dreams. Writing them down helped calm her heart and build her determination as, page by page, her story emerged.

She opened the notebook to the next blank page and wrote today's date at the top, running her hand across the paper as she prepared to write.

I wish I didn't like it here so much. This little beach town in Florida has a wonderful amount of charm and goodness that seems to seep into my soul more and more every day. As lonely as I am, I feel less alone here. Maybe it's because I'm just getting so used to being on my own, or maybe it's the woman who owns the inn, Dottie.

I haven't told her anything about me or what

happened to me, and yet I feel somehow safe with her. I can't explain it. I think it's because she reminds me of Grandma Gigi, which is both happy and sad.

I almost came clean with her the other day, and a big part of me is aching to tell the truth. But I can't do it. What if she thinks the "right" thing to do is alert the police —then Doug will be pounding on my door in no time.

I've come too far to compromise my safety and risk something getting back to him somehow. Dang, it's hard though. Keeping everything to myself is starting to totally break me down. I'm not sure how much longer I can keep the secret in, even though I know I have to try.

I'll be starting as a maid in a couple of weeks, and maybe I'll stay here for about another month or so before moving along. I haven't decided yet.

I do know that my heart is aching for a new life, for companionship of some kind, for a world without fear and anxiety. I long for a life where I don't have to lie or hide or sneak around. Where I can develop relationships with people like Dottie and find trust in others once again.

Maybe I'll get there someday.

Emily looked up from her notebook, the ocean breeze blowing her hair back around her face.

She turned to look down the beach and saw, far in the distance, a figure in white sweatpants and a matching white jacket walking along the water's edge. As she got closer, it was very easy for Emily to recognize the woman striding purposefully along the sand.

"Speak of the devil and she appears," she whispered to Ruthie. "Or angel, I should say."

Dottie spotted Emily only a few seconds after Emily realized who she was, and instantly started waving her arm and picked up her speed excitedly to come say hello. Of course, Ruthie jumped up and trotted toward her, knowing and loving Dottie already.

Emily couldn't help but smile and laugh to herself at Dottie's obvious joy over running into Emily on a morning beach walk. She couldn't remember the last time someone was excited to see her, except Grandma Gigi, of course.

"Well, this is a fun surprise!" Dottie exclaimed as she walked over, her face flushed pink from the sun.

"Good morning," Emily said as she shut her notebook and stood up to say hello. "Enjoying a sunrise power walk?"

"Every day." Dottie nodded proudly. "That and morning yoga keeps me young, you know."

Emily looked past the other woman, way down along the shoreline to the general location of Sweeney House a mile away. "You've come quite a way."

"Mile and a half each way, three in total," Dottie said proudly. "Hello, sweet Ruthie!" She knelt down to play with Ruthie, who gave a tail swish and made a circle in the sand to send her happy message back. "Aren't you just a ball of joy this morning?"

"That she is," Emily said with a soft laugh.

Dottie's gaze landed on the spiral notebook sitting in the sand. "Whatcha working on?"

Oh, you know, Emily thought to herself. *Just quietly documenting my secret escape from my abusive husband, my double identity, and my plans to flee the country in order to finally be safe. Typical Dear Diary stuff.*

Of course, she shrugged nonchalantly and gave the non-answer of, "Just journaling."

"Ah." Dottie nodded slowly, arching her brow just enough to make it clear to Emily that she knew...something.

The woman could sniff out brokenness like a blood-hound, and Emily was cracked in two. How long could she hide it?

"Just boring stuff," Emily added dismissively. "My life is not that interesting, trust me."

"No one's life isn't interesting," Dottie asserted. "You know, Emily, I'm glad I ran into you."

Emily was glad she'd run into Dottie, too, although she didn't fully understand why. Something about the woman's presence was just...peaceful.

"Why's that?" she asked, lifting her hand to shield her eyes from the sun as it got higher in the sky.

"Care to join me on my walk?" Dottie notched her chin toward the shoreline, facing north. "I've got about a half a mile left before I turn around."

Emily knew she had to politely decline. Nothing good was going to come out of building a personal relationship with Dottie Sweeney, who probably had a super-power of drawing the truth out of people.

But loneliness gnawed at her, and even the friendship of a woman in her seventies held a palpable appeal, offering a connection in Emily's dark and solitary existence.

It was a walk. What harm could it do? Plenty. But she'd be careful.

"Sure, I'd love to." Emily let out a sigh as she slid the notebook into her tote bag, slung it over her shoulder, and picked up Ruthie's leash.

Ruthie happily trotted between the two women as they walked along the sand, letting the water splash up against their bare feet with the gentle waves.

"So, Emily," Dottie said softly, lifting her chin and facing forward as they walked. "I see so much of you already, and since you'll be full-time at the inn once it opens in a couple weeks, we will be seeing even more of each other."

Emily smiled, but nerves prickled her chest. "Yes, I suppose we will."

"But there is still much about you I don't know."

Her chest tightened and the next breath was a little harder to take.

"Like I said..." She pushed a strand of hair out of her eyes. "My life really isn't that interesting."

But deep inside—or maybe not so deep—a little ache twisted with the overwhelming desire to spill. Just to unload the burden onto the shoulders of someone else who cared, even just as an employer, about Emily. She shoved that ache aside and walked.

Dottie stayed quiet for a few beats, then turned to Emily, slowing the pace.

"Honey, I'm going to be honest with you right now, okay? Because I believe honesty is important, and, like I told you before, you're part of the Sweeney House family now. And we are just that. A family."

Not really, but she sure craved the idea of a family. "Okay," she replied, purposely vague.

Dottie exhaled sharply, seemingly considering her words before she said, "Look, I know there is something going on in your life. I know that there is more to you than you let on, and I just want to be very clear that I really, really would like to help you. In any way I possibly can."

Emily held her breath, closing her eyes as emotion lodged in her throat.

"I want you to know you're safe here. You can talk to me, and whatever problems you are facing, you don't have to face them alone. If you're willing to be honest with me, I'd love to be there for you however I can. You know what they say..." Dottie turned to her, her eyes glinting with the light of the morning sun as she reached for Emily's hand. "A trouble shared is a trouble halved."

Emily stopped dead in her tracks on the sand, nearly choking on a gasp as Grandma Gigi's signature phrase came out of Dottie's mouth. It was unreal. It was...super-natural.

Was that what this was? Her dear late grandmother trying to speak to her right now, through Dottie. In some bizarre, cosmic way, the spirit of Grandma Gigi was right here, next to her, and Emily could not ignore that.

"My, um..." She shook her head as they continued walking. "My grandma used to always say that."

"Well, she was a wise woman, I'm sure."

"I do have some troubles," Emily admitted, her mind whirring with one question: how much to tell her? Everything? Nothing? A little bit or a lot?

"And would you like to talk to someone about those troubles?" Dottie urged. "I'm sure your grandmother was that person for you and she's gone and...I'm here."

Emily twisted a lock of hair, looking at Dottie, then the ocean, and back to Dottie again. "I can't," she said on a ragged whisper. "I just can't. It's not...smart."

"Emily, sweetheart." Dottie took her hand again. "You need to know that you're safe here. I would never betray you or hurt you. I might even be able to help you, if you tell me the truth."

The words echoed through her mind, and it seemed as if Emily's entire story was sitting on the tip of her tongue, like an avalanche at the top of a mountain. It was only a matter of time.

She needed someone, and that someone was right here.

"Okay. But I need total secrecy," she insisted. "You can't tell anyone. And you have to promise me, Dottie. My life depends on it."

With wide eyes at the last line, Dottie put her hand over her chest. "As God and Jay Sweeney are my witnesses, I will not break your confidence or share a secret."

With a long, slow breath of pure relief, she nodded. "I guess I'll start with the fact that my name isn't really Emily. Well, I was named Emily when I was born, but at six months old I was adopted by Joanna Painter, and renamed Amelia."

Dottie listened, quietly, nonjudgmentally.

Emily let the words keep tumbling out, not that anything could stop her now. "Anyway, my mom was single, but she died when I was really young—"

"I'm so sorry," Dottie murmured.

"Yeah, I don't remember much about her, but her mother, my Grandma Gigi, raised me."

"The wise one."

Emily smiled, her heart feeling warm despite her nerves. "So wise. And about three and a half years ago, I married a man I thought I loved. Doug." She purposely left off the last name, just out of a bone-deep sense of self-preservation.

She couldn't believe she was saying this, but she couldn't stop.

"I hadn't known him for that long, but he was just very charming and charismatic and always doing some wild grand gesture for me. It was very romantic and fast and I thought without a doubt that he was the one. He wanted to move quickly with engagement and marriage, so we did."

She swallowed and took a deep breath to compose herself before sharing the worst parts of the story. "Then things went...sour."

Dottie stayed quiet, calmly listening, giving Emily the time and space to gather herself before she shared the story she'd never before said out loud. "He became violent. Just yelling, at first. Then it quickly turned into physical violence. A shove, a grab. Then a hit."

"Oh, Emily." Dottie fisted her hands, closing her eyes with a grunt. "How awful."

"It was. And then, it got bad. Like, really bad. I've never told anyone this before. My grandma had a sense that something wasn't right, and she saw some bruises on me. But not long after I got married, she got diagnosed with cancer, and it was a long battle. I couldn't weigh her down with this truth. I was sure I could handle it alone."

Dottie turned to her, her eyes misty. "I know we don't know each other that well, but I am here for you, okay? And your secret is safe."

"Okay. Thank you." Emily bit back tears and continued walking side by side with the woman she was now almost fully convinced was an angel. "Anyway, it started to get scary. He hurt me. Badly. Threatened me in every imaginable way."

"And did you tell anyone? A priest or a cop or..."

She swallowed. "My husband is a well-regarded and extremely skilled FBI agent who has connections everywhere. I couldn't go to the police because someone would protect him or alert him. I didn't go to church, I had no friends, and Doug took control of every aspect of my life." She let out a dry laugh. "I know you hear these stories and think, 'Oh, I'd never let a guy do that to me,' but it happened slowly and insidiously. I gave him control, no question, but he abused that control from the day we got married. He used fear and intimidation to get me to quit my job, stay home, cut ties with my friends. Then Grandma Gigi died, and I *truly* had no one."

Dottie put her arm around Emily, pressing her into a hug. "You poor baby. You must have been so scared."

"I was." She swallowed, slowly drawing back, committed to finishing the story. "But when my grandma was dying, she wrote me a letter. And in that letter she told me about a boxful of cash she had, and instructed me to take it and leave him. So, after months of planning, of using my husband's files to find out how to get a fake ID made, of waiting for the opportunity, I ran away. I cut off my hair, dyed it black, and got on a bus and headed to Florida to the town where my fake ID said I lived."

"Fort Pierce."

"I never made it," she confessed. "I stopped in Cocoa Beach because I liked the way it sounded and when I was walking one evening, I saw the sign at Sweeney House that you were hiring a housekeeper. I made up my whole resume, Dottie. I'm sorry."

"Oh, please. I'm...just trying to process this," she said softly. "He hasn't told anyone you're missing?"

"No, which is kind of shocking. I haven't seen one line in the news from the area about a missing woman. And it's been over two months."

"Surely someone misses you!"

Emily gave her a sad smile. "No, he made sure of that. Maybe a neighbor notices I don't bring the dog out, but so far? Nothing. He knows how to find anyone— terrorists, wanted criminals, undercover...whatever. That's his skill. Police departments borrow him to help with missing person investigations. And that's why I'm so scared all the time."

"You think he's looking for you?"

"I'm sure he is." Emily let out an exhale, her shoulders—her whole body, actually—lighter than it was half an hour ago. "That's why I'm living in a temporary place, without a car, no credit card, and..."

"Getting paid in cash," Dottie finished. "I understand."

But did she? When she thought about what this all meant, would she tell the authorities...or ask Emily to leave? She didn't know, but Dottie had asked for trust, so Emily was going to give it to her.

"It's a big, scary mess, and all I want in the whole world is a chance to start over. A chance for a new beginning without any fear or baggage or an abusive control freak hunting me down." She took in a shuddering breath. "I don't know if I'm ever going to get that."

After a moment, Dottie stopped walking, turning to take Emily's hands in hers. "Honey, I can't tell you how deeply I appreciate you sharing your story and being honest with me. I'm sure it took a lot to trust me with that information, and I can assure you that I won't tell a soul."

She smiled, turning to face the other women. "Thank you, Dottie. And I'm sorry for putting that on you, but, wow, I feel better."

"Of course you do, and don't apologize. You've been through a trauma and my heart breaks for what you've suffered." She shook her head. "I am here for you, honey."

"I appreciate that." Emily said. "I still really need a job, so can I still work as a maid at Sweeney House? Even though I lied about pretty much everything?"

Dottie laughed. "Of course. We are happy to have you. And I might just have to throw you a cash bonus for all that hard work you put in on the computer system."

She felt her heart warm with gratitude. "Thank you."

"So, there's truly no one else? Not a long-lost aunt or cousin or anyone you could call and look to for help? Family is so important."

Emily pressed her lips together, the name "Vanessa Young" echoing through her mind. "My grandma left me the name of my birth mother, the one who gave me away when I was six months old."

"The one who named you Emily," Dottie clarified.

"Yes." She nodded. "I looked her up and found her phone number, but—"

"You have to call her!"

"I don't know, I don't think that—"

"Oh, Emily, Amelia, whatever your name is," she joked. "You can never pass up a chance to reconnect with a family member. I know many years have passed, but it could give her a world of joy to hear from you!"

Emily shook her head, hating that it sounded so good and right, but it could go so wrong. "She gave me up. And it was a closed adoption."

"Did you know that my husband Jay had a daughter with his high school girlfriend who was put up for adoption?"

"Um, no. I can't say I did." Emily smiled.

Dottie nodded. "That's right. And my girls, Sam and Julie, reached out to her to make a connection, since they were her half-sisters and all, and that woman is Lori."

"Lori?" Emily turned with surprise. "The one who does the yoga classes in the cabana?"

"That's the one. We didn't meet her until she was well into her fifties and now she, her daughter, and her grandbaby-on-the-way are all as much a part of our family as anyone. Just because Sam and Julie made the bold and impulsive choice to reach out to her. She's started a whole new life here."

"Wow." Emily kicked the edge of the water, watching it gently splash up around her ankles as she thought about this. "That's an amazing story."

"And you'll have an amazing story, too." Dottie placed a gentle hand on her arm. "No matter what happens. You're brave, and strong, and clearly extremely resilient. That much I can tell."

She didn't feel so brave or strong lately, just scared.

"Call your birth mother, Emily. You never know what could come of it. Anything is possible."

Emily took in a long inhale, smelling the salt and the warmth of the sea. She knew Dottie was right. Anything was possible.

Chapter Fourteen

Taylor

"Wait. What? A bridal shop?" Sam held up both hands and slid a glare at Taylor. "I told you I didn't want some blushing bride gown for this wedding. Unless we're here for you."

Taylor laughed softly at that. "Not yet, Mom, but they have all kinds of dresses here. I called and checked, and they have plenty off-the-rack that are not Vera Wang hoop skirts. And I didn't make a huge deal and invite all your sisters and mother and best friend to sip champagne on a white leather couch and pass judgment. No matter how fun that sounds."

Her mother snorted. "Yes, it will be fun when you get married. But..." She turned and looked at the name of the store, her gaze landing on a cloud of lace and tulle in the window. "This isn't for me."

"Give it a chance, Mom." Taylor urged her toward the door. "They have a good selection of a wide range of dresses and the owner told me the tailor could work you in over the next week or so. Wedding dresses usually take months."

"Not if we go to a department store and get something...simple."

"We'll get something simple," Taylor promised. "But it will be for a wedding. Your wedding. Come on."

On a sigh, they walked in, sharing a quick look and a laugh at the white leather sofa. "Okay, I sit and judge, you try on.'"

Half an hour—and one teensy glass of bubbly for Taylor—later, Sam had stars in her eyes and was totally swept up in the moment, allowing the helpful stylist to find a nice selection of elegant gowns that would look incredible.

Taylor leaned back on the sofa and crossed her legs. "Get in there and start the show, Mom."

Sam pointed a finger at Taylor, smiling. "Get your judging pants on, Miss Tay. I want nothing but honest feedback."

"When am I not honest?" Taylor threw her hands up, laughing.

Sam disappeared around the corner to a dressing stall, where the stylist helped her into the first dress and Taylor leaned back and took in the vibe. She wasn't ready for all this yet, she thought, but when her day came, she'd like a small and intimate place like this. Not a major, overpriced name boutique, but something where she could find the right dress for the right man.

Was that Andre? She didn't know, but—

"Okay, here comes dress number one," her mother called.

Taylor did a mock drum roll on her knees. "Dress number one!"

Sam emerged from behind the curtain wearing a

stunningly intricate, lace embroidered mermaid-style dress that hugged her figure. Hugged it maybe a little too much. Whoa, was there any room for...imagination?

Before opening her mouth, she looked at her mom's face, which was glowing with radiance and joy.

If this was the dress she wanted, then what did Taylor's opinion matter? She looked stunning and, frankly, had the figure to carry it off.

"Wow. Mom. It's..."

"Horrible!" Sam finished, and the two of them burst out laughing. "Who do I think I am, Madonna? I can't believe I even pulled it off the rack."

Taylor laughed so hard she almost spilled her champagne. "I was going to say youthful."

"Youthful for a boudoir model, yeah." Sam rolled her eyes, turning to head back into the dressing room. "Moving on."

Taylor chuckled to herself and sipped her champagne, reflecting on how she treasured these moments, even though—especially though—her family had become fractured.

So much about Taylor's life and family was unorthodox, so she knew she had to treasure moments like this—the moments of Sam laughing in a ridiculously sexy wedding gown. Maybe Dad was a lost cause, but Mom would always be her best friend.

"Oh, boy. This one's a doozy," Sam mused from inside the dressing room. "Not sure what we were thinking when we picked it."

"You were thinking fairy-tale wedding," the saleswoman said. "And that's what this one says."

"What it says," Sam said over the swishing of a lot of tulle and netting, "is that I fell into a wedding cake and came out looking like this."

She stepped out in a literal cloud of white, layer upon layer of sparkly netting and taffeta, silk, tulle, lace, and...no.

"It's hard to move," Sam said, biting her lip.

"But you'll look great in the pumpkin carriage, Cinderella."

Sam snorted and attempted to spin around, but the gigantic skirt got caught on the platform and she nearly fell over. "It's *way* too much."

"I love it."

"Seriously?" Sam blinked.

"I mean, if I were to get married, I'd..."

Sam gathered up the material in her hand and turned to the stylist. "Make a note of this one...for the future."

Taylor gave her a wistful smile. "You're sweet, Mom. Now, let's get to that pale pink A-line that you loved."

"Yes, please."

While she did, Taylor walked through a few rows of dresses, plucking some that appealed...for the future.

"All right, you ready for dress number three?" Sam called, a note of excitement in her voice that was impossible to ignore.

Taylor turned just as she walked out in a simple column of the palest pink satin with a barely there layer of chiffon that made it move like liquid mercury.

"Oh." She put her hand to her lips. "Mom. You look beautiful."

She smiled and took a step up to the platform, turning to the endless mirror. "I love it."

"It's elegant and graceful and soft and perfect," Taylor whispered. "A little color, a sweetheart neckline, and everything about it says classy but fun. Frankly, it's you in a dress."

"Taylor!" Sam spun to face her, blinking back some tears. "You're so sweet."

"Do you love this one?"

She bit her lip and turned back to the mirror, a flush deepening her cheeks. "I love this one. It's beach wedding appropriate, but still leaves no doubt who the bride is."

The stylist joined them, clasping her hands. "That was made for you, Samantha," she whispered, bending over to fluff the hem. "Very little alterations and you'll look like a princess."

"A pregnant princess," she mouthed to Taylor in the mirror.

But Taylor didn't see anything but her beautiful, beautiful mother winning at the game of life.

"Is this the one?" the saleswoman asked.

Sam nodded, her eyes misty.

"Then let me go get our tailor for the final fitting."

When she stepped out and left them alone, Taylor came up on the platform, taking her mother's hands and giving them a squeeze. "You deserve this, Mommy," she whispered.

"Oh, Tay."

"I mean it. You deserve to marry a man who adores you, who will be faithful until the end, and who will be as amazing a dad as you are a mom." Tears of joy and pride stung behind her eyes as she looked at Sam, the most beautiful bride. "Do you realize the mountain you climbed? The victory you achieved? The new life you forged when the old one imploded?"

"Taylor," Mom said, her voice thick. "I could never have done this without you. I couldn't have dreamed of doing it without you."

They hugged until the seamstress came out, took a bazillion pictures, and even posed in front of the "I said Yes to the Dress" sign.

They walked out with nothing but a receipt, a promise for the alterations to be done in two weeks, and one of the best memories they'd ever shared.

It occurred to Taylor that, in twenty-five years, she had never seen her mom this happy. And there was no one more deserving of happiness than Samantha Sweeney.

Yes, her family was broken. Yes, her dad made some seriously costly mistakes. But...if it hadn't all happened exactly the way that it did, then Sam would not be this happy right now.

Despite all the pain and sadness that Max had put them through, in a way, he'd actually freed Sam to go and spread her wings and fall in love with her real soulmate, who brought her this kind of joy.

If Dad had never cheated, Mom would never have gotten to have all of this.

"And that..." Taylor lifted her pint glass filled with her favorite raspberry sour beer. "Was my epiphany."

Andre looked at her from across the high-top table on the deck at Blackhawk Brewing, his brown eyes gleaming with amusement as he lifted a glass of water and toasted with her.

"Well, Tay, that is quite an epiphany. I know how much you've struggled with your dad, and rightfully so, but I do think it would do you a world of good to make at least a little bit of peace with him. Because, you're right. As much as things sucked for a while, it all did work out for the best, especially for your mom. She's crazy happy."

Taylor was grateful that he was able to take a half hour away from managing the local brewery tonight to hang with her. Andre Everett was a constant source of reason and steadiness in Taylor's life, and he was also her best friend.

She needed him, and she'd begun to realize she needed him all the time. And she was okay with that.

"I know. It's impossible to deny that Mom is glowing in a way I've never seen before." Taylor took a drink, glancing around to take in the lively buzz of the atmosphere at Andre's brewery. "Remember when you first started this place?"

Andre smiled and it reached his eyes as he held his hand out to take Taylor's. "Are you kidding? It feels like yesterday. This spot wouldn't be a tenth of what it is without my PR guru." He winked at her.

She squeezed his hand. "I'm just so glad it brought us together."

"See?" He nudged her playfully. "Everything happens for a reason, Taylor Parker. And it always works out the way it's supposed to."

She took a deep breath, listening to the soft rock music playing through the speakers and the low hum of chatter and conversation throughout the expansive back deck.

Taylor thought back to that fateful day when she came home early over winter break to find her dad with Kayla. She never, ever could have imagined that working out for the good of anything.

But, somehow, it had. Mom needed a fresh start and a new life in order to find Ethan, and Taylor needed to get away and find a new career and fall in love with Andre. Ben needed to come out of his shell and be surrounded by family and love, and he'd blossomed.

"I..." She brushed her hair out of her face. "I can't believe I'm actually saying this, but I *want* to forgive him. I just don't know if I can."

"That's a darn good place to start, I think," Andre said.

"It's so hard." Taylor shook her head. "They painted over the wall. I mean, can you believe it? I don't know how to get past that."

Andre leveled his gaze on her, still holding her hand tightly. "Babe, you have to talk to them. Both of them. I know how you feel about Kayla, but she's a fact of life if you want to have a relationship of any kind with your dad or Brooklyn."

Taylor huffed out a breath. "I know."

"So, just be honest. Calm and reasonable, but sit down with them and explain why you felt so hurt." Andre lifted a broad shoulder. "There's always a way to make things right, and I think it's pretty obvious that your dad wants to."

"In his own, twisted, annoying Max Parker way... yeah. He does." She took another sip, setting the pint glass back down and running her fingers over the droplets of condensation on the glass. "I just feel like I can't go back there after what went down last time. I mean, I kinda lost it."

"You were upset." He shrugged again. "They understand. I'm sure it would mean the world if you wanted to give it another chance and go back to see them again."

Taylor swallowed, nerves already stretched across her chest at the thought. "I did really like the baby."

Andre laughed, tilting his head back. "See? You've got a heart of gold, Tay. I know you can do this, and you'll never regret mending a broken bridge."

"Why are you so wise?" Taylor angled her head and studied her ridiculously handsome boyfriend with his tight braids and cool clothes. "You're like an old sage."

He snorted. "Tell you what—I'll go with you."

Taylor perked up, eyes wide. "You...you will?"

"I think you could use the support, and not Ben this time. I'm off on Sunday. Let's go together. I'll drive, and that way I'll be there as a buffer and help you keep your cool."

"Andre." Taylor held his hand and beamed at him with gratitude. "That would mean the absolute world to me. Thank you."

"I love you, Tay. I'd do anything for you."

"I love you, too."

And she did. She really, really did.

Chapter Fifteen

Julie

The sun was just beginning to set as Julie, Brian, and the rest of the main team in charge of Wave Haven planning wrapped up their dinner meeting at Sharky's Sea Shack.

Brian had called the meeting and, of course, stated that it would be held at the office. But when it became clear that the only time that worked for everyone was after 6 p.m., Julie suggested they make a team dinner out of it.

To her surprise, Brian happily agreed.

As they finished up, Linda Westbrook slid her laptop into her bag and nodded contently. "Well, everything is on track and it appears our ducks are in a row for this festival."

"Thank you so much for all you're doing, Linda." Julie stood up to give her a hug that she may or may not have wanted, but whatever. Julie liked hugs. "You're an absolute gem."

"Just doing my job, Mayor." Linda smiled.

The other department heads and city representatives said their goodbyes, thanking Julie and Brian and leaving to head home.

Which left, of course, Julie and Brian, sitting directly across from one another in the fading orange sunlight right out on the water.

Sharky's, a local favorite casual eatery, was situated off the boardwalk along the Cocoa Beach Pier, only about a mile north of Sweeney House. The pier, bustling with restaurants, bars and shops extended out over the water.

As Julie glanced across the table at Brian, she suddenly became very aware that this felt a whole lot like...a date.

Should she leave? Should she stay? Should she order a drink or a dessert or ask him if he wanted to go for a walk?

Was he thinking any of the same thoughts, or was he still concerned with the metal detector placement at the entrances of the festival?

"So," Julie said, breaking the silence, wondering if he was going to leave, too, but secretly hoping he wouldn't. "Any other concerns, Chief?"

"None at the moment." Brian smiled. "Considering the short notice of an event this size, everything seems to be very well prepared. We must have someone amazing in charge in this city."

"The washed up, tattooed musician ain't a half bad mayor, is she?" Julie joked.

"The professional, talented, and very much all-business mayor is doing a wonderful job." Brian pinned his steel-blue gaze on her, his eyes dancing with the reflection of the setting sun.

Julie, struck by the sincerity of the compliment,

leaned closer across the table and smiled. "Thank you. That really means a lot."

"Any luck shutting down the haters on the local Facebook whine-fest groups?"

"They've been pretty quiet." Julie sipped her Diet Coke proudly. "I think if this festival is a big success, and I can keep myself out of any kind of controversy or small-town drama and rumors, it should be okay. I just want to be taken seriously."

"You are serious," Brian said. "But you're also seriously *fun*."

"Mayors aren't supposed to be fun."

He inched forward, lowering his voice. "I think they're supposed to be passionate, intelligent, caring, and authentic. Which you are. I've..." He cleared his throat, drawing back as if he realized he was oversharing. "I've come to realize you are definitely competent."

Never one to avoid spontaneous fun, Julie put her hand on his and decided to go for broke. "Do you want to go for a walk? You know, to the pier?" She nodded out toward the long boardwalk.

"Yeah, that sounds great."

Julie stood up, slinging her bag over her shoulder as she and Brian walked down the stairs of the back deck and Sharky's and onto the long wooden boardwalk.

It was a gorgeous night, with the very last hint of the Florida winter giving the beach a cool breeze and the fading light turning the ocean into a million shades of gold and peach.

Julie felt Brian's muscular arm graze the side of hers,

and she didn't step away. She didn't want to. "Can I be totally honest?" she asked.

"Of course. What's going on?"

"I am so freaking nervous about this festival," Julie confessed on a self-deprecating laugh. "I feel like it's my big chance to have everything go right and really, truly prove that I know what I'm doing, but there are so many factors that are out of my control."

"And yet you'll get blamed for them when something goes wrong, even if you had literally no way of doing anything about it," Brian warned, his voice tinged with sympathy and understanding.

"Yes!" Julie threw her hands up. "Exactly."

"Welcome to small-town politics. As the chief of police, I'm pretty sure I get blamed for every crime that happens in Cocoa Beach."

"There are crimes in Cocoa Beach?" Julie asked playfully.

"Sure. Mild vandalism, shoplifting, the occasional underage drinker..." He narrowed his gaze, giving her a teasing nudge. "Some high school kids are just trouble with a capital T. You might remember."

Julie chuckled at that, remembering how she'd watch him from across the music room, studying his varsity letterman jacket and perfect, shiny smile.

They'd lived in different worlds. Crossing paths, only steps away, but a universe of high school expectations and social norms had kept them chasms apart.

"You must have thought I was going to end up in jail when we were back in high school," she mused.

"That's not exactly what I thought," Brian admitted, his voice trailing off as they walked past a bustling outdoor bar with a live band playing on a wooden deck.

"Oh, come on, King Brian." She elbowed him as she sang his old nickname. "What *did* you think of me back then?"

He looked at her, lifting a shoulder. "You first. What did you think of me?"

Julie drew back, facing forward as she pondered the question and they walked along the boardwalk to the end of the pier. "I thought you deserved the nickname. Like my twin brother but even more of a golden boy. Homecoming King, football star, nine thousand AP classes...I thought you were in another league."

Brian nodded, considering Julie's response. "I thought you were fascinating, to be honest."

They reached the very end of the pier, and stopped to lean against the railing at the edge of the boardwalk that hung over the ocean.

The evening was quiet and still, and there was no one around this part of the deck besides them.

"Really?" Julie turned to face Brian, and they held each other's gaze for a few beats.

"Yes," he said with certainty, closing the gap between them a couple of inches. "I know you assume I didn't notice you, or thought you were just some artsy burnout, but that's not the truth, Julie."

Julie's heart hammered in her chest.

Was it possible John was completely right and Brian Wilkes had actually always *liked* her?

It seemed like a silly joke at first, but nothing about this moment between them was silly.

"What is the truth, then?" Julie asked, her voice barely above a whisper.

Brian let out a soft laugh. "The truth is that I had a secret, massive, painful crush on you, and for some reason it's taken me three decades to tell you that. I was riveted by you. I didn't think you'd want anything to do with a dumb jock like me, so I stuck to the status quo."

"Lanie," Julie said softly.

Brian closed his eyes and nodded. "Yeah. And don't get me wrong, I loved her a lot but even in high school, there was always drama and we were on again and off again. Ultimately, even though we got married, I couldn't give her what she wanted. Still, we had Davis and even though it didn't work out, I'm glad it happened."

Julie nodded, knowing she felt the same way about her relationship with Roman. She'd be lost without Bliss.

"I had a thing for you, though, Julianna. A pretty big thing." Brian let out a mock sigh. "There. I admitted it. My sixteen-year-old self can be at peace now."

Julie smiled, shaking her head with disbelief as she studied the man in front of her. "I had no idea. We hardly ever spoke."

"My mistake. It was high school, you know? We were kids and there were labels. Plus, when I was broken up with Lanie, she still had her hounds watching me."

She swallowed. "Too bad. I wish you would have given it a shot, though. To throw the entire high school ecosystem off balance, if nothing else."

Brian chuckled softly. "I always wondered where you were, what you ended up doing. Something wild and fun and amazing, like touring and living in a van."

Julie laughed. "Believe me, that life isn't as idyllic as it seems. Have you ever heard of a composting toilet?"

"Yes and no, thank you." He laughed. "And then I saw you on a billboard for the next mayoral election and it was like fate smacked me in the face."

Julie smiled, her whole chest warm and her head buzzing. "And now...we're here."

"We're here."

She glanced down, then back up at him, considering the man in front of her. He was the opposite of everything she used to think she wanted. Julie liked reckless and impulsive and spontaneous. She fell for men who had a sizable wild streak and didn't know the meaning of commitment.

But now, standing just inches away from her on the edge of the pier, was a man who was the opposite of what she'd always wanted, and yet was, in fact, everything she needed.

"You know..." Julie took a deep breath, leaning close enough to smell the tiniest hint of Brian's woodsy cologne. "It's not too late."

He furrowed his brow, a crooked smile playing at the corner of his mouth. "That's what's so beautiful about this life, Julie Sweeney. It's full of second chances."

On a soft sigh, he leaned in and kissed her, a light and airy kiss that was enough to make the whole world melt away.

For just a few, fleeting seconds, Julie floated on a cloud, her lips pressed to his, everything about him feeling steady and safe.

In a moment, it was over, and she pulled back, both of them quiet as the impact of the kiss hit.

"Do you think anyone saw that?" she whispered, glancing around at the relatively dead end of the pier. "We are, kind of, public figures."

Brian shook his head. "There's no one around. You look absolutely beautiful, by the way. Even, what? Thirty years later? I think you're prettier now than then. And then? I thought it hurt to look at you because you were so gorgeous."

Julie felt her face warm, the world quiet but for the waves softly splashing around them and the distant sound of music from the boardwalk. "Thank you. I never knew how much I wanted to do that until now."

She leaned forward for one more quick peck, thinking that if this was her life's new wild and exciting turn, she was all in for this ride.

"Mom!" Bliss burst into Julie's bedroom at the literal crack of dawn, startling Julie awake. "Mom, oh, my gosh. Is there something you're not telling me?"

Her daughter flounced across the room, her blond hair swishing around her face.

"You have entirely too much energy at"—Julie

squinted in the direction of the clock on her nightstand—
"6:41 a.m. What is going on, Blissy?"

Bliss came and sat down at the edge of the bed,
smelling like youthful, floral perfume and sunshine.
"Well, I woke up early to get ready for school and saw
this!"

Julie had to shield her eyes from the blaring beacon
that was Bliss's iPhone, but the second her pupils
adjusted to the light, her stomach dropped. "Oh...oh, no.
Oh, man."

On the screen was a slightly out of focus photograph
of Julie and Brian kissing on the pier. It was a bit blurry
and dark, but the distinctive tattoo on Julie's left arm was
visible, and anyone who knew Brian Wilkes, which
would be the entire town and all the adjoining ones,
would know that was him.

Bliss's eyes were wide and her mouth gaping open.
"You didn't tell me you were having a secret love affair
with that police dude!"

"Bliss." Julie pressed her palm into her forehead, fear
and anxiety rising rapidly in her chest. "We're *not* having
a secret love affair. It was one kiss, and some jerk took a
picture and... Where did you see this?"

"Twitter. Some anonymous account called Cocoa
Beach Happenings posted it."

"Oh, *man.*" She groaned and fell back into her
pillowing, wishing this were a bad dream.

"It's okay, Mom. He's not married, right?"

"Of course not!"

"And neither are you, so...is it such a bad thing?"

"Well, considering he's the chief of police and I'm the mayor? It's a...questionable thing."

"But you deserve to be happy."

"I do," she agreed, managing a smile for the support. "But I also swore to do a great job as mayor and not, you know, kiss one of my direct reports in the moonlight on the pier."

"Then everyone can just shut up," Bliss said, the rise to Julie's defense very sweet, but naïve.

Julie rubbed her eyes and tried to swallow the lump of fear in her throat that came with the thought of facing the day ahead. "Sweets, it's not that simple. We have a professional relationship, there's politics involved and... oh, man. Facebook is gonna go nuts over this."

"I really don't see the problem." Bliss shrugged. "Two grown—*really* grown—people who like each other. It'll blow over," she said. "Let me read the comments."

"It's unprofessional," Julie said. "He's the chief of police and I'm the mayor. It looks really, really bad for us to be—I believe the word is 'fraternizing,' but I could be wrong—I could get in a lot of trouble, and...ugh."

She climbed out of bed and did a quick stop in the bathroom, brushing her teeth, washing her face, and headed into her closet to get one of the outfits she'd bought with Erica. Bliss was still sitting on the bed, still skimming her phone, and from the expression she wore? The comments were not good.

"I have to call him and get to the office," Julie announced, staring at the clothes but only seeing that grainy image. "And I better do it fast."

She settled on a maroon mid-length dress, definitely the most conservative and the least fraternize-y one of the lot.

Bliss finally put the phone down when Julie turned for help zipping up the dress.

"Well, for what it's worth, Mom, you've seemed exceptionally happy the past few weeks. And if that's because of Brian Wilkes, then I think it's a good thing."

Julie turned around to face her daughter, touched by her empathy and her selfless care. "I really appreciate your support, Bliss, and...I don't know. Maybe one day something could happen, but not now. I'm so new as mayor and my reputation is on shaky ground as it is."

"Who cares?" Bliss arched a brow. "You already got elected. Haters gonna hate."

Julie opened her mouth to protest but couldn't actually come up with a sound rebuttal. "Is Lilly picking you up for school?"

"Yup. She'll be here in fifteen."

"Okay, great." Julie leaned forward and kissed Bliss's forehead. "I have to run. Have an amazing day, babe. We'll talk more when I get home tonight."

"I demand to hear everything, including all details that led up to this moonlight-on-the-pier kiss!"

Rolling her eyes, but secretly smiling at the description, Julie took a little time to slap on blush and lipstick, brush and braid her hair, then slide into some low pumps. A quick look in the mirror confirmed that she looked downright dowdy and not at all like a woman who'd partake in moonlight-on-the-pier kissing.

"I promise all the deets," she assured Bliss. "But now, wish me luck on the battlefield, also known as small-town City Hall."

Julie had barely pulled out of their apartment complex when she was commanding her cellphone to call Brian Wilkes.

After a ring and a half, he answered with two words. "Don't panic."

For some reason, that made her smile. And get a weird, tumbly sensation in her stomach. And, honestly, those two words erased the panic. How did he do that?

"Yes, Chief," she said softly. "What do you suggest I do, then?"

"Think and not react."

Julie gripped the steering wheel as she cruised down A1A toward her office. "But my reputation as a professional is on the line. Possibly the chopping block. Can they recall me?"

He chuckled. "No one is getting recalled, Jules. I know it looks bad right now, and those Facebook trolls aren't going to like it, but I've got a plan."

"You do?" Julie angled her head as she turned into the parking lot of the office. "I sincerely hope that plan includes deleting that picture off the face of the Earth and using your police authority to enact a mass memory wipe on everyone who saw it."

He snorted. "Not exactly, but I've got something."

She pulled into her parking spot, staring at the "Reserved for Mayor Julianna Sweeney" sign through her windshield.

Not for long, she thought to herself.

"What's your plan, then, Chief?" she asked into the speakerphone.

"I have an interview with the *Space Coast Chronicles* on Wednesday."

"To talk about...this?" Julie drew back in horror.

"No," Brian said on an easy laugh that calmed her frayed nerves like balm. "It's been scheduled for weeks. Adrianna Harvey, their lead reporter, is a good friend of mine, and she wanted to do a story about the upcoming fundraising programs for the department."

"Okay," Julie drew the word out slowly. "How does that help us?"

"We spin the story with a friendly reporter. I can address it in the interview, completely downplay the entire thing and make sure it's very clear that we have a strictly professional relationship."

"That includes kissing."

"One kiss. Could have been a hug. Could have been the angle. Doesn't mean anything serious is going on."

An unexpected gut-punch of disappointment hit Julie at the cavalier description of the romantic kiss. Guess they both thought different things were going on.

She cleared her throat and looked hard at the dashboard as if it were his face. Julie Sweeney wasn't coy, she didn't play games, and she was too old not to know the truth of a relationship.

"Is that what you think?" she asked softly. "That nothing is going on?" She didn't regret asking—she had to know.

"That's not what I think at all," Brian said quietly after a pause. "I think something is definitely going on, but we are in unique positions that require us to navigate it very carefully, especially while you're building a solid reputation and gaining respect."

Relief washed over her and she smiled, liking yet another thing about him—he was straightforward and smart. "Okay, good. I agree. Especially if you think you can nip this in the bud with that interview."

"I'm just going to try to get it off of people's radars. I don't want you dealing with any more cyberbullies and keyboard warriors."

Her heart tugged. "Thanks, Brian. I really appreciate that. Let me know if there's anything I can do on the whole damage-control front."

"I sure will. And, for the record, Julie—I don't regret anything."

Now she was really smiling. Full on cheesy grin alone in her car. "I don't, either."

"So, we got this. We'll take it one day at a time, and I'll handle it. Promise."

"Okay." Julie took the keys out of the ignition and swung her bag over her shoulder, opening the driver's-side door. "I'm trusting you, Brian Wilkes."

And she knew, no matter what happened, that he was worthy of her trust. With this, and with anything else.

Chapter Sixteen

Dottie

Dottie Sweeney sure did find herself putting makeup on a whole lot more often these days. Inching back from the magnifying mirror on her bathroom vanity, she tried to make sure her eyebrows were drawn on correctly.

But her gaze lifted and met Sam's, who watched from the doorway with way too much mirth in her expression.

"Are you excited for your date?" Sam asked.

"It is most certainly not a date," Dottie insisted, rubbing one brow that might be just a little too dark.

Sam walked in and leaned against the bathroom counter, giving her mother a sassy arch of her own brow, which was thick and perfect and young. "Franklin Fox is making you a private gourmet dinner, just for the two of you, on a Friday night..."

"We're testing out some menu items is all." Dottie gently stroked one more touch of blush on her cheeks, not that she needed it. She felt flushed every time she saw the man, which was ridiculous at her age.

"Mm-hmm. Right." Sam rolled her eyes. "Why can't you just admit that this is a date and you're pretty darn excited about it?"

"I..." Dottie started, but stopped herself, not knowing what to say or how to explain her feelings.

She couldn't deny that Sam was right. Tonight's plans sure seemed like a date. But for heaven's sake, she was a seventy-two-year-old widow. Who was she to be going on dates? And with a rich celebrity, no less.

"I think he's just being nice, honey, really." She ran a hand through her soft gray curls, happy with the way they looked shiny and full around her face. "I'm still not even a hundred percent certain I can trust the guy as our head chef, let alone as my...date or whatever you think is going on here."

"Mom." Sam leaned down, gently brushing a curl out of Dottie's face. "You look absolutely beautiful. He likes you. Embrace it. Enjoy it. Be happy. You earned it."

"Oh, Sam, I am happy. I have all my babies and grandbabies in Cocoa Beach and now we have the inn and the bistro. I'm as happy as can be."

"Does he make your heart flutter?" Sam angled her head curiously. "Even just the tiniest bit?"

Dottie pressed her lips together before making the admission. "Perhaps the tiniest bit."

Sam laughed and put her hands on Dottie's shoulders, giving a squeeze and holding her gaze in the mirror. "Then why so reluctant to call it a date?"

Dottie took in a slow breath, suddenly overcome with emotion that could quickly turn into mascara-streaming tears if she didn't get ahold of herself.

"Am I...am I ready for this?" she asked Sam. "Is it right that I go on a real date? Jay's only been gone a couple of years, and he was my one and only. I was perfectly happy with that as my future. I never even thought about finding someone else or replacing him or—"

"You're not replacing Dad," Sam said. "You're...stepping into the next chapter of your life. Take it from a permanent resident of the next chapter. Come on in, Mom. The water's warm and full of romance."

"Pfft! Romance. I had my romance, Sam. Had it, loved it, and buried it." Her voice wavered on the last words. "Oh, Sam! Am I doing something terrible and stupid and wrong? Shouldn't I be sad about your father and not able to look at another man in that way?" She dropped her head. "Am I a horrible person?"

"Yes. You, Dorothy Sweeney, angel of Cocoa Beach, beacon of light and graciousness and love. You are, in fact, a horrible person. I'm so sorry it took you this long to figure that out."

Dottie laughed at Sam's endearing sarcasm. "I just...I feel like I shouldn't be capable of this. And yet... I am."

"Of course you are."

"I'm more than capable, actually." Dottie leaned close, squeezing Sam's hands and dropping her voice to a whisper. "I'm pretty darn excited."

"Yay! I'm so happy for you. You're going to have a wonderful night and probably one of the best meals of your life." Sam smiled and tapped her still-flat stomach. "Color me and the little one jelly."

"But is it so wrong?" Dottie asked nervously. "Isn't it

a total betrayal to your father? Why am I not sad? Why am I so okay with this?"

"Because you've healed, Mom. You've grieved your loss, and now your beautiful, wonderful life is continuing on. Dad lives in all of our hearts every single day."

"Of course he does. I think about him constantly."

"I know you do." Sam rubbed her shoulder. "But just because his life ended doesn't mean yours did. He will always be the love of your life. He will always be our daddy, our patriarch, the greatest man we ever knew."

"That he is." Dottie's heart swelled. "Was," she corrected sadly.

"And always will be, but you've honored him and mourned him and now you're capable of feeling new feelings in a completely new and different way. And there is nothing wrong with that."

"It is a new season in my life, I suppose." Dottie sighed wistfully, shaking her head as she pondered the way life rolled out in the most unexpected turns. "It feels wrong to enjoy a season without him."

"Well, it's not. Dad is smiling down on us this very minute, thinking about how stunning you look, and wanting so badly for you to not hide from the world and limit yourself just because he's gone." She squeezed Dottie's shoulder one more time. "Have fun, Mom."

Dottie laughed softly, straightening her back and standing to give her sweet Sam one more quick hug. "I will. I really think I will."

SITTING at the booth along the oceanfront windows of Jay's American Bistro, Dottie was warmed by a rare bout of pride. Not in any kind of egotistical, arrogant sort of way, but the purest pride for what she'd accomplished.

Not just the lovely atmosphere of a new restaurant or the complete overhaul of an aging inn, but her family— kids, grandkids, add-ons—and just in general for this restaurant, and for her own transformation. In some ways, that was even more tangible than the upgrades to Sweeney House.

There had been a time when she'd thought that Jay's death would destroy her. Days when she'd been certain that she'd never truly laugh again, never watch a sunrise without heartache, never wake up in the morning without pain.

But Sam was right. She'd healed. She'd grown. And somehow, through the loss and the change, Dottie Sweeney found herself to be even braver, stronger, and more fearless than she could have ever dreamed.

"Welcome to Jay's American Bistro, young lady." Franklin walked out of the kitchen, fully dressed in a white, double breasted chef's jacket and a *toque blanc* perched on his head.

The hat might look silly on some, but it did nothing to diminish his good looks, and he somehow managed to carry it off with an air of sophistication. But the real appeal of this man was the twinkle in his gaze, the window to his heart, which Dottie had come to decide was sincere.

"Look at you in full uniform." She stood up to give

him a hug. "How lucky am I to have a private dinner cooked just for me by one of the best chefs in the world?"

Franklin lifted a shoulder and gave a humble smile. "I'm not that great. They make the food look better on TV."

"Oh, hush." Dottie waved a hand. "Are you alone in the kitchen tonight?"

He nodded. "I am. Since I'm only cooking for the two of us, I don't need too many hands to help. Also, I like to cook solo when I create a new menu, get a close bond with the dishes before anyone else gets their hands on them."

Dottie sat back down in her booth, flipping the white napkin onto her lap as she settled in. "Okay, Chef. I'm ready to be wowed."

"Appetizers will be out shortly," he promised her. "Can I get you something to drink while you're waiting?"

"You're the server tonight, too, huh?"

"Oh, yes. My boss is running me ragged in this place. It's okay, though, because she's quite pretty." He added a wink.

Dottie laughed and felt her cheeks warm over the charming compliment. She'd always thought he might be just a TV personality, that the producers no doubt played up his charisma and wit for ratings, and then he'd be a beast behind the scenes.

But it all seemed to be authentic, without cameras and an audience of one.

"Just a sparkling water, please." Dottie looked up at him and smiled. "Don't worry, I tip well."

Franklin laughed and walked away, returning with a green bottle of San Pellegrino and a glass. He poured the drink and headed back to the kitchen, chatting briefly, then leaving Dottie to sip and enjoy the view.

After a few moments, he returned carrying a tray with four small plates on it, each featuring bite-sized creations drizzled with something beautiful and garnished with small orchids.

"Oh, my heavens!" Dottie gasped as he slowly placed each of the appetizers onto the table and the aromas tantalized her.

"Don't worry, it's a tasting menu. I figured it's impor- tant that we test out some of these staples for the Bistro and, of course, for Sam's wedding."

"What a wonderful idea, Franklin."

"Plus..." He took the chair across from her, removing his chef's hat and placing his napkin on his lap. "I will be joining you, of course."

"This is absolutely gorgeous." Dottie studied the plates, taking in the color, even the graceful layout of the food against the white. Everything was simply...thoughtful.

"May I present our starters," he said with a formal tip of his head toward the table. "Crab cakes, drizzled with a vinaigrette and chipotle garlic aioli, placed on a bed of Mediterranean marinated vegetables. Next is a pan- seared pork belly, paired with smoked brie and fig jam. Over here are our steamed mussels in white wine and rosemary sauce. And, finally, stuffed mushrooms with Manchego and ground lamb. *Bon appetit.*"

"You know..." Dottie stared at the dishes that looked like they popped right off the pages of a food magazine or gourmet cookbook. "I've never considered myself to be that much of a foodie, but I get it. I get the obsession now. This is fantastic!"

Franklin gave a hearty laugh, lifting his glass of sparkling water. "I'd like to propose a toast."

Dottie raised her cup to touch his.

"To the woman who launched my career as a grandfather."

With a quick laugh, she inched back. "Really?"

"Truly, Dorothy. Your suggestion unlocked a whole relationship with Henry, and seeing how you interact with your grandkids gave me such great insight into what I was doing wrong."

"I'm so glad."

He nodded. "We're making plans for later this week. He wants to show me Kennedy Space Center, since he was there on a field trip recently—"

"Let me know when you go. My daughter Erica can get you VIP passes and a chance to chat with an astronaut."

His jaw dropped. "Henry will love that. Anyway, thank you." He dinged her glass. "You have been an inspiration and I see many...surprises ahead."

The way he said that gave her a little thrill of excitement, and the thought that maybe he didn't mean surprises with Henry, but her.

"That's beautiful, Franklin. Cheers."

As they dove into the first course, Dottie was swept

away into culinary heaven, and Franklin told stories of his travels with the Food Network and his first job as a line cook.

It was impossible to deny that the man was enigmatic and hilarious. With each bite of delicious food, Dottie felt herself slip deeper under his spell, mesmerized by a man who could create a culinary treat, spin a delightful tale, and listen attentively.

Once the appetizers had disappeared and many belly laughs had been shared, Dottie leaned back in the booth, sighing softly. "You are quite something, Franklin Fox."

He angled his head. "How so?"

"The stories, the life, the talent! I've never met anyone like you."

"I could say the same to you, you know." He kept his gaze fixed on hers, his expression serious and real.

"Oh, good heavens. You're a celebrity. I'm a grandma —yes, a good one," she added with a laugh. "But no one wants my autograph."

"No one really wants mine anymore, either," he said with a wistful smile. "And you, Dorothy Sweeney, are so much more than a grandma. I've never met a person with a heart so gold and pure, with radiance that spreads to everyone around. I mean, look at your kids! They're grown and married and still they all flock to you. You're the glue of a wonderful, big, happy family. You created that, and you kept it so close and together all these years. It's much more than I was ever able to do."

She could tell the compliment came from his heart, and it meant the absolute world to Dottie. "Thank you,

Franklin. I never felt like I did anything of great significance. I just tried to be the best mom and wife I could be."

"You are. It's why I'm so drawn to you."

Drawn to her.

Dottie felt a little flutter in her heart, and she didn't instantly try to wipe it away or shut it down.

"I hope this isn't too forward," Dottie said slowly, clearing her throat. "But you are, uh, divorced?"

It had just occurred to her that in all of these conversations with Franklin, she'd never known much about his ex-wife. Nothing she'd ever seen written about him even mentioned a wife.

"Yes, amicably," he said. "Susan and I had a good relationship, but we were young and quite immature. I was very wrapped up in the TV lifestyle and it just got to be too much. We separated shortly after our daughter was born, and I never remarried."

"Dated quite a bit, though," Dottie teased. "Or at least that's what the, uh, tabloids said."

Franklin leaned back and narrowed his gaze playfully. "Wow, Dorothy, you really were a fan."

She rolled her eyes. "My husband liked the Food Network and I...liked your show."

"Tell me about your husband," Franklin said, the statement so direct and bold it caught Dottie off guard.

Was it okay to talk about Jay at this dinner, which was undeniably a date or something very much like it?

Her mind flashed with images of the man she loved, the man she'd always loved, and Dottie waited, as always, for the inevitable pang of grief and sadness. It didn't come.

"Jay was quite a character," she started, shaking her head and actually relishing the opportunity to share memories of him. She wasn't sad. She wasn't broken. She began to talk, and stories tumbled out with laughter and joy. "He had sayings for everything, lots of advice, a huge heart, and unconditional love for his family. And this inn," she added. "Although he never wanted a proper restaurant. That was my addition."

"A good one," he said. "How did you meet him?"

She smiled at the question and the memory, which she shared with just enough detail to keep it interesting, but not too personal. She told him how they moved to Cocoa Beach when Jay was in the Air Force, and how shocked they were when she found out she was pregnant with twins.

She told him about Jay's over-the-top Christmas traditions and his love of New Year's resolutions and his dying wish that all four of his kids would always be best friends.

"Anyway, I'm rambling." Dottie chuckled and waved a hand after finishing a silly anecdote about when Jay pranked the kids into thinking they were going to an extra school class but drove them to Disney World instead.

"You most certainly are not rambling," Franklin said. "He sounds like an incredible man, and makes me feel like a terrible father."

"Well, he wasn't much of a cook."

Franklin laughed. "Seriously, it's no wonder you have

such a wonderful family. Thank you for sharing all of that with me, really."

"Thank you for listening," she said, looking down at her nearly empty plate. "To be honest, I used to think I'd never be able to talk about him without feeling...beyond blue. Wrecked, really. But I've healed from the grief these past two years. Now, I feel grateful for the decades we had together and it brings me so much joy to share those memories. I'm good. And, gosh, I'm sorry for such vulnerability."

"Please don't apologize, Dottie." Franklin smiled at her, his eyes kind and warm. "You have amazing stories. I'd love the chance to hear every last one of them."

Dottie held his gaze for a few beats, feeling more seen and understood than she had in a long, long time. "You know," she said. "When you get older, you start to feel invisible and a bit irrelevant."

"I do know." He pressed his finger to his chest. "Has-been, remember?"

"Well, I just wanted to say..." She swallowed. "Thank you for making me feel visible again."

"Just like making you this dinner, it's an honor and a privilege. Now, should we get on to the salad course?"

"Oh, my goodness, we haven't even had salads yet!" Dottie laughed, leaning back in the cushion of the booth seat and playfully resting her hands behind her head. "I could get used to this."

The night continued on, and Dottie and Franklin spent hours in the candlelit, empty restaurant, laughing and eating and talking the night away.

Franklin finished off the dinner with a classic crème brulée, while she shared stories about all her grandkids and he tried to memorize each of their names, ages, and branch of the family tree.

Dottie had no idea why he cared so much, but it meant the world.

By the end of the evening, she had a full stomach and an even fuller heart. She had no doubt of three things: Jay's American Bistro was going to have the best food in the area, possibly in the state of Florida; Franklin Fox was a trustworthy and sincere man; and, lastly, if this was a date, it was a very, very good one.

Chapter Seventeen

Emily

Emily must have paced a mile and a half back and forth on the ratty carpet of her motel room, clutching her disposable phone in clammy hands.

It was before nine in the morning, and Emily didn't have to be anywhere that day. Dottie had instructed her to take a few days away from the inn to relax, regroup, and...reconnect.

Reconnect with one Vanessa Young, her birth mother.

Emily couldn't really remember how to relax, and never really knew what "regroup" actually meant. But the "reconnecting" instruction was easily the scariest and hardest part of Dottie's advice.

"I don't know, Ruthie." She turned to the creature lounging on the bed, whose pointy nose followed Emily back and forth with every lap across the tiny room. "She gave me up for adoption when I was six months old. Obviously, she hadn't fallen in love with her baby and fought to keep it."

But the truth was, no one knew that story. No one but Vanessa Young.

Ruthie stared back at her, the dog's expressive dark brown eyes wide with interest.

"I know it's been almost twenty-nine years. I know things have changed." Emily ran a hand through her hair, noticing just how terrible a job she'd done at cutting the ends.

Whatever. A bad haircut was the least of her problems. She used to be pretty, and fresh, young, and well put together. Until Doug made her feel worthless and useless and trashy.

She longed for her old self. Would that version of Amelia Painter ever come back? She didn't know, but somewhere, way deep in the recess of her heart and soul, she sensed that a connection with her birth mother could help. But...

"She didn't want me then," Emily continued, shaking her head as she attempted to work out the thoughts that never seemed to have an answer or solution. "So why would she want anything to do with me now?"

Ruthie let out a soft whimper, rolling onto her side in the pillows on the bed.

"Yes, I know she was only sixteen when she had me, so of course it was too much for her to handle. And that's not to say adoption wasn't the right move, because if I had never been adopted, I never would have had Grandma Gigi. I don't harbor any resentment toward her for giving me up. She did what she had to do," Emily explained, knowing all Ruthie wanted was a belly rub, but this was helping her.

The dog blinked a few times, keeping her gaze fixed on her trusty owner.

"And I know she's technically my only family or friend or...person on the planet." She paused her pacing at the bed and rubbed that smooth belly, letting the truth hit her.

She didn't have a soul in the world anymore who truly, truly cared about her. And this woman, the woman who'd brought her into the world, was out there. Emily had done the math. Vanessa Young would be forty-five now, sixteen years older than Emily.

What was she like? What did she do? Would she be thrilled to hear from her long-lost adopted daughter, or would she tell her to never call again?

Was she married? Had more kids?

The thought of Vanessa having another baby and choosing to keep it hurt a little, Emily couldn't deny that as she started pacing again. But, again, she'd been a teenager and it all worked out so that Emily could be with Gigi.

But Gigi was gone, and Emily was so desperately alone.

Suddenly, Ruthie sat up and barked—a sharp, high-pitched noise that startled Emily.

"What? What's wrong, baby?"

Ruthie barked again loudly, and Emily could have sworn the dog was pointing her nose directly at the sweaty disposable phone gripped in Emily's right hand. Or demanding more rubs, but Emily was starved for an actual conversation on the topic.

"You think I should call her, don't you?"

Ruthie whimpered and settled back down, curled up in a C shape on the ugly bedspread.

"You're right." Emily shut her eyes and let out a breath, nerves fraying. "I mean, what have I got to lose? The worst thing that can happen is that I end up exactly where I am now—alone."

Alone *and* knowing that the woman who gave birth to Emily rejected her not once but twice.

Could she handle that pain if that's what it came to?

Emily glanced to the left, catching a glimpse of herself in the foggy bathroom mirror above the sink. She noticed the ratty haircut, the bad dye and her now bony frame, thin from denying herself food while she rationed her cash.

But that skinny girl with the bad hair had escaped using her wits. She took trains and buses all the way across the country, used her own strength and resourcefulness to get a job, and managed to carve out the shreds of a new existence.

She most certainly could handle another bout of rejection.

"Okay, here I go." She typed in the phone number that she'd now memorized for how many times she'd stared at it, and hovered her thumb over the Call button.

The words "Burbank, CA" came up on the screen as the number registered, and a jolt of anxiety zinged down her spine.

She leaned on the side of the bed and rubbed Ruthie's soft, pointy ears for good luck, then quickly pressed the Call button, holding her breath as the line began to ring.

After what felt like an eternity but was actually only two rings, a woman answered.

"Hello, this is Vanessa."

Emily sucked in a breath, all her words stuck in her throat like concrete.

It was her. It was her birth mother on the phone. She'd practiced what to say, she'd rehearsed this a dozen times.

"Hello?" Vanessa said again. "If this is another marketing call, I do not want to upgrade my car insurance or whatever you want."

Emily looked at Ruthie, swallowed her nerves and stood up to resume pacing. "Um, hi, this is...this is Vanessa Young, right?"

"Yes." The other woman sounded *over* it. "Can I help you?"

"Yes. Well, actually, sort of. Not really, I just...um..."

"Is this a sales call?" She sounded annoyed. "A survey or something? I'm sorry, I'm very busy."

Emily could hear something clatter in the background. Voices and noise and...something. She tried to picture this woman who'd brought her into the world, but her mind went blank.

"No, no. It's not a sales call."

"Who is it, then?" She was getting impatient. Emily needed to just buck up and speak.

"This is, uh, this is Emily. Your, um..." She swallowed, squeezing her eyes shut as she clenched the phone in her hand. "Daughter. The baby you had at sixteen. It's, um, me."

For the longest moment, endless heartbeats of time, she heard nothing from the other side. For a moment, she thought the woman had hung up, then she heard her take a shaky breath.

"I thought they changed your name."

"I sort of changed it back," she said slowly, frozen in the middle of the motel room.

"How did you... What are you..." Vanessa's voice was quivering. "I can't believe you're calling me, I...I don't..."

"Look, you don't have to say anything," Emily said, letting go of her tension and deciding to just get everything off her chest. At least that way it would be done. "I got this number from my grandmother, who passed away recently. She was the only family I had, and, she left me money so that I could leave my abusive husband who I'm actually still on the run from at the moment, and she told me about you. She told me to call you. See, my adoptive mother, Joanna, died when I was three, and so Grandma Gigi raised me, but now she's gone. And my husband, Doug, is horrible and evil and cut me off from the world for a long time. I escaped and I'm hiding out right now, and things have just been really hard and scary and I thought I would just take a crazy risk and call you."

She managed a much-needed breath, and when Vanessa didn't respond or hang up, she continued.

"I don't want money or anything like that," she added quickly, suddenly aware that Vanessa might think that's what this call was about. "I just...I don't know what I want. I don't have anybody, and I really, really need a fresh start in life somehow, because things got pretty tough for me. But I do believe in second chances, and I'm hoping to find one of my own, and I just called you because you're my mother and you exist. That's...that's why I called."

The phone line was silent long enough for Emily to second guess, and then regret, this entire phone call in the first place.

"Are you... Are you there?" Emily whispered softly, her heart slamming so loud she swore the sound was echoing through the room.

"Emily, I...I can't believe I'm talking to you right now."

A tendril of hope slid through her chest as she waited for Vanessa to continue.

"But I'm so sorry, I can't do this right now. I have to go. Thank you for calling and I'm sorry for your situation and...I'm sorry. I can't."

"I'm at the Sweeney House in Cocoa Beach, if you ever want to—"

The click of disconnection was like a visceral punch to her gut. Emily winced, nearly sinking to the floor with disappointment, but she caught the edge of the bed and perched there. She stared at the phone, defeated, then let it thump to the floor from her clammy hand.

She shouldn't be this sad. She had nothing to lose. After all, she didn't even know the woman. But...

That was her mother. And she didn't want to talk to her.

The bitter, metallic taste of disappointment made her wonder if she might be sick, but after a few deep breaths, she stood.

"She gave me away for a reason, I guess," Emily whispered, her voice cracking as the rejection and abandonment crushed her soul. "I should have known. I never should have called. I don't even know what I was hoping to get out of that."

She snuggled close to Ruthie, scratching the fur on her neck and wiping some unexpected tears that fell down her cheeks.

Was there going to come a day when Emily could accept her fate as a lone wolf? When she could just be glad she survived that horrible marriage and made it out at all?

When would she stop longing for connection, for family, for a new chance at life that was clearly not in the cards for her?

She sat up abruptly, wiped her tears with the heel of her hand, and drew in a shuddering breath.

Hope was not lost for her life, but in this particular instant, it sure felt hopeless.

She slipped on Ruthie's leash, shoved her feet into some sandals and walked outside, fighting some sobs.

The Florida sun warmed her skin as she marched with Ruthie down the street toward the beach.

When they got there, Emily flipped her shoes off and ran with her dog straight into the water. It was colder than she expected, but it felt refreshing and cleansing.

As she waded around, Ruthie sat patiently by the

shoreline, watching Emily closely as always to make sure she was okay.

She walked around as the thigh-high water wet the bottom of her shorts, then she went back to the sand, plopped down, and wept.

There had to be another future for her, a better one. There just had to.

Chapter Eighteen

Taylor

The drive into her childhood neighborhood was only slightly less weird today than when she'd come with Ben, but it was a massive relief to have Andre with her. He brought a level of comfort and security to Taylor that was hard to describe.

With him, she felt like she could handle anything.

"Have I told you how much I appreciate you doing this with me?" She turned to him from the passenger seat and smiled, looping her arm through his.

"About a hundred times." He winked. "Tay, I love you. I really want to help you navigate this tough situation with your dad. I know there isn't really that much I can do, but I hope me just being here with you helps at least a little."

"It helps a lot." She leaned her head against the window as they cruised in through the front gate of Hibiscus Landing after checking in at the guard station.

As they got closer to the house, her nerves began to kick up a bit.

She wasn't showing up unannounced, of course. She'd called her dad and simply asked if she could stop by today to see the baby. He seemed stunned, but quickly agreed.

"It's this one right here." She nodded at the home, which looked less and less like the one she'd grown up in. The landscaping had been updated and the shutters painted. Little by little, Kayla was transforming the home into her own.

She thought once again of the painted-over wall and felt some anger and hurt rise in her heart. She squeezed Andre's arm and let it go.

"Nice house," he remarked, putting his Subaru in Park in the driveway. "You ready for this?"

She scrunched up her nose. "I guess so. I know this is hard to believe, but I don't want to fight with him."

"I know you don't." Andre took her hand. "So don't."

"I just...I get so sad and angry about everything, and every time I try to let it go, something new arises, like them painting over Ben's and my growth wall. And I feel erased all over again."

"I know." He leveled his gaze on hers, his handsome, espresso-colored eyes keeping her heartbeat steady. "But listen, Tay. You've been through a lot. You've grown, you've learned, and you're exactly where you're supposed to be now. With me," he teased, "and your mom and grandma and aunts and uncles and working at John's office. You've come such a long way since everything happened, and I really do think you're capable of forgiving him and letting the past be the past. Maybe your dad has come a long way, too."

She let out a soft sigh. "I guess I can't deny that it was kind of nice to talk to him last time. He does seem more chill and is really interested in my life, which is new."

"See?" Andre lifted a shoulder. "Everyone can change and grow. This could be the first step in a new future for you. Your baby sister, your dad—they can be a part of your life."

She closed her eyes, emotion tightening her chest. "I'd actually really like that. I just...I'm scared I don't know how."

"You have a heart of gold, Taylor Parker. And forgiveness is a beautiful thing. Plus, I'll be with you the whole time."

Taylor leaned over and kissed him, awash with affection and love. "Okay. Let's do it."

This time, after Taylor rang the doorbell and her dad answered it, she wasn't struck by how different the house looked or how all of Mom's touches had been replaced and discarded.

It was just...the new house. Where Dad and Kayla lived.

"Taylor, I'm so glad you came back." Max held out his arm, offering her an awkward side-hug that she accepted.

"This is my boyfriend, Andre." She gestured at Andre, who held out his hand and gave Dad's a firm shake.

"It's a pleasure to meet you, Andre," Max said with a smile that seemed genuine. "I've heard great things. Mostly from Ben," he added with a laugh.

"Love that kid." Andre smiled, glancing at Taylor with a reassuring nod. "It's so nice to meet you, Dr. Parker."

"Please, call me Max." Dad waved a hand and guided them down the hall and toward the living room. "Kayla and Brooklyn are in here."

"We don't move much these days," Kayla said softly, lying in the same recliner she'd been in at Taylor's last visit, holding the bundled-up baby in her arms.

"That's not true. You took a long walk this morning." Max walked over and took the baby from Kayla. "You don't give yourself enough credit."

"I feel like a lazy lump." Kayla slowly got out of the chair, looking closer to her normal svelte self than last time. "Hi again, Taylor."

"Hey, Kayla." Taylor noticed an apologetic look on Kayla's pretty face—a shadow of shame as she glanced away from the eye contact. "This is Andre, my boyfriend."

"Andre, hi." Kayla shook his hand. "I'm so glad you could make it today."

For a few moments, it was silent but for Brooklyn's soft coos as Max held her and bounced her gently against his chest.

"She's beautiful," Andre said with a smile. "Can I hold her?"

"Of course." Dad handed the baby to Andre and he gently and effortlessly took her in his strong arms.

Taylor couldn't deny that the man looked even cuter holding a baby. He'd be an amazing father one day.

"She likes you!" Kayla mused with a smile, as little Brooklyn stayed quiet and nestled into Andre's arms.

"She has good taste," Taylor teased.

After a smattering of small talk and the offer of iced teas for everyone from Kayla, the four of them and the baby—who was now attached to Andre—settled into the living room.

Tension stretched through the room, like they all knew *the big talk* was right around the corner. But with her strength and support sitting by her side adorably holding her baby sister, she was ready for it.

Max took a deep breath. "Tay, can we—"

"Look, I'm sorry." Taylor blurted the words out, and all three sets of eyes flew to her. "I acted like a child last week when we came here. I know that you're trying." She turned to Dad, then to Kayla. "Both of you. And I really see that you guys want to include me in your new life and your new family and you don't have to do that. You could have dropped me and decided to never call again, but you didn't. You made an effort. And I haven't reciprocated that effort because I've been too fixated on the past."

"Taylor." Max's eyes were wide with hope and shock, and Taylor could have sworn she saw tears in them. "First of all, you're my daughter. I would never drop you. And you have every right to be hurt and angry about all the things that happened with this family. I was a terrible father, a bad excuse for a husband, and believe me, I live with those regrets every day."

Taylor nodded, her eyes stinging with tears.

"But, Taylor," Max continued, "when Brooklyn was born, I knew that all I wanted in the world was a fresh start with you and Ben. I wanted you guys to get to know Kayla. She's an amazing person."

Kayla shook her head, smiling. "We want Brooklyn to grow up knowing her older siblings," she added.

Max scooted forward on the loveseat, his gaze serious and sincere. "Your mother and I...we had a lot of problems. We grew far apart and the differences we overlooked when we were young just couldn't be ignored anymore. We've both gone on to find our person, and that's a good thing."

Taylor couldn't deny that. Mom was meant to be with Ethan. Heck, they were getting married in a week!

"But the way that I acted..." He ran a hand through his hair. "The decisions I made...I'm beyond ashamed."

"Me, too." Kayla lifted her hand slightly, swallowing hard. "I never intended to break up a family. It was so dumb and thoughtless, the way things happened. I love your father, but we did not go about it in any sort of the right way."

"Well, we can all agree on that," Taylor joked, easing the tension a bit. "Dad, Kayla..." She looked back and forth between her father and stepmother. She could feel Andre's steady presence by her side, like a rock of unwavering strength. "I forgive you. And I really mean it. I'd love to have a relationship with you both, and of course with little Brooklyn. I hope we can start a new chapter, and I promise to leave the past in the past."

"Ohh." Kayla fanned her face, a tear falling down her cheek. "I've wanted this so badly, you have no idea."

Taylor glanced at Andre, breathing out a physical sigh of relief. "Me, too," she whispered. "I just didn't know it yet."

"Come here." Max stood up, extending his arms. "Both of you. Andre, you're part of this family now, too. And even if you're not, I think you're Brooklyn's new favorite person, so you can't leave."

Andre laughed and stood up, still holding the baby as he glanced at Taylor, giving her a proud nod. "Happy to be here."

"Bring it in." Kayla stood up, too, and the four of them hugged with little baby Brooklyn right in the center.

Taylor felt the weight of the world leave her shoulders in that moment. There it was. The pain, the anger, the resentment...it floated away into the twenty-foot ceilings of Dad and Kayla's two-story living room and disappeared.

Kayla drew back, looking at Taylor. "And, as for the wall in the TV room upstairs—"

"Don't worry about it," Taylor said.

"I just want to make sure you know that it was all me," Kayla said. "Your dad wanted to keep it. It was the only thing he asked me not to change. And one night when Max was working late, I went in and just stared at it. I felt like I could never compete with the family he'd had before. Like I was just an imposter and I was so ashamed of myself and... in a fit of jealousy and pregnancy hormones, I painted over it. It's sort of why I redecorated the entire house. Your mom had done a beautiful job, I just...I couldn't take the constant reminder of what had come before me and what I'd so carelessly messed up." She shook her head. "I was wrong, and I'm so sorry."

"I get that." Taylor held her arms out and gave Kayla one more hug. "I forgive you," she said, and truly meant it.

Every person on Earth was filled with mistakes and regrets, Taylor realized. Family, at the end of the day, is family. And if there was one thing she'd learned this past year since moving to Cocoa Beach, it was that family is truly the most important thing in life.

So, even if hers didn't look perfect and was a bit broken, she valued them. She valued Brooklyn, and her dad, and even Kayla. They mattered, and they were part of her.

They spent the afternoon hanging out on the patio, playing a few rounds of the game of *Life*—weirdly, Dad's favorite board game—and obsessing over every facet of perfect Brooklyn.

Taylor learned that Kayla intended to go back to school once Brooklyn was a few years old, to get her nurse practitioner license. She also learned that her new stepmom had a secret passion for knitting, which was funny and surprising, but she happily accepted a gift of a turquoise throw blanket that she suspected would get a place of honor in her apartment.

Dad told stories about when Taylor and Ben were really little, and spent a good amount of time getting to know Andre and hearing about what he did at the brewery.

Taylor talked about working at John's agency and how Aunt Julie was the mayor of Cocoa Beach and Grandma was dating a celebrity chef, which everyone got a huge kick out of.

The day turned into a pleasant one, and once they said their goodbyes and Taylor and Andre headed out to the car, her heart felt a hundred pounds lighter.

Andre wrapped his arms around Taylor, planting a kiss on her forehead. "I'm so proud of you. I know that wasn't easy."

"Actually..." She drew back, brushing some hair out of her eyes and shielding her face from the sun. "It was easier than I thought it would be. It's because I had you with me."

"Oh, come on." He opened the car door for her, as he always did, and she slid into the passenger seat. "I didn't do a thing, Tay."

"You didn't have to," she said, turning to face him as he settled into the car and started the engine. "You've helped me overcome my past and learn the power of forgiveness and second chances. You and my mom and my grandma and...everyone. It feels good to let go."

He placed a loving hand on her leg as he drove out of the neighborhood and onto the main road to head back toward the East Coast.

"The future looks bright, Taylor Parker." He gave her knee a playful squeeze. "And I'm just so glad we have each other."

"Me, too." She laced her fingers through his, spontaneously deciding to roll down the window and let the warm breeze flow through her hair.

For the first time since that horrible day three years ago, Taylor was truly free.

Chapter Nineteen

Julie

"You have got to be freaking kidding me."
Julie stared at the headline of the online news article, her jaw gaping.

Conflict of Interest?
Romance Rumors Spark Between Cocoa Beach Mayor
and Chief of Police

Amber cringed as she read the computer screen over Julie's shoulder, slowly setting a latte down on her desk. "Oh, boy. That is...not good."

This was what Brian thought would be a friendly interview? Julie dropped her head into her hands, letting her hair fall around her face. "This is not going to help my reputation at all."

"It's never good when there's even a hint of scandal, no matter how innocent or perfectly fine between two adults." Amber rested her hand on her pregnant belly and gave Julie a sympathetic smile. "What can I do to help mitigate this? Other than wait until it blows over, because it will, I promise you."

"The picture might have blown over, but an article in

Space Coast Chronicles?" She groaned and leaned back in her desk chair, staring at the ceiling. "I don't think there's anything you can do, hon. Just help me weather the storm."

"Brace yourself for ruthless Facebook comments." Amber rolled her eyes. "But you are not doing anything technically wrong. Two single people, put together through work, and you've known each other for decades. Please. People are allowed to date."

"All true, but it looks unprofessional." Julie sipped her latte. "I'm so new, and I've got a lot to prove to this community. They took a chance by electing me, and I really don't want to blow it."

Although Julie was afraid she already had.

"You won't." Amber placed a reassuring hand on Julie's shoulder. "Let's think about how to address it—if at all—at the press conference this afternoon."

She groaned at the thought of facing the small group of intrepid local reporters who were supposed to be helping the city of Cocoa Beach build enthusiasm for Wave Haven. The festival was four days away, and Julie wanted to bring together the leaders of the team to share important information about safety, road closures, traffic redirection, parking instructions, and many other fun and exciting things.

But "the leaders" meant Julie and Brian would be together in front of cameras and microphones the day this article came out.

"I'll start writing up some key messages and your talking points," Amber said. "And your job will be to deliver them and keep the content focused on festival logistics."

Julie pinched the bridge of her nose, hoping she could pull that off. "Thanks, Amber. I better call Brian and give him the same instructions. I'm sure he's seen this and is feeling sheepish that his plan backfired."

"Right?" Amber turned around from the office doorway and gave Julie a sympathetic glance. "You think they're friendly reporters, then wham. They smell blood in the water."

"Evidently a juicy article is more important than what he described as a solid friendship," Julie said. "I'm gonna call him."

"Good luck."

Julie clicked his name in her recent calls and held the phone to her ear while it rang.

She wasn't mad at Brian in the slightest—she truly believed he'd done his best to mitigate the effects of the scandalous kissing picture.

Perhaps it was just Julie's fate that she'd never be taken seriously as a professional or a mayor or...an adult. Maybe that was just her lot in life, that people judged and misunderstood her, and no matter what she did, she could never manage to prove them wrong.

"Hey, Jules. Please don't freak out. I promise you, I did not tell her to write—"

"I know, I know." She couldn't help but laugh softly at his instant desire to calm and steady her. "It's okay. I just don't understand how she could publish this. I thought the interview was about the fundraising program?"

"It was," he insisted. "We talked about the fundraiser for almost the entire time. Then, at the very end, she said she want to address the 'elephant in the room.'"

"Oh, boy."

"And she brought up the picture, of course. Which I was honestly a little relieved she brought up, because I figured I could use it as an opportunity to address the rumors and squash them before they got too far out of hand."

Julie stared at the words on her computer screen. "I fear they are not very squashed."

"No, they aren't." He sighed. "I was very clear. I said that Julie and I have a professional relationship and nothing more. That photo caught a moment where we were acting in a less than professional way outside of working hours, but I can confidently say there is nothing going on between us besides a friendly work relationship."

"She, uh..." Julie scoffed. "Put quite the twist on that."

"No kidding," he agreed. "And we need to be prepared for questions about this at today's press conference."

"I know. Amber's writing up my talking points right now in hopes I'll be able to keep the focus solely on festival logistics."

"I imagine it will be relatively easy to do that," Brian assured her. "The people running this conference aren't local sleuths posting on Facebook and Nextdoor about rumors and drama. They just want us to give detailed information and instructions so the residents know what to expect this weekend."

"So we just pretend like nothing happened?" Julie guessed, not entirely sure that strategy was going to work, but willing to try anything.

"Do you think it's possible?"

She winced. "Considering the fact that I'm literally terrified to open Facebook this morning, I don't know. Is the professional thing to do just ignore it?"

Brian was quiet for a few beats. "Don't worry, Julie. Really. I think I have an idea about how to handle it."

She scanned the article on the screen again. "Don't take this the wrong way, Chief, but, uh...your last idea kinda blew up in our faces."

"I know," he said, chuckling softly. "But can you trust me just one more time?"

Julie leaned back in her chair and took a deep drink of her latte. "I don't think I have a choice."

❧

For someone who had spent her life chasing the thrill of a cheering crowd and the adrenaline rush of being on stage in front of hundreds of people, Julie was surprisingly nervous when she had to address the people of Cocoa Beach.

Without the guitar in her hand or the drumbeats to drown out the world, she was overwhelmingly aware of the pressure and importance of her words in these types of moments.

Goofing around, playing music, and expressing her passion as a kid and as a young woman was fun and thrilling, but never too serious.

And that passion—for the city of Cocoa Beach—was what had won her this election. But this was a local presser about safety and logistics. It didn't get much more serious—or boring— than that. Not to mention the fact that Adrianna's article was circulating through cyberspace at the usual breakneck speed.

Brian was certain the reporters at this press conference wouldn't bring up the silly rumors or the article, but Julie wasn't so sure.

The conference was held in front of City Hall, taking advantage of a dreamily beautiful day. There were already several cameramen and reporters waiting for Julie and Brian to walk up to the podium and talk about... logistics. Just logistics. Only logistics.

No...kisses.

She took a deep breath, attempting to smooth down her hair despite the Florida humidity. She'd opted for yet another Erica-inspired look—a black pencil skirt with a long-sleeved, light pink blouse, pearl necklace, and low black heels.

Tattoos were sufficiently covered, and Julie had even opted to wear her glasses instead of contacts, because Bliss said they made her look scholarly.

"Hey." Brian's gentle touch on her back startled Julie, and she whipped around to meet his gaze.

"Hi."

"You okay?" he asked softly, dipping his chin low to study her face, his brows pulled together with concern.

Julie shook her head. "Sort of. Not really."

"Relax, okay? I promise everything will be fine."

She glanced out at the reporters setting up their recorders and microphones. "Can you promise me they won't ask about the article?"

"No promises, but I highly doubt they will. These aren't the personal interest reporters. Their beat is town events, police activities, and, your favorite, parking problems."

She chuckled. "Okay. So no silly gossip."

His brow flicked. "Silly? I think we're clear, Jules. But if they do ask a question about it, let me take it. I'll handle it."

She nodded, her gaze shifting down to the file folder in her hands. Inside it was the printed-out bulleted list of talking points that Amber had written up for her. Julie had read them over and over, memorizing each. But they weren't song lyrics and she could forget.

Before she knew it, it was time for them to take the podium, and a couple of camera flashes startled her as she walked out and set her file down in front of her.

"Hello, everyone," Julie said into the microphone, clearing her throat. "As you know, I'm Mayor Julie Sweeney, alongside Chief of Police Brian Wilkes and a few members of our teams. We have a very big event coming to town and today, we'd like to review the timing, logistics, details, and updates that will impact our residents and the thousands of guests we're expecting. Safety is first, fun is second, and we sure do want everyone to leave with a positive impression of our town."

She turned to catch Brian's gaze, and he gave her a reassuring nod, making her nerves ease.

"Chief Wilkes will address the safety and road changes." She stepped away and Brian took the mic.

"Thank you, Mayor. Let's start with closures. All Cocoa Beach residents and visitors should know that A1A spanning from Tenth Street on the south end and Ocean Street on the north end will be blocked off and closed. Detour signs will be posted, but we recommend taking an alternate route on Saturday. My department has prepared a detailed map that has been emailed to you and we ask that you share it with your readers and viewers."

While he spoke, Julie admired how calm and authoritative he was at the microphone. Unfazed, he shot out information with clarity and the precision she'd expect from a former Marine.

And no one was going to question *him*.

What had she been so worried about? It was just a stupid article. Maybe no one even saw it.

But as she watched him, thinking about his terrible sax playing in high school and his secret crush on her and his garage band and the Diet Cokes, she realized just how crazy about this man she truly was.

Focus, Julie! she thought to herself. *If you keep staring at him with stars in your eyes, it's going to be entirely too obvious that the article was, in fact, completely true.*

She faced the gathering and planted her most serious and un-crushed look on her face, listening as Brian started on parking, moved to foot traffic, and on to the placement of his patrol cars and police officers through the crowd.

When he finished, Brian turned to her, his gaze warm and steady. "And I'll go ahead and hand it back over to Mayor Sweeney for the next question."

Julie straightened her back and glanced down at her talking points.

"Question for Mayor Sweeney!"

Julie looked up and nodded to the woman with her hand raised. "Go ahead."

"Isabelle Hunt with CBTV News," she announced. "Mayor Sweeney, this is a bit of a topic divergence from Wave Haven..."

Oh, no.

"But there have been some reports of a potential romantic relationship between you and Chief Wilkes based on a photograph that has been circulating online as well as a recent article in the *Space Coast Chronicles*. What can you say to calm concerns that this type of unprofessional behavior could lead to shaky leadership for our great city? Are the rumors true? Can you speak on your relationship with Chief Wilkes?"

Julie froze, the blood in her veins turning to ice. "I... um..." She looked at Brian, who she expected to be as ghost white as she felt, but he looked calm and prepared.

Brian leaned forward. "I can go ahead and speak on this, Ms. Hunt. Thank you. First of all—"

"Respectfully, this question was directed to the mayor, Chief Wilkes," Isabelle said forcefully, then murmured, "No mansplaining necessary."

The comment sent ire up Julie's back, enough that she lifted her chin, placed her hands on either side of the podium and spoke into the microphone. "Chief Wilkes and I work very well together to help keep this city safe and secure for everyone. Our relationship is cordial. We've known each other since we both attended Cocoa Beach High School and, as locals, we know what matters to this city."

"How do you explain the photograph then, Mayor Sweeney?" the slimy little Isabelle continued. "It was very clear that you two were kissing at the pier."

Julie clenched her jaw but Brian leaned in.

"Nothing was clear in that photo," he said. "Including the credit for the photographer. For all we know, it was doctored."

"Well, you'd know if it was doctored," the reporter fired back. "Did you kiss her or not?"

Julie wasn't breathing as she watched him, a thousand thoughts racing through her mind at once.

What was he going to say? How would he spin this? Surely, he'd tell everyone that none of it was true, that there was nothing going on and never had been and never would be.

But that wasn't the truth. At least Julie really, really hoped it wasn't.

Brian cleared his throat, gave Julie one last reassuring nod, and leaned close to the microphone on the podium.

"I have always considered myself to be an honest man, and I place a high value on transparency, especially with the community that I've spent the better part of my career serving."

Where was he going with this?

"I think it's only fair that the people of this wonderful little city know what's really going on."

Julie's heart hammered.

"I..." He paused and inhaled slowly, turning to Julie. "Have a crush on the mayor."

A soft chorus of gasps and laughter swirled around the lawn, but Julie stayed perfectly still, her jaw slack with shock as she blinked back, staring at him.

"As I'm sure you are all aware, Julianna Sweeney is an incredible woman who has already done a fantastic job as mayor of this city. She was born and raised here, and, as she mentioned, our friendship goes back many decades." He tipped his head. "Many more than us fifty-somethings want to admit."

Julie laughed softly, frozen in place as she attempted to process what he was actually doing and saying right now.

"I don't talk about my personal life and neither does she, but at the moment, we are both single, so there's no scandal. We have discovered that we might have genuine feelings for one another. Or at least I have them for her." Brian looked at her and smiled, his blue eyes lighting up.

Julie shook her head in disbelief, smiling through her shock.

"So, yes, that was us kissing in the photograph, and,

yes, there has been a bit of a romance that has developed, but we both took an oath to perform our duties to the very best of our abilities, and nothing that goes on in our personal lives will change that."

"Absolutely," Julie chimed in suddenly.

Brian looked at her and their gazes locked. "Anyway," he continued, "that's the truth. I think we're great as individuals but I think we're even better as a team. Our personalities might be polar opposites but that's only drawn me to you even more. I want to be with you, for real, and see where this goes." He paused, taking a breath. "And I really hope you want that, too."

Julie nodded, stepping off of the podium toward him, her hands shaking as she held her arms out. "I do want that," she said quietly.

Julie was vaguely aware of the cameras flashing and the soft cheers going on around them.

"Give her a kiss!" someone called.

"Show us you mean it!" another person yelled.

He took one step closer, lifted her hand and brought it to his lips.

"Do better!" a reporter shouted.

With a quick laugh, he drew her in and lightly kissed her, then put his lips to her ear. "I heard somewhere once that the best way to shut them up is get them to root for you."

There was a low-grade cheer, only a little louder than the clicking of cameras.

"We need a movie!" a woman called out. "The mayor and the police chief forever!"

"I think it worked," she whispered.

"Did it?" he asked.

She just blushed and he had to know the answer was yes.

They separated, laughing as she pressed her forehead to his.

"Okay, Cocoa Beach," she said into the microphone. "Let's talk about the music festival, shall we?"

Julie had found her guy, the calm to her crazy, the logic to her dreams. All these years, she'd felt a piece of her was missing. She'd searched for it in crowds and on stages, she'd searched for it by traveling the country and seeking out every imaginable adventure.

Everything she'd thought she wanted had always been right here, waiting for her, at home.

Chapter Twenty

Dottie

I t was Friday, the day before the music festival, and two days before Sam's wedding and the grand reopening of Sweeney House.

Dottie was *crazed* with things to do.

But she and her daughters had decided that Friday night was the perfect night to throw a little bridal shower for Sam, something small and fun at the cottage to honor her and, well, *shower* her with love!

It was early, and no one would be arriving for at least a half hour or so—well, except for one person—so Dottie was warming up the hors d'oeuvres that Franklin had prepared for her and setting out champagne flutes for mimosas.

She hummed to herself as she floated about the cottage, her heart as light as a feather and her mind unable to resist going back to her lovely date with Franklin the other night.

It had been far too long since all of her girls were together in one room, and Dottie knew they had much to catch up on.

She laughed to herself, thinking about Julie and Brian Wilkes, kissing on the local news yesterday. And the response had been overwhelmingly positive. Turns out, Cocoa Beach residents liked a little romance in City Hall.

As Dottie was carefully adorning her cheese board with olives and seasoned nuts, she heard a knock at the front door, and knew exactly who had arrived.

There was only one person who she'd told to be there a half hour early, and it was also the only woman who would knock instead of just walking into the cottage.

"Emily." Dottie smiled widely as she opened the door and saw the young woman standing on the other side, her eyes downcast. "Come on in."

Ruthie, her precocious little companion, trotted by Emily's side and happily hopped up onto the sofa in the living room.

"Hi, Dottie." Emily lifted her gaze, and Dottie could instantly tell that something had happened.

From the moment they met, Emily had been mysterious and often seemed sad, but this look was different, Dottie could tell.

"Thank you for inviting me." Emily sat down on the edge of the sofa and crossed her legs as Ruthie placed her head on her owner's knee. "I'm not sure if I'm going to stay, though. I'm not really in the mood to meet new people, and—"

"Emily, honey, what's wrong?"

Dottie had told her to arrive early because she knew that Emily would likely need to talk. Just a sense.

"I, um..." Emily looked up, her eyes instantly filling. "I called my birth mother. Vanessa Young."

Dottie gasped softly, but her excitement was quickly quashed by the pain and sadness written all over the girl's face. "And? Did you talk to her? You must tell me everything."

Emily sniffed, scratching her dog's head. "Yeah. I mean, sort of. I told her who I was and she kind of went silent. So I figured I might as well just get it all out in the open, so I just started...rambling." Emily shook her head. "I told her a very brief version of my life story, and I said I didn't want anything from her I just...wanted to call."

"Well, what did she say?"

"Nothing." Emily swallowed, clenching her jaw. "She said, 'I can't do this right now, I have to go,' and she hung up. And that was that."

Dottie's heart ached for this sweet woman, so tragically alone after going through unthinkable trauma.

"Emily." Dottie got up and hugged her. "I am so, so sorry. I can't believe that's all she said but I'm sure you stunned her and she wasn't at all prepared for the call."

Emily shrugged her shoulders and took a deep breath. "It's okay. I don't know what I expected. I mean, she didn't want me then; why would she want me now?"

"Because things change, and life takes unexpected turns." Dottie placed a hand on her arm. "Don't let this break you, okay?"

Emily met Dottie's gaze, her eyes dark and rich and full of way too much pain for any twenty-nine-year-old to know. "How can I not?" she whispered, her voice shaky.

"Look, I know this is going to sound like a platitude, and I completely understand that. But life is always,

always full of surprises. You really do never know what's around the corner."

Emily sniffled and kept her eyes fixed on Dottie.

"Take it from a woman who is seventy-two and still continuing to be shocked by the surprises of life all the time. Anything can happen, and something completely and totally unexpected could be waiting for you."

She gave a sad smile. "Well, I hope it's not my husband."

"He isn't going to find you."

She nodded, brushing some of her jet-black hair behind her ear. "Thank you, Dottie. And thank you for everything. You've been so kind to me. I'm glad to be here and work at the inn, even if it's only for a little while."

"You are welcome to work here as long as you can and need to." Dottie gave her hand a squeeze. "Just don't give up hope, okay? Promise me. You never know."

Emily smiled, nodding. "I promise."

"Now, are you sure you don't want to stay for mimosas and charcuterie and a very last-minute, poorly thrown together bridal shower? We'd love to have you."

"I really appreciate it, Dottie, but I'm just going to bring the mood down."

"That's nonsense, but if you prefer to rest and be alone, I do understand."

"I do." She got up and held her arms out, giving Dottie a big hug. "I'll see you early Sunday morning to start setting up for the wedding. I'm ready to work."

"Splendid." Dottie walked her to the front door, and

Ruthie followed. "I'll see you then, and we'll have a lovely time."

"Thanks again."

"Remember." Dottie narrowed her gaze. "Surprises are on their way."

A fact that Dottie knew all too well, considering she was a seventy-two-year-old widow who had just been on a date with a celebrity chef.

As EVENING FELL over Cocoa Beach, the cottage hummed with joy, excitement, and family as all the women who loved and adored Sam gathered together to share gifts, stories, and support.

Nothing made Dottie's heart happier.

She took a second to look around the living room, which was packed. They'd brought in some of the outside furniture and a few people were sitting on the floor.

Sam was in the middle of the sofa, laughing with Annie, who sat to her left. Along the couch were Julie, Erica, Lori, and Imani, sharing conversation and mimosas joyfully, while Taylor sat on the floor giggling about something with Amber and Bliss.

Dottie assumed her spot in Jay's old recliner, her heart as full as her living room.

"Okay, okay." Taylor stood up and clinked her champagne flute with a plastic fork. "As the daughter of the bride and maid of honor, I have something very important to say. Many things, actually."

Dottie looked at Sam, who was watching Taylor with misty eyes.

"Mom, you're incredible." Taylor laughed tearfully as she turned to Sam. "I know I can speak for every woman in this room when I say that you are one of the most amazing people on this planet. You are the picture of self-lessness and grace, and your resilience is truly inspiring."

Dottie glanced around to see hardly any dry eyes in the room. Sam was so deeply loved.

"I can't thank you enough for being the greatest role model and best friend I could ever ask for. And now, you're marrying the love of your life, and there is no one who deserves true, real, eternal happiness as much as you." Taylor lifted her champagne glass, and the rest of the group followed suit. "I love you, Mom. Cheers to the bride!"

"Cheers!"

"Woo!"

"Love you Sam!"

Dottie clinked her glass to everyone's and they all laughed and sipped and basked in Sam's effervescent pre-wedding glow.

They played games, told stories, and Sam opened a slew of hilarious, romantic, and heartfelt gifts.

Everyone took turns making speeches about Sam. Lastly, it was Dottie's turn.

She stood up out of Jay's recliner and walked over to Sam, reaching for her hand and squeezing it tightly. "It's just so beautiful to have all of you wonderful ladies together in one room. I am a blessed woman."

Sam laughed tearfully.

"Well, at risk of getting too sappy, I just want to tell you, Sam, how much you mean to me."

"Aw, Mom." Sam wiped a tear.

"You know, I often get told that I'm the glue of this family. Not to toot my own horn or anything," Dottie added with a playful flip of her curls. "But in the last nine months, I've come to realize that my role as the glue has been passed down. Sam, you're the glue, now. You're the one who brings us all together. You're the person who guides every member of this family and close friends through good times and bad. And when you moved here last June, you revived me. Your light and your persistence and your excitement about this new chapter brought a new chapter alive for me, too. I'm so happy for you, and so grateful for you. Ethan is a lucky, lucky man."

"I love you, Mom!" Sam jumped up and hugged Dottie tightly, and Dottie squeezed her sweet daughter right back, every ounce of her filled to the brim with gratitude.

"Okay, so..." Erica shifted in her seat. "If I also may say something."

Sam gestured to her. "Please do."

Erica continued. "Sam, babe, you know I love you more than anything and I'm so happy to be at your bridal shower. But is it okay if I shift the attention to Julie for a second? Because we all are dying to know what is going on with you and Brian Wilkes—"

"Yes!" Sam gasped. "Tell us! We all saw the kiss, and when we texted you about it, you went ghost."

"For real." Imani lifted a shoulder. "John was telling me about how the chief had it bad for you in high school. I'm dying to know the full story."

"Okay, okay." Julie held her hands up, setting her glass down on the coffee table. "The reason I didn't answer all the texts is because I knew we'd all be together here tonight, and I wanted to tell you all in person."

"You must," Dottie insisted.

"I will." Julie pointed at her mom. "But only if you tell us what's going on between you and Chef Fox when I'm finished."

The gasps and oohs were now moved in Dottie's direction, and she tried to stifle her smile as her cheeks went warm. "There is nothing going on, my silly girls. He is working at the inn now and he and I have become... friends. That's simply it."

"I don't buy it," Sam tsked. "But...Julie first."

"Yes, Mom, tell us!" Bliss pumped her fist. "I already know the story, but I want to hear it again."

"All right." Julie told the room how she and Brian knew each other in high school, were polar opposites in every way, and now found themselves working side by side to run the city of Cocoa Beach.

She shared about their opposite yet wonderfully complementary personalities, their time playing in his garage band together, and how they'd connected on a deeper level recently.

"Did you know the kiss was coming?" Sam asked. "At the press conference?"

"Not in the slightest." Julie shook her head, laughing

and glowing almost as brightly as Sam. "I assumed he'd deny it and downplay it, but he surprised me."

Dottie's heart tugged as she watched a look form on Julie's face that she had never seen before. "Life is full of surprises these days."

"It was completely epic how he did it on TV like that," Amber added. "So romantic."

"I was shocked," Julie said on a laugh.

"So you two are..." Annie shimmied her shoulders playfully. "Together, now?"

"Yeah." Julie smiled widely, her eyes shiny and clear. "We are. And I think it's...really good."

Bliss got up and walked over to Julie, giving her mom a big hug. "It *is* really good, Mom."

Dottie pressed her hand to her heart, appreciating the beauty and strength and joy of the women in these rooms. "My girls," she whispered.

The celebration continued as the sun went down and the desserts came out. Cupcakes, of course, made by Annie and decorated to perfection featuring all of Sam's favorite flavors.

The noisy and festive dessert was interrupted by a sudden knock at the door.

"Who's here that's not supposed to be here?" Taylor asked, frowning with confusion as she licked a drop of pink icing off of her fingertip.

"Let me get it." Dottie rose to answer the door, wondering if perhaps Emily had changed her mind and wanted to join the party after all.

But when she opened the front door of the cottage,

she was greeted by...a giant bouquet of flowers held by a delivery man.

"Oh, my heavens!" Dottie gasped. "These are gorgeous. They must be for the bride."

The man glanced at his signature device. "Dorothy Sweeney."

Dottie blinked back. "For me?"

"If you're Dorothy. Would you sign here, ma'am?" He held out the device.

Dottie scribbled a signature with her finger on the touchpad and took the monstrous bunch of roses and lilies by the glass vase.

She thanked him and walked back into the living room, where all eyes were on her.

"Someone sent flowers." She chuckled with amusement as she set them down on the table, noticing a white envelope sticking out of the top of the colorful and elegant bouquet. "Probably to give to Sam."

"Oh, I doubt it," Sam teased. "I think we all know who sent you flowers."

Dottie rolled her eyes and flicked her fingers dismissively, although the thought of it made her heart flutter.

She plucked the little envelope out of the flowers and opened it up, her eyes scanning the words so fast her mind could hardly keep up.

Dorothy – I hope you enjoy these flowers, which are as colorful and gorgeous as you are. It would be a great honor to accompany you to your daughter's wedding as your date for the evening. I'll be done in the kitchen in time for the reception, and I'd love nothing more than to dance with you. Yours truly, FF

"Oh..." Dottie held her hand to her mouth, unable to hide the smile that pulled at her cheeks and came straight from her heart. "Oh, my."

"What is it?" Taylor rushed over.

Sam stood up, walked to Dottie, and craned her neck to read the card. "What did he say?"

Within seconds, every woman in the room was on her feet as they surrounded Dottie, clamoring to read the card.

Finally, Erica plucked it right out of Dottie's fingers and cleared her throat, reading the note out loud.

"Oh. My. Gosh," Bliss squealed, clasping her hands together. "Grandma! He wants to be your wedding date."

"Well...I mean..." Dottie laughed softly, flustered by the attention and the card. "He's already going to be there, but he'll be working, so I don't see how..."

Imani shook her head. "He says very clearly that he'll be done in the kitchen for the reception. No slithering your way out of this one."

"He likes you, Mom!" Erica nudged Dottie. "This is so sweet and romantic."

"It's amazing," Sam agreed, taking Dottie's hands. "How do you feel about it?"

Dottie pressed her lips together, pondering the question. She hardly knew what to say or think or feel.

Shouldn't she be sad? Shouldn't she be horrified by the idea of dancing at Sam's wedding with a man who wasn't Jay Sweeney? Shouldn't it feel wrong on every level?

It...didn't. In fact, it felt right. It felt exciting and fun and made Dottie feel beautiful and young and like this last chapter of life could be entirely unexpected and different and more wonderful than she'd ever dreamed.

"When Franklin first walked through the doors of Sweeney House, I was shocked," she told them. "After I got over my initial reaction, I was determined not to trust him due to his status and wealth and fame. I thought surely he had some ulterior motive for coming to work at our little bistro. But, in time, I've grown to know him, and I've learned that he is a deeply good-hearted man. And I think I will accept his invitation."

Dottie hugged all her girls in a huddle of laughter and support, in a moment that felt too good to be true.

Her life did not end when Jay's did. It merely continued to surprise her.

Chapter Twenty-one

Julie

J ulie realized something on the first Saturday of April. Music festivals, whether she was playing, attending, or running them as mayor, were most definitely her element.

The morning had been a hectic blur, and Julie was all over the place at Wave Haven, delegating, instructing, and keeping track of her responsibilities for the festival. So far, everything had gone off without a hitch, and the crowd seemed to be having the time of their lives.

The Wave Haven company reps were spot-on with their timing and management of the artists, and now, in the late afternoon, everything was right on track.

Logistically, Julie felt like she'd truly done her job in planning the city's management of this kind of event. Parking was organized, crowds were controlled, and Brian, of course, had oodles of officers exactly where they all needed to be.

As Julie walked down the long strip of roads and beach access that had been blocked off to cars for the day, she savored the warm sunshine and the glorious weather. The music from the main stage echoed through the city, and the street was full of festivalgoers in fun outfits, taking pictures, buying snacks, laughing and dancing and enjoying the true magic of live music that Julie knew all too well.

As she headed down the street, she spotted Linda Westbrook standing on the street corner with her cell-phone to her ear.

Julie waved and walked over.

"Mayor, hello!" Linda finished her call and put her phone away, giving Julie a big, contented smile. "Everything is going so well! No issues so far that I'm aware of."

"Same here." Julie looked around, the setting sun cooling the air. "It seems like Wave Haven is a pretty big success, and I can't even imagine the tourism revenue it's brought in for the city."

"I know." Linda grinned. "We might be able to finally put some funding in to expand the parking garage by Ron Jon's."

"That's exciting," Julie said, oddly meaning it. She glanced down at her watch. "It's 6:30. Don't the Space Kittens come on in an hour?"

"I believe so." Linda nodded. "I haven't heard anything about headliner preparations, though. I'm going to call the Wave Haven rep and make sure all is well, and see if they need anything else from us city planners." She held up a finger. "Be right back."

"Take your time." Julie wandered off, weaving through the crowd and smiling at the lines outside of restaurants and bars and even clothing stores.

Her little city was alive tonight, that was for sure.

She pulled out her phone and sent a quick text to

Brian, making sure everything on the security and safety side of things was going just as well.

"Mayor!" A woman ran up to Julie, waving her hand.

"Yes?" Julie smiled.

"Hi. I'm so sorry to bother you, I'm sure you're busy. My name is Carrie, and I just wanted you to know that I voted for you, because your story about your daughter was really touching, and I think you're doing a great job."

Julie inhaled slowly, warmth filling her chest. "Oh, wow. Thank you so much, Carrie. That means the world. I really just want to give back to Cocoa Beach."

"I know, and I know you might get some pushback for this, but I personally think you and Chief Wilkes are adorable together." Carrie laughed. "It was a pleasure to meet you!"

Julie felt her face flush. "Thank you." She shook her head. "Nice to meet you, Carrie. Enjoy Wave Haven!"

"Julie!"

She whipped around at the sound of another person in the crowd calling her name. As Julie turned, she saw Linda Westbrook running full speed with a look of pure horror on her face.

Oh, no. Maybe it *was* all too good to be true.

"Linda? What's wrong?" She rushed over and took Linda aside on the sidewalk.

"We've got problems." The woman caught her breath. "I just got off the phone with a company rep from Wave Haven."

"Yeah?" Julie frowned, waiting for her to continue as her heart rate picked up more and more every second.

"The Space Kittens aren't here."

"The...you...*what?*" Julie felt the world tilt under her feet and she struggled to stay standing. "Linda, there has to be some sort of mistake. The Space Kittens are the headliner. They're going on at 7:30. Of course they're here!"

Linda pressed her lips together and shook her head. "The whole night is going to be a disaster. Trina Tribelli had some last-minute breakdown and flew the whole band back to L.A. on her jet."

Julie felt her jaw go slack. "There's no headliner?"

"There's no headliner," Linda repeated softly. "And I want to remind you that, as mayor, this isn't really your problem. You did your part in preparing the city, handling event logistics, etcetera. Just because some prima donna singer freaks out and doesn't want to play the show doesn't reflect badly on you."

Julie felt disappointment rock her as she leaned against the side of a building. "I know that, and this is obviously Wave Haven's problem and not Cocoa Beach's, but...we really put our hearts and souls into planning this event. And now it's going to be a total disaster, and we're going to look like fools for thinking we were capable of pulling off something of this caliber."

If this crashed and burned, then future events wouldn't want to come to Cocoa Beach. Even worse, the Facebook mafia would find a way to make this completely Julie's fault.

"I don't know what to do." Linda shook her head. "The Wave Haven people are blowing a gasket."

"I'd imagine," she scoffed dryly, running her hands through her hair.

No headliner? People were going to be so upset, and the city's biggest musical event ever would go down in history as an epic failure.

"I need to talk to Trina," Julie insisted.

Linda arched a brow. "Good luck getting access to that diva. Plus, they're halfway across the country right now. They aren't coming back."

Julie racked her brain for answers or solutions of how to possibly get that band on that stage tonight...but there simply weren't any.

Was this it? Did she have to just accept defeat and, once again, try to find a way to explain this to her community and all the people who'd paid for tickets and travel plans?

They'd blame her. Surely they would.

Linda glanced down the street toward the stage. "I'm going to speak with the Wave Haven organizers and see if they have a backup band or anything. I'll call you." She headed off to go attempt to put out this fire, which seemed unlikely.

"Good idea," Julie said, though she wasn't hopeful. She knew how these things worked, and there weren't generally backup bands waiting on deck.

"Hey!"

Suddenly, just as all hope was lost, Julie looked up to see Brian jogging toward her and Linda, wearing his police uniform and looking almost handsome enough to make her smile. Almost.

"Did you hear the news?" Julie asked on a deep sigh. "The Space Kittens have flown to Mars. Well, L.A. There's no headliner and this whole festival is ruined."

"No, it's not," Brian asserted, his eyes piercing her with a look she was starting to recognize.

"Don't tell me," she joked. "You have a plan to solve the problem."

"I kinda do," he said with a laugh.

"What do you mean?" she asked hopefully, already knowing how those plans usually worked. "Did you talk to the band manager? Are they on their way back to Florida?"

"No, not exactly." He scratched the back of his head.

"Then what is it? How are you going to get the Space Kittens to play the show?"

"They're not going to play the show." He held her gaze intensely. "We are."

What did he just say?

Julie could hardly choke out the laugh in her chest, she was so stunned and confused. "We...as in...we? The garage band?"

"Keith, Tony, and Rob ran back to my place to load up the gear into their trucks. Get your singing voice warmed up, baby, we're on at 7:30."

"Brian." Julie shook her head, closer to speechless than she'd ever been. "We can't...we can't *headline* Wave Haven with your garage cover band."

"It's either that or no headliner, Jules." He wrapped his arms around her waist, tucking her behind the side of the building and away from the crowd. "In case you haven't noticed, I'm a bit of a rule-breaker."

She snorted. "Oh, completely."

"Let's put it this way—I don't believe in the word 'can't.' I think we can. And we will. And it'll be...interesting. And fun. And we just might save the whole festival, or at least make it the most memorable event this city has ever held." He planted a quick kiss on her lips that made her head spin. "So, what do you say?"

"I say you're crazy." She ran a hand through his hair. "And I love crazy. Let's do it."

THROUGHOUT JULIE SWEENEY's entire adult life, she'd chased a feeling she aptly named "euphoria." She'd had glimpses of it—fleeting moments on stage or with Bliss, playing music to a big crowd and feeling them adore it.

But euphoria was always just a tiny tease of the fulfillment she'd always wanted as a musician. She'd been certain she'd find it as a rock star. She'd always thought she just needed her big break, her chance, and she'd get famous and then life would be constant euphoria.

That never happened. She never found that existential high of playing on stage and entering a state of musical perfection and magic felt by everyone in the crowd.

That was, until now.

On the stage of Wave Haven, in front of a massive outdoor crowd under the setting Cocoa Beach sun, Julie played cover after cover of her favorite rock classics with Brian and his band, and her heart was so full she swore it was going to burst.

Yes, there was a small exodus when it was announced that the Space Kittens wouldn't be playing due to a Trina Temper Tantrum. That actually got a laugh and the crowd was just mellow enough to accept the local classic rock cover band made up of some cops and the mayor.

They didn't have any original songs, so they let the crowd shout out suggestions and, if they knew it, they'd play it. They knew a lot, and people went wild.

From "Sweet Child of Mine" to "Rocket Man" with a lot of decades in between, Julie sang her heart out while Brian and the guys nailed every note behind her. They should rename this band Rise to The Occasion, because that was exactly what they did.

The energy was palpable, and by the time they announced that this was their last song for the night, the crowd had almost forgotten about the missing Space Kittens entirely and were visibly enjoying watching the mayor and four cops play with all they had on every song.

Brian, Keith, Tony, and Rob were still in their police uniforms, which no doubt made for some social media gold, and Julie had changed into jeans and an "I love CB" T-shirt. Not the black leather getup she was used to performing in, but she felt more like herself than ever.

"One more!" Julie pointed at the crowd, wiping some sweat from her brow. "We can do one more song. Who's got one?"

Some shouts echoed through the crowd, but the name of one song in particular stuck out to Julie.

"'More Than a Feeling'!"

She turned to Brian and the guys. "You guys know it?"

"Of course." Tony lifted a shoulder. "Better than Boston, if you ask me."

"Perfect." Julie held the microphone to her mouth. "'More Than a Feeling' it is!"

Cheers erupted through the crowd, and Tony counted off into the first few gentle guitar riffs of the rock classic.

As Julie sang the words, she closed her eyes, letting the moment wrap around her and hold her.

"It's more than a feeling," she sang, glancing at Brian, who looked at her with stars in his eyes. *"I begin dreaming..."*

The song was unfiltered euphoria...or maybe that was the saxophone player standing next to her and improvising a killer solo that people went nuts for.

As the song finished, the cheering erupted, and Julie walked right up to Brian, giving him a big hug and a kiss. He wrapped his arm around her waist and spun her around, then leaned into the mic.

"Let's hear it for our mayor! Isn't she incredible?"

"So are you." She laughed and kissed him again while the crowd broke into a chant of *"Ma-yor! Ma-yor! Ma-yor!"*

Julie threw her head back with a laugh, then gave a

very exaggerated bow. "I love you, Cocoa Beach!" She waved her arm. "Good night!"

They headed off the stage, and Julie felt like she was floating on a cloud.

Brian kissed her again as they ducked behind the curtain, holding her waist in his arms as his gaze locked with hers. "You saved everything, Julie."

"Are you kidding? It was your crazy idea."

"You taught me how to have crazy ideas."

She laughed, raising a shoulder playfully. "I guess I can take credit for that."

He gently touched her face, running his thumb along her cheek. "I'm falling in love with you, Julianna Sweeney. Maybe I'm already there, since I pretty much fell in love with you in eleventh grade."

The euphoria continued, getting even stronger as her head spun with emotions and joy. "I love you, too. No one has ever made me feel so safe and so happy." She tilted her chin up and kissed him again.

"Mom!"

Julie and Brian both whipped around to see Bliss running over, blond hair flying, with the entire Sweeney clan in tow.

"Baby!" Julie rushed over and hugged her daughter tightly.

"That was literally the coolest thing ever!" Bliss exclaimed. "Best show you've ever done."

"You must be Bliss." Brian held out his hand. "It's a pleasure to meet you, and I just want you to know that I am completely crazy about your mother. I hope that in time you can trust me and we can get to know—"

"Brian!" Bliss leapt forward, surprising him with a hug. "You don't need to use formalities with me. I've never seen my mom this happy before! I also never thought she'd date a cop, but I guess it's good to have someone keeping her in line."

"Okay, Bliss." Julie laughed and rolled her eyes.

Within seconds, every other member of the family and close friends were rushing to hug and congratulate Julie and say hello to Brian.

It was a full-on Sweeney family love fest, which would undoubtedly continue into the next day at Sam's wedding.

"Jules!" Erica pushed through the crowd of hugs and selfies to get to Julie. "Look at these Facebook posts."

"Oh, gosh," Julie groaned. "I'd rather not. I'm sure rocking out to Stevie Nicks is definitely not the professional and proper way for a mayor to conduct herself. I don't want to see it right now."

"Umm..." Erica laughed softly, holding her phone out. "It's quite the opposite, actually."

Julie's eyes widened with shock as she scrolled through the Facebook pages on Erica's feed, one post after another with pictures and videos from the show.

Coolest. Mayor. Ever.

I was wrong about Julie Sweeney...she's awesome!

I didn't know how much I needed to see the mayor and chief of police play classic rock.

The Cocoa Beach mayor > every other mayor

"Holy cow." She held her hand to her mouth, laughing with disbelief. "They love it!"

"They love *you*," Erica said, squeezing her sister in a tight hug. "And how could they not? You are, in fact, the coolest mayor ever."

Julie laughed, engulfed in a sea of love and family, with her incredible daughter and the man she adored by her side.

She'd finally found her euphoria, and this time, it was never going to end.

Chapter Twenty-two

Taylor

"How do I look? One last check?" Sam whispered anxiously to Taylor, twirling in her elegant dress as the music started up outside on the beach.

"You look like a dream, Mom." Taylor hugged Sam, fighting what had to be her tenth round of tears that day. "I'm so happy for you."

"My Tay." Sam stroked Taylor's cheek, her eyes misty. "I don't know where I'd be without you."

"You'll never have to." Taylor took her mom's hands and squeezed them both. "You ready to get married?"

Outside, the violinist and cellist duet started to softly play the melody to Elvis Presley's "Can't Help Falling in Love," and Taylor knew that was her cue, as maid of honor, to begin her walk down the aisle.

They were hidden away in a suite on the ground floor of Sweeney House, which had a path laid out directly through the lobby, out the back, and to the beachfront wedding, where forty-five of Taylor's dearest loved ones waited to watch her mom get married.

"I better go," Taylor said with a sniff, handing Sam her bouquet. "I love you, Mommy. I'll see you out there."

Sam nodded, joy emanating from her brimming smile. "Taylor," she said quickly.

Taylor looked back from the edge of the door, just before she made the turn where the entire ceremony would see her.

"I'm so proud of you."

She didn't have to specify why. Taylor knew it was because she'd finally, truly forgiven her dad.

And life had felt so much better ever since. "Thanks, Mom."

Step by step, Taylor walked down the aisle, holding her delicate bouquet and taking her time with each stride.

She'd assumed she would be nervous, thinking to herself, "Don't trip, don't trip, do not trip," the entire walk. She figured she'd be worried about her posture or the way her dress was flowing in the breeze.

But as she walked, none of that even crossed Taylor's mind. She couldn't wipe the smile off of her face as she floated down the aisle, her gaze moving from Annie to Lori to Imani and all of their other loved ones.

Her breath caught in her chest as her eyes fell on Andre, sitting next to her Uncle John and beaming at Taylor like he was looking at the sun and moon.

Taylor couldn't help but imagine herself, one day, as the bride.

But it was a fleeting thought, because today was Mom's day, and that in and of itself made it one of the happiest days of Taylor's life.

After a little wink to her boyfriend, she looked to the

end of the aisle, where Ethan stood in front of the beautiful wooden arch he'd made with his own hands, now draped in vines and white lilies.

When she reached it, she gave Ethan a big hug.

"Welcome to Crazytown," she teased.

"Taylor." He nodded, clearly holding back some tears himself. "It's an honor to become your stepfather today."

She swallowed, brushing a strand of hair out of her face. "The honor is all mine."

She assumed her spot next to where mom would be standing, and shut her eyes for a moment, the ocean breeze wrapping around her like a warm blanket of home and comfort.

Finally, finally, everything was right.

The music paused and changed keys, and the whole audience stood and turned to watch Sam walk down the aisle on Ben's arm.

There was not a dry eye on the beach as Samantha Sweeney, beloved daughter, sister, mother, and friend walked down the aisle between the sea of people who adored her.

Ben walked tall and proud next to Mom, and though he'd deny it to his grave, Taylor watched him wipe a tear as they rounded the corner.

Taylor turned her gaze, watching Ethan watch Mom, and that was the moment she knew for sure.

This man was her mom's forever, and everything happened so that this could all work out perfectly. There was no more bitterness, resentment, or regrets. Taylor couldn't waste another second wishing things had been different, because the look on Ethan's face said it all.

She knew that her mom would be happy and safe for the rest of her days.

Through a tearful laugh, Taylor hugged Sam when she reached the end of the aisle, and she took her bouquet of flowers so Sam could meet Ethan at the altar.

The ceremony was flawless—a beautiful celebration of a love so real that everyone on the beach could feel it.

Sam and Ethan exchanged their vows and rings, and Taylor listened carefully to the words.

"For better or for worse, in sickness and in health, for richer or for poorer..."

She glanced into the crowd and found Andre, his gaze locked on her. Taylor's heart did a little flip when she made eye contact with the man she loved so dearly.

For better or for worse.

No, no. She was getting ahead of herself. She had wedding brain and was under the spell of Mom's magical and romantic day. She and Andre were going at their own pace and their time would come.

"I now pronounce you..." The minister—a dear friend of Grandpa Jay's who was a pastor at the local church and had known the Sweeneys since they were kids—held up his hands. "Husband and wife. You may kiss the bride!"

Everyone cheered and Taylor let out a whoop as Ethan and Sam shared their first kiss as a married couple.

The music picked up and they walked back down the aisle beaming brighter than the evening sun.

After the ceremony, Taylor found Andre in the crowd.

"I have to say..." He smiled at her, looking ridiculously handsome in his "casual wedding attire" of a button-down, tie and khakis. "You are the most beautiful maid of honor I've ever seen."

Taylor laughed and looped her arm through his. "My duties have officially ended. Now it's party time."

The crowd headed into Sweeney House for the reception, a small, classy, and undoubtedly fabulously gourmet dinner followed by dancing and cake and fun.

"Wait, Tay." Andre took her hand, stopping her on the beach as everyone else headed indoors to begin the festivities.

Taylor turned around, her hair blowing around her face in the ocean breeze. "What's wrong?"

"I just..." He pressed his lips together. "I love you so much. And I know that we're young and still figuring everything out, but I just want to be really clear about something."

She angled her head, inching closer to him. "What is it?"

"I want that"—he gestured back at the wedding ceremony space, the rows of chairs and the aisle and the beautiful arch—"with you. And I don't want to wait that much longer."

She could practically feel her heart doing somersaults in her chest. "Andre..." Taylor wrapped her arms around him, looking up to meet his loving gaze. "I want that so bad with you, too. And there's no rush, but..."

"But soon." He took her chin in his hands, delicately tilting her head up to kiss her. "Really soon. You're next."

Taylor's head was spinning, thinking that she might be the next bride in the family. "I like the sound of that."

"Did you get cake, Tay?" Annie sat in an empty chair at Taylor's table, her eyes shiny with joy. "I just want to make sure everyone got a slice, because I see some hooligans already diving in for seconds."

They all turned to face the cake table in the corner of the restaurant, where cousins Ben, Damien, and Liam looked awfully guilty as they held their dessert plates.

"I got my piece, Annie, don't worry." Taylor grinned. "It was to die for."

Next to her, Dottie smiled. "You made a wonderful choice with the raspberry compote."

"I must agree," Franklin added, lifting his glass of water and glancing at Dottie with a smile that seemed almost only between them. "It was light and refreshing, but still decadent. A wonderful balance of flavors."

"Wow." Annie grinned, her cheeks flushed pink. "Praise from Franklin Fox! I'm speechless. Thank you, sir. I'm a huge fan."

"Please." Dottie waved a hand, a playful smile lighting up her face, which Taylor couldn't help but notice looked younger and brighter than it had in years. "Don't inflate his ego. That's the last thing we need."

Taylor looked around, studying the entirety of the

room and drinking in a moment she knew she'd want to vividly remember forever.

Sitting at the table with Grandma, Franklin, Julie, and Annie. In the middle of the restaurant, a dance floor had been laid down and was being put to good use.

The kids, of course, were having more fun than anyone. Jada was dancing wildly with Ellen and Riley, Annie's boyfriend's daughter. Andre was deep in conversation with Brian Wilkes, Julie's now boyfriend, laughing about something over a beer in the corner of the room.

The new bistro had been beautifully decorated with flowers, tablecloths, centerpieces, and string lights that hung everywhere.

Sam was in the center of the dance floor, arm in arm with Aunt Erica and Aunt Imani as they shouted the lyrics to some oldie Mom loved. Uncle John, Uncle Will and Ethan were having a painful-to-watch dance-off.

"Look at Uncle John," Taylor cackled to Annie.

"A trainwreck." Annie shook her head as they watched John attempt to shake his hips. "I don't want to look, but I can't bring myself to look away."

Emily, the new maid who seemed to be everywhere, walked up to the table, dressed in black slacks and a black shirt. "Can I get you guys any drink refills? More water?"

Taylor looked at the young woman who was only a few years older than she was. She didn't know much about Emily, but Grandma seemed to like her. "I think I'm good. Thanks, though!"

After Emily gave a shy smile and walked away,

Taylor turned to Dottie. "I thought you said she was starting as a maid."

"She is, but we needed all hands on deck for this wedding, so I had her come in as a server." Dottie sipped her drink. "She's quite competent and I know she could use the extra cash."

"There's the blushing bride!" Julie exclaimed as Sam sat down at the table with them.

"I need a dancing break." Sam drank some water and laughed. "These Sweeneys are relentless. Did you see John?"

"We can't *unsee* him," Julie cracked.

"How are you feeling, Mom?" Taylor asked. "I mean, I know you're on Cloud Nine, but with the, you know, baby and everything, I just want to make sure you're okay."

"Tay." Sam reached her hand out and placed it on top of Taylor's. "He's having the time of his life."

"Wait a second." Dottie held up a hand, her gaze widened dramatically. "Did you just say *he*?"

Sam put her hand over her mouth. "Whoops. I was going to wait until after the wedding. We found out a few days ago. I'm kind of surprised Ethan's feet have touched the ground."

"A boy!" Taylor exclaimed.

"How exciting!" Annie clasped her hands together.

Julie leaned over and gave Sam a big hug. "I'm so happy for you, sister. Congratulations."

"Thank you." Sam sighed wistfully. "I had a feeling this one was a boy."

"So..." Dottie leaned forward on the table, her eyebrows lifted. "Any ideas for names?"

"We, uh, we actually already chose a name." Sam looked around the table, everyone sitting there waiting intently with anticipation.

"Oh, please don't be one of those people that keeps the name a secret until the kid is born," Julie whined. "Because I will literally sit here, holding you hostage and guessing names until you crack and tell me what it is."

Sam laughed, waving a hand. "Don't worry, I won't make you guess. We're naming the baby Joseph." She swallowed. "But we're going to call him Jay."

Taylor gasped softly, turning her attention to Dottie, who instantly teared up.

"Sam." Dottie got up and hugged Sam tightly, wiping a tear. "That's just wonderful."

The group continued talking, enjoying this little sliver of time together in the midst of the craziness of the wedding day and evening.

Taylor quickly understood what Grandma loved so much about Franklin, who proved to have that magical combination of dry wit and genuine charm. She could definitely get used to having him around.

Annie gushed about the food and Julie told the full story of how Brian decided their band was going to play Wave Haven, and Taylor locked eyes with Andre from across the dance floor, her mind echoing with thoughts of, "Really soon, you're next."

"You guys." Julie leaned forward, lowering her voice

as her gaze narrowed. "Who is that guy? A friend of Ethan's?"

They all turned their attention to the entrance to Jay's that attached to the lobby of the inn. Standing there was a man, tall, muscular, and unfamiliar.

Sam frowned, angling her head. "No, that's not one of Ethan's friends. I know them all, and I've never seen that guy in my life."

"A wedding crasher?" Annie suggested, her eyes wide.

Taylor glanced at her mom, instantly seeing stress and worry rise in Sam's expression.

"I got this." Taylor stood up, placing her hands on her mother's shoulders. "You relax, be the bride, soak in your night. I'll deal with Mr. Random."

Sam looked up with gratitude. "Thanks, Tay."

As she moved to the doorway, Taylor watched the man. He was scanning the room, intently searching every inch of it as if he were on a mission. No question, he was looking for someone.

A coil of worry crept up in her chest, but she squashed it. Surely he was some distant relative of Ethan's or someone who'd wandered into the wrong place.

"Um, hi. Can I help you?" Taylor forced a smile, but could instantly feel that the vibes were way off with this guy.

He hardly noticed her, his narrowed glare fixed intently on the far corners of the restaurant floor.

Taylor frowned. "Are you here for the Sweeney-Price wedding?"

"I'm looking for Amelia." He flicked his eyes to Taylor. "Is she here?"

Amelia? Who the heck was Amelia?

"Um, no, sorry. I think you're in the wrong place. There's no one on the guest list here named Amelia."

He pressed his lips together in a thin line. "All right then. Sorry about that."

"Okay..." Taylor gave a weird, awkward laugh and walked back to her table, sitting down and leaning closely so that Dottie and Julie could hear her. "I don't know who he is. He said he's looking for someone named Amelia. I told him that I don't think there's anyone here named—"

"Oh, no." Dottie gasped in sudden fear, her hands flying to her mouth. "I know who he is."

"What?" Taylor asked. "Who is he?"

But it was obvious that Dottie didn't have time to explain. She turned to Julie. "Get Brian," Dottie commanded.

"Grandma, who is he? What's going on?" Taylor felt fear and worry rising in her throat, looking around the room. She spotted her mother slow-dancing with Ethan, blissfully unaware of the stranger or any sort of drama.

Taylor prayed it would stay that way.

Dottie stood up suddenly, a look of protective determination on her face. "I need to find Emily."

Emily? The woman who was just here? The new maid? What did she have to do with this?

Julie rushed off to follow Dottie's orders and find Chief Wilkes, and Taylor knew that if her grandmother's first instinct was to get the police, there was definitely something going on.

Whatever it was, it could not ruin Mom's wedding.

Taylor glanced around, searching for a clue or answer or piece to this bizarre puzzle.

Her eyes reached the back corner of Jay's, the small side entrance to the kitchen, and spotted Emily, who stood frozen in place, her face bloodless.

Taylor whipped her head back around to see if Mystery Man was still in the doorway, and she watched him slip out as soon as she looked.

Something was *not* right.

Chapter Twenty-three

Emily

Run. Run. *Run.*
But she couldn't.

Emily froze instead, suddenly realizing how utterly sick of running she was. Sick of fear and the constant undertone of low-frequency anxiety, sick of the sort of trembling worry that never seemed to go away.

Sick of Doug Rosetti looming over her life and ruining it.

But if she didn't run...he'd kill her.

That was enough to signal her body to unfreeze and get moving, to whip around and plow toward the back door. She had to get back to her motel, get Ruthie, and get *out* as fast as humanly possible.

Wiping her brain of every other thought but the need to stay alive, she pumped her arms and moved her legs, running to the point where she could hardly breathe or see straight.

She sprinted the whole mile down the beach, dodging people, ignoring everything, focused on getting to safety. The damp sand was tough to power through in the sneakers she'd worn to serve at the wedding, but nothing was going to stop her.

Run. Run. *Run*. Next town, next city. Maybe she could find a way to get on a plane.

Maybe she could make it out of the country, even just to the Caribbean or Mexico. He'd have a harder time finding her there.

But as she tore down the beach, gasping for air, the harsh reality of her life crashed into her like a tsunami.

He would find her. He'd found her once, and he'd do it again. Doug Rosetti was not a quitter, and he'd go to the ends of the Earth to get what he wanted, and what he wanted was to kill his wife.

The realization sent tears streaming down her face, which was burning hot. She wiped them away, trying desperately to catch her breath.

"Thank...God..." she wheezed to herself as the motel finally came in sight.

Without breaking stride, Emily dug the card key to her room out of her pocket and finished her sprint right up to the door of her room.

With her hand shaking uncontrollably, she managed to slide the card into the reader and watched the light turn green as the lock clicked open.

She was safe. For now, at least.

The room was completely dark as she opened the door and closed it behind her, leaning her back against it as she struggled to catch her breath.

Through her spinning thoughts, Emily was vaguely aware that Ruthie wasn't barking or jumping at her feet like she normally would be.

Still trembling from adrenaline and fear, Emily

reached to the right and flipped the light switch on the wall.

"Hey, Amelia."

Her blood turned to ice at the sight of Doug sitting on the edge of the bed, holding a whimpering Ruthie.

Emily's stomach felt like liquid and a blood-curdling scream threatened, but nothing came out of her body. No sound, just...terror.

"Don't be scared." Doug stroked Ruthie's head, the motion making Emily sick with fear. "I'm not going to hurt you."

How did this happen? How did he know where she was staying? How did he get in and...

It didn't matter. This was his superpower, which was why she'd never, ever be safe. If she even got out of this room alive.

Well, she had to try.

She spun around and grabbed the door handle. She barely had her fingers on it when one hand clamped over her arm and the other crushed her mouth to prevent a scream.

Ruthie whined and darted under the bed.

"Let me go!" Emily mumbled, trying to bite him, but he was too skilled to let that happen.

"Like hell I'm letting you go," Doug growled, his familiar voice sending ripples of hatred through her body. "You think you can just leave me, Amelia? You think you can lie to my face and get away with it?"

Sensing that she was too defeated to scream, he eased his hand and let her breathe, but all she could do was let out a sob. "You're evil, Doug. You're an abusive, violent man and if I didn't run away from you, you would have killed me!"

"I ought to kill you now for how disrespectful and dishonest you were to me." He whipped her around and shoved her against the wall, getting right in her face.

She writhed and tried to escape, but he kept her pinned, then yanked her around and threw her on the bed.

Closing her eyes, she started to cry, full sobs quaking her body.

Her arm screamed with pain and she glanced at it, his fingerprints bright red and stinging.

This was going to get worse, and fast. She had no phone on her, no way to call for help. She was trapped in a motel room with her abuser and she had no escape.

Who could help her? Who?

Suddenly, Grandma Gigi's words echoed through her mind, and in her desperation, Emily remembered her favorite Bible verse.

"I sought the Lord and He answered me, He delivered me from all my fears," she whispered to herself.

"What's that?" Doug loomed over her. "You think *praying* is going to help you out of this? You did this to yourself, Amelia."

"No, you did this to me!" she shouted through her tears, her bones shaking.

"I did this?" He threw his head back, letting out a truly evil laugh. "I gave you every woman's dream, Amelia. You didn't have to work, you didn't have to do anything. I *provided* for you, and all I asked for in return was a little bit of respect, but you couldn't even give that to me."

I'm seeking you, Lord. Please deliver me.

"You don't deserve respect," she said, her voice low. "You're a coward, Doug Rosetti."

"What did you call me?" He stood up, towering over her with anger and fury radiating from him.

He raised his arm, and Emily gripped the bedspread, her whole body cringing in anticipation of the blow. She squeezed her eyes shut and repeated the words to herself.

Just before Doug could swing his arm down and strike her, loud and aggressive banging on the door startled them both.

"Cocoa Beach Police, open up!"

Was that real? There was no way. Emily had to just be so terrified she'd begun hallucinating.

But clearly, Doug heard it, too, because he lowered his arm and got right in her face. "You called the cops?" he hissed. "You think they're going to do anything to me?"

More banging. "Open the door or we're kicking in down!"

Please kick it down, Emily pleaded silently.

Doug grabbed her neck, shaking her hard. "What did you do, Amelia?"

The fear in his eyes almost made her smile.

"That's it, we're coming in!" the man's voice from outside shouted, just before a harsh bang and a crash.

Doug released Emily's neck and turned around. She

sat up on the bed to see the motel door smashed in, and three police officers rushing into the room.

The skin on her neck screamed with pain, and she could already feel deep bruises forming.

With the officers was Brian Wilkes, still in his suit from Sam's wedding, speaking into a walkie as his guys charged toward Doug.

One of them grabbed his arms while another got out a pair of handcuffs.

Emily felt like she was dreaming.

"Are you Doug Rosetti?" the cop asked forcefully.

"Yes, but..." Doug sputtered. "I didn't do anything wrong. I'm FBI. This is some sort of mistake. This—"

"You're under arrest for domestic assault, battery, and stalking." One of the cops secured the handcuffs behind Doug's back and yanked him toward the door. "You're going to jail."

Emily decided that those were the four most beautiful words she'd ever heard.

In a state of quivering shock, Emily crouched down and reached under the bed, pulling Ruthie out and clinging to her tightly. She held the dog close, watching as they shoved Doug into the back of a cop car and slammed the door.

The red and blue lights flashed through the room from outside, lighting up her world as she comforted Ruthie and stared in disbelief at the scene in front of her.

She watched the squad car speed away, with all of her fear and pain and suffering in the back seat—gone forever.

"Are you all right?" Brian Wilkes rushed to her, handing her a blanket. "I'm glad we got here in time. Did he hurt you? Do you need any kind of medical attention? Your neck is bruised."

Emily shook her head as Brian draped the blanket over her shoulders and Ruthie snuggled close. "No, I'm... I'm okay." She looked up at Chief Wilkes, his kind blue eyes like an ocean of comfort and peace. "I'm going to be okay."

"You absolutely are, Ms..." He angled his head, waiting for her to supply her last name.

Preston was the last name she'd arbitrarily chosen for her fake ID, when she decided to go by Emily once she made a run for it.

But the name had no meaning to her, and it wasn't who she was.

"Young," she said, surprising herself by choosing the last name she'd been born with—the last name of her birth mother. "Emily Young."

"Ms. Young." Brian nodded. "We'll need you to come down to the station and give your statement to the authorities, and we can provide you with a place to stay, if necessary."

Emily shook her head. "I have someone I can call."

"Dottie, I'm guessing?" Brian tipped his head and smiled.

"Yeah." Emily laughed softly.

"She's got a room ready for you, I'm sure." He nodded and stood up. "Take your time. I can drive you over there when you're ready."

"Chief Wilkes?" Emily asked as he was heading out through the broken-down door.

"Yeah?"

"Is he really going to be put away?" She swallowed, toying with Ruthie's ear.

"Yes." Brian nodded. "He's gone. There's more than enough evidence to give him a long sentence, plus investigators will go through all of his files, finding who knows what other kinds of shady stuff. You're free. There's nothing to be afraid of anymore."

Emily shut her eyes and took a deep breath.

Thank you, Grandma Gigi, for the verse and the strength. He delivered me from all my fears.

⬩

"HERE, HAVE SOME MORE COFFEE." Dottie poured some steaming brew into Emily's empty mug, sitting down at the kitchen table next to her.

Ben was at school and Sam and Ethan had gone on their honeymoon—an Alaskan cruise, which Emily guessed was where Florida residents who lived in tropical paradise took their vacations. Dottie had brought Emily into the cottage for a place to stay. It was quiet this morning, and safe, and warm.

Honestly, she could stay in this little house on the beach forever.

"Thanks, Dottie." Emily wrapped her hands around the warm mug, closing her eyes as she inhaled the rich scent of the coffee.

"How are you feeling this morning?"

Dottie, obviously, had been filled in on everything that went down last night, and Emily was beyond glad to have someone here looking out for her this morning.

"I'm okay." Emily smiled. "It was traumatic—"

Dottie snorted. "I'll say."

"But my heart feels lighter than it has since...well, since I married him." Emily looked out through the sliding glass doors of the cottage onto the sunny beach. "I'm in desperate need of a fresh start, a new life after everything that's transpired."

Dottie placed a hand on Emily's. "I completely understand that, and you have my full support in whatever you want to do. You're welcome here as long as you'd like to stay. And Ruthie, of course."

Emily laughed softly, looking down at Ruthie, who was sound asleep on the light wooden floor.

It was almost as if she, too, knew they were finally out of danger.

"Thank you, Dottie." Emily squeezed the older woman's hand. "For everything."

"You are quite welcome, my dear."

A knock at the door made Emily jump, and she had to remind herself that he couldn't come back. He couldn't come after her anymore.

Dottie stood up. "I'll go see who that is. Franklin was planning on stopping by this afternoon. Maybe he changed his plans and came early."

Emily wiggled her eyebrows. "You two really *are* a cute couple, by the way."

Dottie waved a hand, her kind face blushing as she shook her head and walked down the hall to go answer the front door.

Emily took a deep drink of coffee, letting out a long sigh as it warmed her throat. She leaned against the back of the chair, closing her eyes and feeling the sun pour onto her skin.

She had no idea where to take her life from here, but just like Dottie had told her, anything could be waiting around the next corner.

"You're who?" Dottie's voice echoed through the house, forcing Emily to spring into awareness.

From the sound of it, the person at the door was not Franklin Fox, or any one of the many family members who dropped in all the time.

"Oh...oh, my goodness," Dottie said. "Is she expecting you?"

Who was at the door? Who was the "she" Dottie was referring to? Surely it wasn't Emily.

Curiosity won out, so Emily got up, clutching her coffee mug and wrapped in the warm fuzzy robe that belonged to Sam. She tiptoed out of the kitchen and down the hallway, creeping toward the open front door where Dottie stood talking to a woman Emily didn't recognize.

"Um, Emily..." Dottie turned around as she realized Emily was behind her. "This is quite the unexpected surprise but this woman...this is Vanessa Young."

The Earth rocked so hard under Emily's feet that she had to press her hand against the wall to stay standing.

Vanessa Young. Her birth mother. The woman who gave her up after six months. The woman who hung up the phone a week ago.

Emily could hardly think or breathe or talk. "You're... you...what?"

"Hi, Emily." Vanessa was tall, lean, with caramel-colored hair that framed a lovely face. She looked...like Emily, only a forty-five-year-old version. "I'm so sorry to show up unannounced like this, but could we talk? Would that be okay?"

Emily felt her jaw go slack as she looked from the woman to Dottie and back to...her mother. The woman who looked so much like her, it was uncanny. The same bow in her lips, the same shape of her nose, and exactly the same brown eyes. Even their eyebrows arched alike.

Was she still asleep? Was this part of her dream?

"Emily, honey." Dottie placed a hand on her shoulder. "You should talk to her."

Emily blinked, trying desperately to gather her thoughts and make sense of the last twelve hours, but it was nearly impossible.

"I can't believe you're here." Emily shook her head, choking on a laugh. "I'm...I'm just so shocked and confused."

"I know," Vanessa said, her voice calm and steady. "I can't imagine."

Emily took a deep breath and glanced at Dottie, who gave her a hopeful, reassuring nod. "Come on. Let's go sit outside." Emily gestured for Vanessa to follow her through the house and out to the back deck.

Dottie smiled and winked subtly at Emily. "I'll be over at the inn if you need anything."

"Thanks, Dottie." Emily smiled, her hand still shaking from the shock as she pulled open the sliding glass door and stepped out into the warm sun on the back deck.

The ocean breeze was refreshing and salty, and the sounds of seagulls echoed softly through the morning air.

Vanessa sat on the edge of one of the chairs, fidgeting nervously with hands that had long, pink acrylic nails and pretty gold rings decorating them.

No wedding ring, though, Emily noticed.

She was beautiful, dressed in an expensive outfit, everything coordinated and classy, like she'd stepped out of a magazine.

"Look, I know this is probably crazy for you." Vanessa inhaled sharply. "It's crazy for me, too."

"Why did you hang up?" Emily asked, the question falling off her tongue before she had a chance to think it through.

Vanessa shut her eyes and pressed her lips together. "Because I was in shock."

"Kind of like I am now," Emily retorted with a dry laugh.

"Yes, exactly like you are now." Vanessa laughed, too, a sense of relief in her voice that the ice was maybe beginning to fracture. "Only you can't hang up on me."

"I wouldn't even if I could," she said. "What are you doing here? If you wanted to talk to me, why not just call back?"

"I tried," Vanessa explained, shaking her head. "It said the line was disabled. I assumed you just blocked my number or something."

Of course. The burner phone. She'd deactivated it a couple of days after calling Vanessa for fear of Doug tracking her down.

"Oh, that was my bad." She waved a hand. "I didn't block you, it was a disposable phone. I was on the run... long story."

"I heard it," Vanessa said. "The long story. About your husband and the abuse and your escape. I listened to every word you said and I was so stunned and moved that you'd found me I just...I couldn't speak. I wanted to gather my thoughts before I approached you again."

Emily swallowed, picking at a loose thread on the robe. "Well, good news. He's in jail. He found me last night but they arrested him and took him away."

"Oh, thank God." Vanessa placed a hand on her heart. "You've been through so much."

Emily lifted a shoulder. "I could use a fresh start, that's for sure."

"You and me both." Vanessa looked out at the ocean, the breeze lifting her silky hair away from her face.

"Why's that? It's so weird...I don't know anything about you."

Vanessa turned to her. "Well, we can start with the fact that I just lost my job. A big job that I'd worked at for a very long time. I actually got the news right before your phone call last week, which was another contributing factor to my total freeze up."

"Oh." Emily frowned. "I'm so sorry."

"You mentioned that your grandmother passed? That she raised you after Joanna died?"

Emily winced, shocked at how little Vanessa knew about her life. "Yes, she passed recently, right before I ran away."

"Oh my." Vanessa pressed her lips together and suddenly looked like she was about to cry. "Emily, I've... I've spent my life wondering about you. Thinking about you all the time. I was just a kid when I had you, but I've thought about you every day. I never did anything to try and find you because I didn't know if it would break the contract of the adoption, and, I didn't want to just barge into your life."

"I understand." Emily smiled. "I had a wonderful childhood. Grandma Gigi is my angel. She gave me her dog, Ruthie, and the money to get away from Doug." She gestured at the little creature, who had joined them on the deck and was sunbathing on her side.

Vanessa laughed softly. "She's precious, and I'm so glad to hear that."

"I'm sorry for catching you off guard with the phone call," Emily said, her eyes downcast.

"I'm sorry for catching you off guard by showing up," she replied with a chuckle. "But I'm not sorry that we're finally talking."

Emily looked up, her heart lifting a bit. "Me either. So what was the job? The one you lost?"

"I am—er, was, I should say—a celebrity stylist."

"What?" Emily drew back. "That's so cool!"

"It used to be cool, back when *I* used to be cool. Now I'm old and washed up, according to the industry. They all want these young TikTok people now, and I basically got aged out." She shook her head, shutting her eyes.

"That's so unfair. I'm sorry." Emily pursed her lips. "I used to be an administrator before Doug made me quit. I love computers. Then I was a fake hotel maid. And now I'm...well...I don't know what I am."

"I don't either." Vanessa inched forward on the chair, her eyes bright with life. "But...Emily, I have a crazy idea."

"Okay..." Emily laughed slowly. "What is it?"

"You and I, we don't know each other, but we are mother and daughter."

"Weird but true."

Vanessa took in a breath. "I'm starting a new life, in a new place. And...I want you to come with me."

She sat back on the sofa, let out a sigh, and listened as this beautiful woman who had given birth to her delivered the biggest surprise yet.

Chapter Twenty-four

Dottie

By the time Franklin arrived at the inn, Emily and Vanessa had been on the deck talking for hours.

Dottie was not lurking by any means, but she couldn't help but peek outside and look next door at the back deck of the cottage every now and then. They'd been laughing, talking, totally lost in conversation.

Was there anything more beautiful than a reunion?

"Would you quit stalking, Dorothy?" Franklin chuckled, standing in the lobby of the inn as Dottie peeked her head out the back door to take another look at the scene.

"I am not stalking," she insisted, stepping back inside. "I am simply looking out for Emily, although she seems to be very much enjoying her time with her mother. Birth mother, I suppose."

"Now that was a shocking turn of events, I imagine." Franklin nodded toward the beach. "It's a beautiful day. What do you say we go for a walk along the ocean?"

Dottie smiled. "I suppose it will help ease my temptation to stalk next door. Let's go."

Franklin laughed and gestured for her to head out first, and she did.

It was nearly noon, and the sun was sitting high in

the vast blue sky, without a single cloud in sight. The waves of the ocean were calm and steady, and the air was just cool enough to make the day utterly perfect.

"Well," Dottie said as they got in step and started heading south along the water. "That was one heck of a wedding."

"It was a marvelous time," Franklin agreed. "And everyone seemed to really like the food, which I'm happy about."

"*Like* the food?" She turned to him, arching a brow. "I had at least twenty of our guests come up to me and tell me it was the best meal of their lives. You hit it out of the park. If the food at Jay's is always that good, we're going to have reservations booked out months in advance!"

"As you should." Franklin turned to her, the sun glinting in his eyes. "You've created a uniquely comfortable, classy, and simply lovely restaurant. It honors your late husband tremendously, and I do hope that my cooking can complement its greatness."

"Jay's would be nothing without your talent, Franklin. We're very, very lucky to have you here."

He laughed. "I'm the lucky one. Did I tell you that Henry and I have plans to spend next Saturday together?"

"That's wonderful!"

"He suggested it. He actually called me and asked if I could take him to EPCOT on Saturday so we could ride Test Track. I guess that's some sort of horrendously fast racing ride, but I don't care." He shook his head, smiling joyfully. "I'd get on any roller coaster in the world if it means that my grandson wants to spend time with me."

"See? You haven't even been here that long and he already knows how awesome you are. I'm so glad for you, Franklin."

"It's wonderful. When we were on the phone, he even mentioned something about wanting to cook dinner for his parents. My daughter and son-in-law have a wedding anniversary, and Henry was looking for my help to surprise them with a cooked dinner."

"Oh, now he's dangerously close to your wheel-house," Dottie teased. "He sounds like a very sweet kid."

"I'd love for you to meet him." Franklin turned to Dottie as they walked, the water gently splashing up around their ankles. "In fact, I'd love for you to meet my daughter, too. We've been repairing our relationship too, since I've been spending more time with Henry."

"I'd like that very much." Dottie nodded, joy rising in her heart. "You met basically every person I'm close to last night."

"Well, my family is much, much smaller." Franklin laughed. "But they'd adore you. Almost as much as I do."

The last part nearly stopped Dottie in her tracks, the sincerity in his voice rolling over her with impact. "Oh, Franklin. That's very sweet."

"Dorothy..." He took a deep breath and stopped to face her. "I know you think that I'm just some old celebrity chef with an inflated ego, but I have to tell you that you have changed my life."

She felt a gasp in her throat and butterflies filled her stomach. "I don't think you're—"

"I know you didn't trust me when I first showed up here, and I cannot say that I blame you." He laughed softly, lifting a shoulder. "But you have shown me kindness and the purest heart I've ever seen. I've enjoyed spending time with you more than I've enjoyed anything in a long, long while."

"I feel the same way," she whispered, her heart beating quickly. "When Jay passed, I...I truly thought I'd never know happiness again. But you...you showed up in my life and gave me no choice but to be happy and excited."

His eyes lit up. "You make me feel young again, Dorothy."

"Me, too."

"We have a lot of good years left, and..." He reached his hand down, threading his fingers through hers and holding her hand tight. "I'd very much like to spend them together."

"Franklin..." Dottie felt a laugh bubble in her chest, overwhelmed with joy and excitement at her new and wildly unexpected future with Franklin Fox. "Are you asking me to go steady with you?"

He laughed, tilting his head back as the wind blew his thick hair around his face. "I don't think the kids say that anymore but, yes, Dorothy. If I had a letterman jacket, I'd ask you to wear it."

"And I would. Proudly."

He draped an arm around her shoulder and they

continued their walk, every step making Dottie feel like she could float away with joy.

She was certain that Jay sent him to her. The solitary life she'd been preparing for had been flipped upside down and turned into something completely different. But Dottie Sweeney loved surprises.

And this was the best one yet.

FRANKLIN HAD LEFT to go watch Henry's soccer game, and Dottie was attending to last-minute things at the inn, since Monday was the first day of opening, and every single suite was booked.

Puttering around, humming to herself, she felt entirely too giddy and so happy she could hardly sit still.

Dottie sat down at the main computer at the desk and shook the mouse to wake it up.

Emily must have changed the background picture when she was spending all that time setting up the software, and her choice made Dottie tear up.

On the screen was a photo taken at a family dinner a few months back—it was Dottie surrounded by her grandkids, every single one of them. And now, there was another on the way.

Baby Jay.

"Oh." Dottie held a hand to her face as she felt a lump in her throat.

Her life was filled to the brim with joy and blessings. Every single baby and grandbaby was here with her. And now she had a wonderful new man in her life and the inn of her dreams to manage and enjoy with Sam.

How had she become so blessed? How had everything, even the hardest times, turned into goodness and beauty?

Dottie leaned back in the desk chair, her eyes fixed on the photo as she wiped a tear of joy away.

That very moment, the front doors of Sweeney House swung open, and Dottie turned and gathered herself to greet whoever had arrived.

To her surprise, it was Emily and Vanessa, with Ruthie trotting at Emily's heels.

"Well, hello!" Dottie stood up and walked over to the women. "How are you two? An unexpected reunion after twenty-eight and a half years. All good?"

Emily and her mother shared a look, and they both smiled—looking more like sisters than mother and daughter, and so shockingly similar in appearance.

"Dottie." Emily inhaled slowly. "You told me a few days ago that you never know what surprise life has in store around the next corner."

"I was just thinking that." Dottie chuckled.

"Well..." Emily pressed her lips together. "I have a surprise. Actually, Vanessa does, and I've said yes."

"Yes? To what?"

"A new life," Vanessa said. "As mother and daughter."

"Oh, that's wonderful! What are your plans? Where will you be?"

"I'm going...home. To Rosemary Beach, up in the

panhandle. It's where I grew up. I haven't been back in decades, but..." Vanessa said. "My father is very sick, so I want to see him. But, also, I need a new start. My family is there. We're a bit estranged, but...I can fix that."

"And I need a new start, too," Emily chimed in. "We're going to rent a beach house, and...start our lives all over."

"Oh, my heavens." Dottie reached her arms out and gave Emily a big hug. "You will be deeply missed, sweetheart, but I am so happy and excited for you." She turned to Vanessa. "I'm very sorry to hear about your father. I'm sure he'll be so thrilled to see you."

"Let's hope," Vanessa whispered, her voice a bit strained.

Emily held Dottie tightly. "Thank you for everything," she whispered. "You saved me."

"You saved yourself, my girl." Dottie pulled back and studied the pair, the reunited mother and daughter starting a crazy adventure together. "You must keep me posted and stay in touch."

"I'm sorry to leave you without a maid for your opening."

"Pfft!" Dottie flicked her hand. "We'll fill that slot, but we will miss you. And Ruthie! When do you leave?"

"Now." Vanessa said. "I want to see my dad as soon as possible."

"Of course," Dottie said with a nod.

Emily smiled at Dottie tearfully. "I will never forget how good you and your family have been to me."

"And I promise to be a good mother," Vanessa said,

wrapping both of them in a hug. "It's going to be quite an adventure. A new beginning. For both of us."

More hugs, kisses, and goodbyes followed as Dottie saw out the newly united pair and wished them the absolute best on their journey.

Coming back inside, she walked toward the wall of glass that looked out over the ocean, seeing the boardwalk, the sand, the blue sky, and turquoise waves. So many chapters behind her, so much laughter and love, some heartache, and much hope. That was life, that was the rich tapestry of this thing called life.

She wouldn't change a single thing and couldn't wait to see what the future held.

Would you like to follow Vanessa and Emily to Rosemary Beach? Don't miss the first book in the Young at Heart series **New Beginnings in Rosemary Beach**. Entire series coming soon in digital, paperback, audio, and in Kindle Unlimited! Sign up for my newsletter to stay updated on new releases and more.

The Young at Heart Series – Coming 2024!

New Beginnings in Rosemary Beach – book 1
Old Friends in Rosemary Beach – book 2
Golden Sunsets in Rosemary Beach – book 3
Blue Skies in Rosemary Beach – book 4
First Summer in Rosemary Beach – book 5
Second Chances in Rosemary Beach – book 6
Sweet Memories in Rosemary Beach – book 7

Read the completed Sweeney House series!

Cocoa Beach Cottage - book 1
Cocoa Beach Boardwalk – book 2
Cocoa Beach Reunion – book 3
Cocoa Beach Sunrise – book 4
Cocoa Beach Bakery – book 5
Cocoa Beach Cabana – book 6
Cocoa Beach Bride – book 7